FLOOD
TIDE

Enid Mavor

Published by Lyvit Publishing, Cornwall

www.lyvit.com

ISBN 978-0-9957979-3-2

To my daughters, Fiona and Alison,
and to my grandsons, Matt, Tom, Jake and Louis

FLOOD
TIDE

To Mary
Love from

Enid Mavor

PROLOGUE

She finds it hard to breathe. He is heavy. A dead weight. Breathless, she pulls harder on the legs of the crumpled body. The harsh light of the florescent strip shows up the chaotic cellar; the great heap of coal, boxes of kindling, wooden pallets, the open trapdoor in the floor... Suddenly she is afraid. Not of what she has done, no, that was no more than he deserved; she is afraid the space beneath the floor will be too small. Terrified, she drags the body towards the hole. She will make it fit. Panting, she pauses and wipes the sweat from her forehead. She can see down into the hole now, the wedge-shaped space. She pushes him but as his legs drop down, he gives a low moan. She freezes. He *must* be dead. If he comes round *she* will be the one lying on the cellar floor. Driven on by terror, she pushes his body down until the space is filled. But his head and shoulders are still just above the floor level. She grabs the heavy trap door and slams it down, turns, and drags a pallet over until the hole is secure at last. She slumps to her knees but seconds later is on her feet again. This great heap of coal must be shifted to bury the pallet and the trapdoor before the rising tide seeps through and spreads across the cellar floor and washes away her footprints. And then she'll have his boat to deal with. And an anonymous phone call to make...

CHAPTER ONE

So. I was on the train to Cornwall. At last I'd escaped, thanks to my son's determined efforts. He'd scoffed at my suggestion to find work in a different hospital. 'He'll find you in no time,' he said. 'You need to be somewhere off the radar. A live-in post looking after someone disabled or whatever.'

And Katherine Avery, my nursing officer and long-time friend agreed with him and a few days later she called round. 'Right,' she said. 'I've found you a place in Cornwall. To care for a Mrs Rogers, an elderly wheelchair user woman who lives in Falmouth. She sounds grumpy, but there, we're used to that. You speak to her and if you feel up to it, we'll tell everyone at work you've gone to Scotland. Then if *he* turns up and asks for you, he'll be looking in the totally wrong direction.'

And now, just thinking of him sent a cold shiver down my spine because I knew he would surely track me down in time. But for a while at least, I was free. I watched the countryside fly past the window. A dull February day, but still such a 'green and pleasant land'. I read and dozed until at last I had to change trains for the single-track line to my destination.

The small train was busy with schoolchildren on their way home. I found them amusing and smiled when one of the boys' paper darts landed on my lap. I read the message, took out my biro and scribbled a few words and sent it flying back. Two girls grabbed it and laughed as they read 'Takes one to know one'. The boys too grinned and when the train drew to a halt at the tiny station named 'The Dell', they came and helped me with my luggage. When I looked round for a taxi, one of the boys said he'd get Stan.

They all ran off down the slope and I was suddenly alone on the small platform, in the damp mist. The air felt soft and clean and I breathed deeply. And on my lips I tasted salt.

The boys were soon back with a cheerful Stan in tow and as he hoisted my bags into the boot, I told him where I wanted to go. He straightened, his face losing its smile. 'Ah, so you're Mrs Rogers' new nurse then.' Silently he opened the passenger door for me as I thanked the boys for their help and then we drove off.

And I wondered what it was about Mrs Rogers that had brought about this abrupt change of attitude from the chatty Stan. I supposed I'd soon find out.

The driver found his tongue before we'd gone very far. 'Where you're going might seem a bit strange to you, my dear. Mrs Rogers' old house was built like a lot of others back-to-back against the shops in the street so your only windows are at the rear. Still, you may know that if you've been here before.'

'No,' I said. 'This is my very first visit to Cornwall.'

'Ah well, in February 'tis pretty quiet down here but

soon the evenings will be pulling out.'

Through the mist and murk of the dusk we seemed to turn and twist pointlessly until the taxi swung into a narrow street, mounted the pavement and came to an abrupt halt. 'Can't park here for long, me dear, but I'll get your cases out for you.' And he hauled them from the boot while I clambered out. 'This way,' he called over his shoulder as he turned down a narrow sloping alley paved with uneven cobbles. 'Mind how you go,' he added and I cautiously followed him. There were no windows of course, and only one door halfway along where Stan pressed the bell.

The door opened and a burly man stepped out. 'Mrs Sands, is it? You'd better come in.' Stan lifted my heavy case on to the doorstep and placed the holdall alongside and I quickly dipped into my handbag and handed him a note and told him to keep the change.

Stan shook his head. 'No, that's too much for such a short trip.' and he handed me back a couple of coins. And as I thanked him, he gave me a card. 'Here, hang on to this. I'll come if you want me. Anytime. Don't forget.' And as I turned back to the door where my cases stood, I wondered if I'd imagined the note of caution in his voice.

CHAPTER TWO

The man still stood at the open door. 'Come in then.
I'm Bertram, Mrs Rogers' nephew. My wife and I keep
an eye on her. Here, I'd better take that.'

Gladly I relinquished the heavy case. 'Go through to
the kitchen, they're in there,' he said as he hauled my
case off along the hallway.

I could hear voices from behind an open door so I
tapped and entered. The kitchen was large and old-
fashioned with a pine table in the centre and an Aga at
the far wall. My patient sat in a wheelchair at the head
of the table talking to the wife of grumpy Bertram who
rose to her feet and came towards me, hand
outstretched. 'Ah, you'll be Mrs Sands. Do come in.
I'm Cynthia, Aunt Edith's niece. And this is my aunt
herself.' And with a flourish she waved me towards the
woman who was to be my charge for the weeks and
months ahead.

Edith Rogers sat stiffly upright and stared at me with
unsmiling eyes. She was very thin, her face deeply
etched with lines of pain. Or bitterness. I stood
awkwardly before her, murmuring a greeting, waiting
for some response. Her eyes were very dark and there
was still some black amongst the grey in her short,
scraped-back hair. Then, when the pause was becoming
embarrassing, she waved me towards a chair at the
table and spoke. 'You'll be wanting a cup of tea after

5

that journey, I suppose. Cynthia.'

In response, Cynthia went to the big stove and busied herself making a fresh pot of tea and as I sat down the nephew came in and flopped down heavily opposite me, red-faced and breathing noisily. 'Don't know what you've got in that case of yours. Women!'

Cynthia laughed her bright tinkling laugh. 'Oh Bertie! You know how heavy our cases always are.'

'Speak for yourself,' he grunted. 'Where's that tea then?'

As he spoke I could feel Edith Rogers watching me intently with those dark and deep-set eyes and I became conscious of my own appearance. Of my casual trousers and hair that hadn't seen a comb for hours; brown hair that used to be thick and shiny but was now limp and scraped back into an unbecoming knot that made me look older than my thirty-nine years. The niece was pretty and well groomed and Bertram also immaculately dressed. Only Edith seemed indifferent to my appearance, her eyes probing my face, reading the lines of strain and stress written there by the last three years.

The tea was good but as we all sat at the table, Bertram looked at his watch and Cynthia, on cue, gave a little cry of dismay. 'Oh goodness, look at the time! I'd better show Nurse Sands round and then we must be going. That train being so late has quite upset our plans!'

As I stood to follow her, I said, 'Nurse Sands sounds

so formal – all my colleagues call me Lisa, so you may as well do the same,' and I smiled across at my patient as I spoke. The response was a long silent look and I guessed, correctly as it happened, that Edith Rogers would never use anything other than my full title. That is, when she bothered to call me anything at all.

But Cynthia smiled and rolled her eyes as we went along the hall, shaking her head at Edith's stiff-necked disapproval. She opened the first door on the left to reveal a well-fitted cloakroom. 'That's the downstairs loo, and this next room is the laundry and store. It used to be a pantry.' She switched on the light and I saw a tumble dryer alongside the washing machine. There was a vacuum cleaner and bottles and boxes stood tidily on the shelves. The door opposite opened into a large high-ceilinged sitting room with a dark blue velvet couch and armchairs facing an ancient television set. A great sideboard stood along one wall and navy brocade curtains were drawn across the window. The patterned carpet was dark grey and under the central light the room looked cold and comfortless despite the central heating. I was struck by the absence of pictures or photos. I had the impression of a room rarely used, no scatter of books or magazines. No flowers. No feeling of welcome and comfort…

We went back to the kitchen and I collected my holdall and handbag and followed Cynthia up the stairs. She gestured to the electric stair-lift installed alongside the steep staircase and laughed. 'I like to ride up on that sometimes. P'raps you'd like to try it!'

'No thanks,' I said dryly. 'after sitting in the train all day I need a little exercise.'

'This house isn't very big and it's very old and I hate it,' Cynthia prattled as we climbed the stairs. 'But Aunt Edith will never leave. You'd think she'd be only too glad to move into something light and modern.' We reached the upper landing, a wide passage with doors opening off on either side. 'All these doors! Yet there are only two proper bedrooms. Yours is en suite. Mrs Green, your predecessor, insisted on her own bathroom and I don't blame her. Aunt Edith's is full of all that equipment, lifting gear and stuff.' I'd already been told this by the agency but was glad to see the invalid's bathroom was large, the hoist and rails gleaming, white tiles reflecting the bright light.

'Those two doors alongside the bathroom are the linen room and a box-room. They've got no windows. In fact all the windows here are at the back – you probably noticed we're behind the shops on the front street. Aunt Edith's door is that one,' she waved an arm towards the first closed door on the right while she opened the second. 'This is your room.'

The large bedroom we entered had ancient mahogany furniture and heavy green curtains across the window. The bed however was a modern divan and Cynthia opened another door, narrow and unobtrusive and beckoned me over to show me the en suite bathroom my predecessor had ordered. It was fitted with both bath and shower and once again, the room was spotlessly clean. As if reading my mind, Cynthia said, 'Aunt Edith has a woman in to clean for an hour each morning. Mrs Green would never do cleaning. Said she was a nurse, not chief cook and bottle washer. I don't know why Aunt Edith put up with her all those years. And when Mrs Green broke her hip, we had to find someone else for a few weeks. But then she decided not to come back and she's gone to live with her son in Cardiff, poor man!'

My case stood on the floor beside the bed and I put down my holdall and laid my handbag on the duvet. At least my worries about accommodation were over. How I would get on with my new employer was another matter.

As we went back down the stairs, Cynthia glanced again at her watch. 'Well, that's the lot apart from the cellar and I'm not going down there in these shoes. The steps are a killer.' She pointed to a narrow door in the hall. 'It used to be full of coal but I don't suppose it's ever been used since the central heating got put in and that was years ago, not long after her husband died - well, drowned, apparently. This is a small house though the rooms are quite a decent size. But Aunt Edith would be a lot better off in a little bungalow, somewhere she could look out and see a bit of life. This place...' she shuddered.

Bertram stood up as we entered the kitchen. 'Well Edith, we'll be off now. I'm sure Mrs Sands will look after you. We'll drop in again next week sometime.'

Edith Rogers barely acknowledged their goodbyes and started speaking to me before the door had closed behind them. 'I've already eaten but there's food in the refrigerator. I'll go along and watch the television while you sort yourself out. I'll ring when I want you.' As she spoke she was manoeuvring her electric chair towards the door. I made some sort of reply but it was obvious she wasn't looking for conversation so I turned back and went over to the tall refrigerator and explored its contents, suddenly hungry.

There were several packets of M & S foods and I put together a salad with cheese and buttered a crisp bread roll. After eating the snack and drinking another cup of tea, I stacked the crockery in the dishwasher alongside the porcelain sink and went to join my patient. I already knew from our correspondence and phone calls that she'd suffered from multiple sclerosis for many years and now depended on a wheelchair for movement and needed constant care.

As I entered the sitting room, she switched off the television set and told me she wanted to have a bath and go to bed. So I helped her onto the stair lift and up to the bathroom. Despite her thinness, I was glad of the lifting apparatus; I'd put my back out more than once hand-lifting a slippery wet patient from a bath.

It was over an hour before I finally closed Edith Rogers' bedroom door. She now lay comfortably propped up on her pillows watching a more modern television set. I wondered how long it would take to get through her barrier of reserve, indeed, if ever. And just as I knew she would never use the diminutive 'Lisa' I knew she would always insist on the formal 'Mrs Rogers'.

I collected my mobile phone and went downstairs to the kitchen. Though the chairs were not very comfortable, the stove gave the room a feeling of homeliness and I settled down and phoned my son Josh. When he answered I could tell his room mates were with him from the background noise. He told me to hang on a sec and I guessed he'd gone to the landing to sit on the stairs for our chat. I could hear the laugh in his voice as we spoke, the relief he felt that I'd actually managed to give my tormentor the slip. We chatted for several minutes, but as we rang off I wondered how long it would be before my trail was picked up once more…

It was still quite early, but I thought I might as well follow Edith Rogers' example and go up to my room. I unpacked my bags and by the time I'd put Josh's photo on the dressing table, as well as a couple of snaps of my nursing colleagues, and with my MP3 player playing quietly, the room began to feel a little more mine.

Finally I switched off the light and went to the window and drew back the curtains to find they concealed a pair of tall french doors. Outside the mist seemed to have thickened and all I could see was the pale blanket of fog against the panes of glass. Over these last traumatic years I couldn't bear the thought of hidden eyes watching me from the darkness. So now I drew the curtains back together with a swish. I would wait for the morning to discover what lay beyond my bedroom window.

CHAPTER THREE

Edith Rogers rang her bell twice during the night. Once at two o'clock and again at six-thirty when I made her comfortable with a cup of tea. She told me then she'd sleep until at least nine o'clock. 'You might as well have a lie-in,' she remarked with a slight thawing of her manner.

Back in my room I found I was no longer tired so I had a shower and after I dressed I went over to the window. As I pulled back the curtains I caught my breath in astonishment and delight, for in the faint light of the breaking day I could see the mist had vanished and a sheet of water lay before me, pale and shimmering.

I fumbled with the catch of the french doors as I saw a wooden balcony outside and I could hear the water lapping. But the doors were locked and I couldn't find a key. No doubt Edith Rogers would give it to me later. It was still not light enough to see very far but I hugged myself with pleasure at being so close to the sea.

Downstairs I made myself some tea and went along to the sitting room to draw back those curtains too. Once again, I found french windows leading to a balcony, and this time the key was in the lock. I opened the doors and stepped outside, delighting in the quiet greyness of the dawn and the clean cool air on my cheeks.

With a mug of tea in my hands, I leaned against the railing and breathed in the salt air. A number of vessels were moored a little way out in the harbour and some boats were already moving. As I stood there, the blurred shape across the bay slowly revealed itself to be low wooded hills and fields, and to the left a village lay along the water's edge. To the right, I could see a pier and beyond that, ships and cranes in the docks I'd read about.

I stood there, revelling in the quietness, until the morning chill finally turned me back. Inside the warm kitchen, I was just finishing some toast when Edith's bell rang and I went upstairs.

'I can't get back to sleep. You might as well get me ready now and I'll have my breakfast downstairs.' I wondered if her abrupt speech was partly due to reserve and would change as we became familiar, but I was soon to find it was her normal manner.

As she ate her breakfast, I mentioned I couldn't find the key to the french doors in my room. 'Don't know anything about that,' she snapped. 'Mrs Green must have put it somewhere. It'll turn up sometime. Anyhow, the fanlight above the doors will open if your want fresh air.' I could tell it was far too soon to start making waves about the missing key. 'I want to go through the town this morning as 'tis not raining.' she went on, and presently we set out. After negotiating the chair down ramps and up the cobbled alley it was plain sailing. The chair, electrically propelled (another of

Mrs Green's "musts") made my job almost unnecessary and we sped along with barely a pause.

The street followed the sea's edge, and I caught several tantalising glimpses of the harbour through a series of other narrow steeply-sloping alleyways. Each time when I stopped, enchanted, I found I had to run on to catch up with the impatient Edith. 'I want to go up past the castle. 'Tis quite a way. How are you for walking?' she asked when I rejoined her for the third time.

I laughed. 'Fine. Haven't had a lot of exercise for a while so it'll do me good. And if I get tired, you can always give me a lift on your lap.' And that flippant remark went down like a lead balloon.

But the views along our walk more than made up for my morose companion. Although it was still cloudy, the air was soft and there was a clarity of light that seemed to hint at sunshine not far away. I kept taking great breaths, filling my lungs. And Edith Rogers at last became more human as she pointed out landmarks, this way and that. Frigid though she seemed, there was no doubting her deep feeling for this town of hers.

And as we reached the top of the hill on which the castle stood, the sun came out and the sight of the glittering expanse of the great harbour took away my breath. I could see the tumbling sea all around. Across the wide mouth of the bay stood a smaller castle, and dancing over and through the waves were craft of all sizes, a tiny yellow-sailed yacht, fishing boats, a small ferry ploughing its way and several great lumbering tankers out in the bay.

Exhilarated beyond words, the long walk back through the town seemed to be over in no time and just before we reached her home, Edith turned her chair onto the pier to speak to some acquaintance. She didn't introduce me and as I looked around I spotted a fisherman selling mackerel. I asked him if they were fresh. 'Fresh my handsome?' he replied, 'They was still whistling at the girls ten minutes ago. Can't get much fresher'n that.' And I bought a couple for our evening meal. Edith had some colour in her cheeks from the stiff breeze and as we turned down her alleyway I was still smiling about my fisherman. She too looked secretly pleased and I wondered if she felt my delight in the town would help to ensure I stayed with her. If only she knew why I wouldn't, couldn't, leave…

We finished off the M&S food for our lunch and as we ate, she suddenly asked why I'd taken this post. 'It says in your letter you've been a nursing sister for years. What made you give all that up to take on a job like this?'

I stood up and went over to the sink to fill the kettle, and with my back towards her, said 'I was attacked by a patient a month or so ago. It's made me nervous. I thought a break would be good.' This was the story I'd planned to tell. And it was true, as far as it went, but I'd no wish to go any further. Even so, I felt the prickling of hair on the back of my neck, the weakness of my legs. I took a deep breath and tried to follow the advice of the doctor, 'Forget the past, live in the present, until you're strong enough to face up to it.' Easier said than done.

'Did you get to speak to your son last night?' Edith asked abruptly.

Relieved, I said I had. 'It's partly because he's away at college that I'm able to do this. Two nurse friends of mine are renting my flat and Josh is going to Spain in the summer. Then he has another two years before he graduates. So I'm free for the first time since he was born. His things are all stacked up in our box room and my friends have a bedroom each. He says if he ever needs to doss down while I'm away, a sleeping bag on the floor will do.'

And because I'd been a little curt earlier, I added, 'My husband died in a road accident when Josh was only two and my mother-in-law asked me to move in with her. It made sense. She looked after Josh while I finished my training. And we put the accident compensation towards buying her council flat later on.'

'So you never got the chance to marry again.' She spoke flatly, having heard much more than I'd intended with my words.

I went back to the table with the teacups and sat down. 'You said it! But there, she was good to us and Josh was very cut up when she died a couple of years ago. When he went off to college, I let the spare room to one of my colleagues.' I didn't tell her I'd asked my friend to move in because I was afraid to be alone any more. I didn't tell her of the triple-locking system I'd had installed and the chains. I didn't tell her how fearful I'd been to leave the building every day…

It started to rain heavily that afternoon and we watched an ancient film on the television set in the sitting room which Edith called the 'front room' regardless of the fact it was well and truly at the back. Even though talking and thinking about the past had briefly disturbed me, I found myself relaxing, ready to believe that perhaps *he* really couldn't reach me now.

I cooked the mackerel that evening and to my surprise Edith said she'd enjoyed the meal. After seeing her settled in her front room, I opened the kitchen window to let out the cooking smells and as I listened to the sea slapping against the wall below, I promised myself that soon I'd go through that door at the end of the alley and walk along the little jetty and out on the wooden walk-way visible from the balcony. Leaning through the window, the water seemed to be a long way down. Then I remembered Cynthia talking about the cellar. Of course, this was a three-story house. But when I mentioned to Edith what I'd like to do, she told me abruptly the door in the alley was always kept locked and anyway, those old wooden boards were too rotten to walk on.

Soon afterwards, Edith decided to go to bed, and once I'd got her settled I had my first long evening to myself. The house was silent. Even in the daytime, the slow-moving traffic could barely be heard. I walked into the sitting room and went over to draw the curtains across the dark panes. Although I knew that out there was just the moving water and the moored boats, I couldn't get rid of my fear of watching eyes. I snapped the curtains together and sat down to read until the pleasant lassitude of the day's exercise called for another early night.

I found myself enjoying the next few weeks as I became familiar with my employer's routine. My first impression of her hardness and bitterness didn't change, but I could see that at least she was fair and knew that many of the things I did were far more than my contract demanded. Cooking for instance. I delighted in using that great cooker. Edith too enjoyed the meals I made, and I kept the glass jar on the dresser filled with my biscuits.

Then, one night as I drew my bedroom curtains, a key fell from the rail. Pleased, I tried it in the lock and with a loud squeak of the hinges, the doors opened. Smiling, I stepped out to the balcony rail when two sounds cut through the air: the ping of Edith's bell and the crack of timber beneath my feet. I froze. Felt the slightest tilt of the balcony floor. Heard the bell ring again.

I turned, hardly daring to breathe, and took one careful step. A slight shudder ran through the planks. Another step brought an ominous creaking. Almost there. One more step and I'd reach the bedroom doors. But the floor tilted again and I slipped on the mossy wood and fell. Lying in the darkness on the sloping wet boards, I could hear the fierce slap of the sea against the wall below and froze again, dreading to fall into those dark depths. The bell rang once more. I reached out my hands until they found the door ledge. I gripped it with both hands and hauled myself towards the safety of my bedroom floor. Everything seemed to be happening in slow motion but at last I found myself lying on the carpet, inhaling its dusty smell. That bell again. She was keeping her finger on the buzzer. Fuelled by adrenalin and a mounting wave of anger, I scrambled to my feet and went straight to Edith's room.

CHAPTER FOUR

Edith was sitting up in her bed, rigid with tension. 'You opened the window. You mustn't go outside. The balcony floor is dangerous.'

I found myself shaking. 'Dangerous!' I exclaimed. 'It almost collapsed into the water
and I thought it was going to take me with it. Why on earth didn't you tell me how bad it was!'

But before I could say anything more, Edith's face drained of all colour and her breathing became laboured and rasping. And of course my years of nursing kicked in and
I hurriedly fetched her inhaler. It was several minutes before she began to breath more normally and by that time my own pulse rate had slowed down and I could no longer be so angry with such a sick woman.

When I felt she was sufficiently recovered, I made a pot of tea and poured us each a cup and sat with her as we both rather shakily drank it. As she handed me her empty cup, she actually said thank you and then went on to say she would get in touch with a carpenter next day and get the balcony repaired for me.

It took a while for both of us to relax enough to get some sleep. And in the morning I was surprised when Edith phoned someone called Maud and asked her to send her son down to take a look at the nurse's balcony. They spoke for a while and Edith put the phone down with a look of satisfaction. 'She says she'll see he comes down as soon as he can.' And then she said we better hurry up and get out and make the most of the sun which had just come out.

As I'd been told, a woman came in each weekday morning for an hour to clean. This was Susan, and though she was very thorough, she hardly opened her mouth to speak and I soon learned she preferred to be left alone to do her work. Sometimes I popped out to the shops while she was there, but I knew I couldn't expect her to attend to my patient if it should become necessary, so I was never away for long.

In any case, I'd soon grown to know my way about the town from our daily outings. The weather had often been cold and damp as we moved into March, but Edith insisted that wrapped up snugly in her wheelchair she was fine. So we covered miles each day and I began to get some idea of the size and shape of the great harbour. One day when the sun briefly shone, I had wondered aloud which of the several beaches I'd seen would be best to swim from when summer came. Edith replied with a dry rejoinder that she had no idea; in her day people had better things to do than cavort on the beaches half naked.

So my days were all busy and I usually slept well, accustoming myself to the brief awakenings in the night to attend my patient. And for hours at a time, no thoughts had been entering my head of the stalker who had turned my last three years into an on-going nightmare. But of course, every now and then in the street, I'd turn to check for traffic and some man passing by, oblivious of my very existence, would for a second become transformed into the dreaded body of my shadow. No, it would not be easy to erase those fears. And despite my resolution, I still wondered how long it would be until he tracked me down once more.

But I could feel already that the fresh air and exercise and general lessening of tension, were building up my strength. Indeed it was only now that I could see how close to a total breakdown I had come before taking the drastic step to flee from my old life. And it was these thoughts over breakfast that drove aside my last-night terrified thoughts of leaving this disagreeable old woman for almost causing me a very nasty accident.

Instead, I sighed to myself and got her ready for our regular morning walk. The sun had indeed come out and we went for a long walk round the castle headland but on the way home we had to hurry to get back before a threatening shower fell. I settled Edith in the kitchen and went into the cloakroom to take off my coat and as I turned, I saw my reflection in the mirror and drew my breath in surprise. The walk had brought colour to my cheeks, and I was smiling to myself at some blackly-humorous remark Edith had just made. So it was a bright-eyed woman I saw staring back at me. The dark circles which had shadowed my eyes for so long had gone and my hair, teased though it was by the wind, looked shiny and healthy. For a long time now, all I had done was scrape it back into a ponytail or sometimes into a rough pleat. Now I shook it loose and decided to ask Edith if someone could cover for me so I could get it cut and styled. I thought how pleased Josh would be to see me now, looking once more like the mother he grew up with instead of the pale and haunted woman of the past three years. My hands came up to my cheeks and I murmured his name and thought with sadness of what I'd put him through.

I ran up the stairs to my bedroom and pulled out the make-up case I hardly ever used these days. Ten minutes later, with a light touch of eye-liner and lipstick and with my hair swept up into a pert top-knot, I went back into the kitchen. Edith looked up, her gaze sharpened for a moment, then she turned away and said a cup of tea would be welcome if you've got the time with all the titivating. I smothered a laugh as I turned to put on the kettle but used the moment to say I would like to get my hair cut one day if she could get someone to cover for me. This was the first time I'd brought up the matter of the relief which had been promised in our earlier conversations. Edith looked put out at first, but presently said I'd better fix up an appointment first, and she would get someone to come in. 'Come to that, if you're not going to be too long, I can manage on my own for an hour or so, as you know very well. You're free to go out by yourself every day once you've seen to me.' All this consideration for me was, I felt, because she'd guessed how ready I'd been to leave after my overnight scare.

Pleased, I went over to the small table I'd set up in the kitchen and switched on my computer for Edith to use. In a telephone conversation with her before I'd arrived, I had told her I would like to have access to the internet and she'd agreed to getting broadband installed as I assured her that she too would be able to use it. Since I'd arrived, I'd also shown her how to use my digital camera, a parting gift from the nurses I'd worked with, and on our walks she liked to scroll through the pictures we'd taken. She was amazed at the ease with which they could be e-mailed to my friends and my laptop and printer now stood in the kitchen rather than in my bedroom, so she could watch me at work.

I think we were both surprised at how quickly she gained confidence practising her new skills. Luckily for her, only one of Edith's hands was badly affected by weakness and she used her good hand on the keyboard of the laptop with growing dexterity. And I was glad to be able to use it myself in the kitchen, because it was the only room in the house I liked. My bedroom and the large front room were still too impersonal and unwelcoming, and downstairs, I found the corridors and storerooms, with their high and shadowy ceilings downright creepy. But there was always something to do and gradually familiarity had bred an indifference to the chill atmosphere. And I knew it would be much more pleasant when the weather was better and we could have the french windows open and make use of the balconies - that's if mine was ever actually repaired.

One evening I'd called Katherine Avery, my old friend. We chatted for a while, catching up on the goings on at the hospital and love-lives of some of the nurses, and then I asked her, 'Has *he* been around?'

The slight pause before she replied made my heart sink. 'Well, yes, he has been around a bit. Asking for you. Trying to find out where you've gone. I've told all the girls on reception you've gone to stay with an aunt in Scotland. They actually think that's true so even if he does manage to get round them, that's what he'll hear.'

My stomach churned. 'How was he?'

'Quite calm, according to Stacey on the desk last week. Perfect gentleman, she said. She wished she had a Hugh Grant look-alike coming round after her like that.'

I bit my lip. 'If only she knew, Katherine. God, I just don't know what I'll do if he turns up here.'

'You're settling in then? You like it?'

'Oh, I can't tell you. The town curls right along the edge of the harbour and spreads up the sides of the hills. And boy, are they steep! But the views at the top are fantastic and I'm getting calf muscles like a body builder.'

'Lisa love, keep on going like you're doing and I think even if he does turn up, you'll be able to sort him out. You sound really strong and positive. Like you used to be in fact. You know what Doc McAlister said about having to lose the victim mentality. I think you're beginning to do just that. And remember, as soon as you're ready to come home, your job is here waiting for you.'

And now, as I thought of Giles Christchurch-Smith and how he had devastated my life, I felt a surge of anger. How dare he. How dare he do this to me and mine. And when staring at my reflection I knew Katherine was right, I was getting stronger and getting things into perspective so *that man* could no longer twist my life out of shape. I was much more my old self. And one day I would be able to get the better of him.

Whatever. Each day I never tired of gazing from the windows overlooking the harbour, watching the busy traffic on the water and the changing colour of the sea as the tides rose and fell against our outer wall. I wished I could paint; I'd taken many photos but wasn't satisfied with the results when I brought them on screen. Nothing could convey the brightness of the light, the freshness of the air and that tang of salt on my lips whenever the wind blew in from the sea. I couldn't wait for Josh to come and see for himself.

We passed the rest of that day in our usual way, but I found Edith was a little less curt with me than usual, her manner almost conciliatory. I knew she'd had several agency nurses caring for her after Mrs Green had her fall, and I also knew not one of them stayed more than a couple of weeks. So I decided this change of attitude was due to her fear that I'd leave because of my narrow escape. Hence the swift arrangements to get the balcony looked at. Whether she would follow it through was yet to be seen.

Edith asked for bed earlier than usual, tired no doubt by the strain we still felt on our relationship. I had just got her into bed when the doorbell rang. 'That'll be Maud's boy. I'm alright. You go on down and let him in and bring him up here to my room.'

There was no spy hole in the door and I felt that all too familiar rush of fear as I went down the stairs. I paused and the bell rang again. This time I forced myself to undo the catch and open the door.

A man stood in the alley, hands in pockets. He turned to face me. 'I'm Jack Edwards. Mrs Rogers is expecting me I think. I'm to take a look at the bedroom balcony.'

I stood back and let him in, and as he stepped inside, I saw a man of about my own age, with fair hair and tanned skin and as he glanced at me, I saw a flash of surprise and, perhaps, admiration, in his look. And for once I didn't react with that familiar shudder of horror. In fact I was glad of the touch of make-up and that I'd still left my hair swinging on my shoulders, the henna rinse I'd used bringing out copper lights in the dark brown.

Into the suddenly charged silence, I spoke. 'I've just this minute got Mrs Rogers to bed but she said for you to go straight up.'

He took off his boots and coat and as we walked up the stairs, I said, 'I'm Lisa Sands, by the way. The new nurse.'

He nodded and smiled, that brief flash of pleasure in his eyes again, and then he went ahead of me into Edith's bedroom. She told him about the balcony and he turned and padded along the landing in his thick socks and crossed my bedroom to the french window. 'Here, let me,' he said as I struggled with the stiff catch and then he leaned out.

'I was standing over there at the rail when I heard the crack. I thought the whole thing was about to fall into the harbour,' I said, watching as he shone his torch where the light from the bedroom failed to reach.

Then he opened the second door and put one foot carefully out on to the creaking boards. As he cautiously added his weight, the floor of the balcony tilted even more and he quickly withdrew. 'Phew!' he turned to me and grinned. 'You better not have your coffee out here just yet. I'll go and take a look from the other balcony down below. You carry on with what you're doing, Mrs Sands. Mrs Rogers knows me. Don't worry.'

I went back to Edith's room to relay this information and she said to sit down and wait until he came upstairs again. A few minutes later he tapped lightly on the door and when she called, he came in and stood unconcernedly beside the bed while he told her what needed to be done. 'I'll have to rig some scaffolding and replace all the supports and the floor boards. And from the look of it, your downstairs balcony is going the same way. I'll have to sort that too. But don't go out on this top one again, Mrs Sands' he gave me a grin as he spoke, 'not unless you're keen on that first swim of the season.' His eyes were very blue. He turned to Edith. 'I can't leave the job I'm on this week, Mrs Rogers, but I'll drop round at the weekend.' He answered her questions about his mother saying she'd just returned from her trip to Germany, and then he said goodbye and I followed him down the stairs to let him out. On the step he turned and said goodnight, and once more our eyes met and there was a moment of charged silence. Then I croaked my own goodnight and closed the door behind him.

Upstairs, the air in my bedroom still had the tangy salt smell of the harbour let in by the opened windows and I was sorry they were tightly closed again. I imagined how it would be with the balcony fixed and the windows open all night when summer came. But summer was a long way off and when, after settling Edith for the night I finally switched out my light, I was lulled to sleep by the steady pattering of rain against the glass. And I dreamed a muddled dream of wheelchairs and balconies and boats, and of a man with blue eyes and laughter lines pale against the tan of his face.

CHAPTER FIVE

On Saturday morning I answered the doorbell to find a young girl standing on the step. She gave me a wide smile and said, 'I'm looking for my dad. Is he here yet?' Then, seeing my bewilderment, she added, 'He's Jack Edwards. He's coming to fix your balcony or something.'

'Oh, yes,' I smiled back at her. 'No, he's not here yet but you'd better come in.'

'Great, thanks. I'll go and say hello to Mrs R. Haven't seen her for ages.' And she skipped past me and went into the kitchen.

Edith Rogers gave the child what could almost be described as a smile. 'We're waiting for your father, Katie. He said he'd be here this morning.'

'Yeah, he's already set out in the boat. Wayne's helping him today.' She turned to me with a smile. 'He's a boy we know, he likes to earn a bit of cash at weekends. They should be here in about ten minutes I think.' She gave me another wide smile and after the briefest of pauses, asked me if I was any good with hair.

'Depends what you want done, I think,' I said cautiously.

'Could you do these plaits for me properly d'you think,' she said, tugging at the fine plaits which hung down over her eyes. 'They always stick out when I do them.'

'Let's have a look,' I said. 'Well, it'd help if you used more than four hairs at a time. Can't make a good plait with less than six.' I tweaked the plaits loose and started again. 'How do you fix the ends anyway? You can't just leave them loose like this? What d'you use, blu-tack? Or bubblegum?'

She giggled. 'No, I've got these. Didn't have time to do my hair properly before I left. I had to find my music and stuff'. She fished in her anorak pocket and pulled out a handful of little beaded rubber bands and while I worked she chattered away, asking me my name and how long was I staying until Edith interrupted and told her not to be so nosy.

For a moment she was deflated but then, patting her hair she asked 'How many can you make, d'you think?'

'I'm on number three. Is there a time limit then?'

'Well, yes. I've got this piano lesson with Mrs Oakes at nine o'clock. But I've got to see Dad first. Oh, listen. I think that's his boat now. You'll see him if you look out the window.'

I quickly finished the third plait and the child leapt up and went to examine my handiwork in the hall mirror. 'Wow! That's really great.'

I went past her to the front room and peered out. A boat was grounded just below the kitchen window on the patch of gritty mud left by low tide and the builder was hauling out scaffolding poles and handing them to a lanky youth who stood with mud half-way up his wellington boots.

'Here, you'd better unlock that door down the ope for them,' called Edith from the kitchen, and as I came in she opened the table drawer and took out two keys. 'The other one's for the cellar. He'll be wanting to store his gear there.'

'I'll show you the way,' Katie ran ahead of me down the cobbled alley to the door at the seaward end and put the key into the lock. It was stiff, however, and she handed over to me and it took all my strength to turn it but at last we got it open and found ourselves standing on a small stone jetty with a flight of broad steps leading down to the walkway I'd seen from the window.

Her father and the youth looked up as we started down the steps. 'Well, pigeon. What are you doing here? Work experience week is it?' Jack Edwards was smiling up at his daughter and gave a friendly wave in my direction.

She paused on the bottom step looking uneasily at the seaweed encrusted wooden walkway. 'Hi Wayne,' she waved to the youth and then to her father, 'I need a fiver, dad. Mum never had any change and she was too busy with Sammy to come to the shops so she told me to ask you.'

'Same old story. But don't come any closer, sweetheart. Those planks aren't safe. Only way you can get your money is go upstairs and lower a bucket on a piece of string.' He grinned again and Wayne laughed.

'Oh dad. Come on. I'm supposed to be up at Mrs Oakes' place, like, well, ten minutes ago. Can't you bring the boat round?'

'Be a lot simpler if I lend you a fiver, wouldn't it?' I smiled at her from my perch at the top of the steps.

'Oh could you do that? Yeah, great. Bye then dad. See you,' and she hurried ahead of me to the house. In the kitchen she went over to the small blackboard, another of Mrs Green's installations, and wrote with yellow chalk, 'I 0 Lisa £5 Jack Edwards' and added the date with a flourish.

I gave her the money and she rushed off, calling 'Be back later I expect,' to us both and as she went up the alley she called back over her shoulder, 'Toby said you're cool.'

'Who's Toby?' I asked in surprise from where I stood at the door.

'He put your suitcase in Stan's taxi,' she shouted as she disappeared round the corner.

I went back indoors laughing and found Edith Rogers in a better mood than I'd yet seen. 'You'd better go round to the bakers and get some saffron buns for them. They'll want something to eat when they come up for a cup of tea dreckly.'

So off I went to get the buns and other things she wanted, but before returning to the house with the shopping, I went down through the gate at the end of the alley to see how the men were getting on. They had some scaffolding erected on either side of the lower balcony so it looked as if that one was to be fixed first, which made sense as it was easier to reach.

I went back indoors and was told by Edith to shout down and find out what time the men wanted their tea. Or coffee. Orders taken I made a pot of each and presently they came in, having shed their boots in the alley outside the door. 'If anyone wants to pinch them,' said Wayne, 'they're welcome. They'd have to be some hard up is all I can say. You should smell that mud when it's been stirred a bit.' And in fact there hung about them that unmistakable tang of sea, salt, ageing seaweed and the rest of the undefineable odours left behind by the receding tide. Quite a nice smell as long as it wasn't concentrated as it must be in the thick blobs on the men's boots outside the door. I was glad they'd left them there, in 'the ope,' as they called it, as Edith herself did.

It was a cheerful break. Wayne tucked into the buns like a starved wolf. From the look of his bony frame he'd not eaten for a week. 'Not so,' Jack told Edith when she said the boy was half starved. 'He eats enough in one day to keep me going for ten.' Then Jack spotted the message on the blackboard and pulled a crumpled five pound note out of his jeans pocket and smoothed it out apologising for the state of it.

I went over to the board and wrote across Katie's message, 'settled in full', and added the date and my signature. 'That's in case Katie comes back to check on you, Jack.' I said. He grinned and said he was pretty sure she'd do just that before the day was out. Edith said how much she'd grown, but there, they're like that at her age, and I asked how old Sammy was. Jack hesitated and then said a little sheepishly, 'Eighteen months, give or take,' and Wayne said it's no use asking him highly technical questions like that this time of the morning.

Presently I saw Edith look at the kitchen clock but in the same moment Jack was pushing back his chair. 'Well, thanks for the refreshments, ladies. But now we'd better be getting back to our Regeneration Falmouth project.'

After they'd gone back to their work, I found myself smiling at some of the nonsense they'd tossed about during their break and later Katie came back towing a girlfriend with her but this time staying only a few minutes. Both girls now had their hair in many more tiny plaits and with their sawn-off denims and skimpy sweaters they looked like teen-age girls anywhere. I don't know why I'd expected Falmouth girls to look any different but I said something about it when the men were back in the kitchen eating their lunch and they both grinned. Wayne said, 'All you up-country lot still think we're a lot of hicks in the sticks, don't you?'

And when I protested he said, 'Just think back to that petrol strike that happened years ago. All the powers-that-be were staggered that a few country bumpkins with mobiles and no organisation could almost bring the country to a standstill. And as soon as they'd made their point, they called it off again. Democracy at work.'

'But it's not that we 'up-country lot' think we're better, Wayne. It's just that we think things must be different, better, in a quiet backwater, in such a remote corner of the country,' I said.

'Quiet backwater! Wait till throwing-out time at the pubs to-night! Ask the local police about joy-riding and drugs and vandalism.' Wayne was in full cry.

Jack intervened. 'No stopping him now,' and to me he added, 'Wayne's head of the student union at the college. This is his Saturday job.'

'Yeh,' Wayne grinned. 'Got to get the dosh to feed my habit, you know.' I laughed too and felt my mental gears crashing as I adjusted a few more stereotypes.

By the time they left it was getting dark. The scaffolding to the lower balcony was still in place and they were coming back next day. 'You'll be able to sit out there in safety next week,' quipped Wayne. 'Forecast isn't good mind, but as long as you wear a wet suit, it should be OK to have your coffee on the balcony.'

They'd put some of their tools down in the cellar and I heard Edith tell Jack he'd better keep the key. Jack said 'Right, I'll keep it safe. We've stacked our stuff up on the pallets because there's the spring tide tonight.'

I exclaimed in surprise. 'But surely the water doesn't come inside the cellar, does it?'

The three of them looked at me and Jack said,

'There's a lot of people in the old flats along the front here who have their electric and gas meters in the cellars and believe me, if it's high tide and the gas runs out, they need put their wellies on to go and top up their meters'.

I was interested and would have liked to go down and take a look at this strange cellar where the tide came in and out through the walls. But they were just about to go, and as Jack now had the key, I would have to wait for a more convenient time to satisfy my growing curiosity.

CHAPTER SIX

That night Edith Rogers slept badly. She rang for me the second time at three o'clock and I made her a cup of tea. 'You'd better find one of those sleeping pills for me,' she muttered. 'I don't believe in them really, but I'm desperate.'

I found the pills and put one into her hand. 'Take it with your tea. And you needn't worry about taking them, you know. The doctor only prescribes what you need.'

Propped on her pillows she took the tablet and held the cup cradled in her hands. 'I'd like you to hire Tom Pooley's car tomorrow. I don't want to have to listen to all that banging and sawing all day long. Pooley's number is in the book by the phone. We can get away after they've had their tea break. And we'll need that folding wheelchair that's in the store room and you'll have to push me.' She glared at me as she spoke in case I should argue that I wouldn't like that. But of course, we wouldn't be able to put her electric chair into the boot of a car and I'd already been aware of that and told her it'd be OK.

For an hour or so after she'd been settled, I sat up in my own bed before slipping along to her bedroom to check she was alright. I could hear her breathing, quiet and steady but it was a while before I could get back to sleep myself. I wondered why Edith should suddenly be so desperate to get away when she'd seemed to enjoy the chat and banter of the men the previous day. But still, I doubted whether I would ever know this deeply introverted character or understand the reasons for her swift changes of mood.

Next day the men arrived early. Each morning before I dressed I liked to look out of my bedroom window to check on the weather and see what was going on in the harbour, because no matter what the hour, there was always some activity out there on the water. Today the sky was pearly-white and the surface of the water was shadowed and wrinkled, a sweep of pale grey velvet, with the pile brushed this way and that by the wind and currents playing their complicated games. Only one vessel chugged down from the Penryn river, crumpling the water ahead of its bows and trailing the widening pleats of its wake. I looked more closely and recognised Wayne's bright red and white sweatshirt. I stood for a while watching the boat approach. Then I swiftly showered and dressed and since Edith was still asleep I went downstairs and made a pot of tea and took the laden tray along to the front room.

The windows now opened easily as Jack had been busy with an oil can and it was pleasant to feel the coolness of the morning air on my face. Wayne and Jack soon appeared on the scaffolding and grinned their thanks for the tea. 'We'll get this lower balcony finished today but you still won't be able to use it properly because we've got to rig the scaffolding on it to get to that top one.'

As we sipped our tea, Jack strolled round pointing out all the wood that needed replacing.

'Looks OK until you start poking about. Then you find half of it has rotted at the ends. Still, it'll be nice when it's all done.'

I told them I have to go and see about hiring a car as Edith wanted a day out. I thought both their faces fell a little when I said this, but Wayne said that yes, Tom Pooley would be up and about by now. And when I phoned, Tom himself answered and said he'd bring the car down at eleven o'clock sharp.

When she was dressed and breakfasted, Edith sent me out to fetch some more cakes for the men's tea break and pasties which could stay in the warming oven for their lunch. I was surprised to find shops open on a Sunday morning, In fact there was more choice than I'd have found in my own suburb back home.

When the men came into the kitchen for their morning break, I was busily preparing a flask and picnic. Wayne said why didn't we just go to a pub for lunch. Edith was looking at her note pad and ticking off what I'd already assembled: rug, scarf, hat, umbrella... She glanced up, 'Never know what those places are like till you get there. I don't like the music, can't hear yourself think. Best be independent. And the birds can have what we don't eat.'

Wayne laughed, 'Make sure you have plenty of scraps, Lisa. I've heard seagulls are very partial this time of the year.'

Just then someone banged on the door and Tom Pooley materialised. 'No need to rush, Mrs Rogers, I'm early.' He eyed the teapot and I put another mug on the table and filled it. 'I'm parked up on the pavement but there's no wardens round this time of the day.

They're still in bed, wardens are. Comes of not being able to sleep nights from their guilty consciences slapping tickets out, left right and centre.'

But I noticed he refused a seat and drank his tea quickly. I'd packed everything now and Wayne took the bag and Jack manoeuvred Edith's wheel chair down the ramp and up the cobbles to the estate car.

Edith was helped into the front passenger seat while Jack folded the chair and stowed it in the boot and Tom handed me the keys. 'You don't have to drop me back at the garage 'cos I'm going up the road to my daughter's place. Mrs Rogers will tell you where to go. Enjoy yourselves.'

I hadn't driven for months and this car was bigger than my old Polo. And I was only too aware of the three men standing back grinning to watch me take away on the slope. I took a deep breath, determined not to make a fool of myself in front of this particular audience. I switched on the ignition, gingerly put the car in gear and slowly released the clutch. Too many revs. I eased off the throttle so they'd not have cause to call me a boy racer. Then, gently, gently, I edged the car forward. Off the pavement with barely a bump and slowly we moved ahead. I heard a cheer and some clapping from behind and gave a royal wave from the window as we turned the corner and they disappeared from view.

Edith directed me, giving her instructions in good time and with careful warning of what might lie ahead. There were so many unaccustomed hazards and despite the years I'd been driving I was nervous. The most disconcerting thing was the way a narrow road would suddenly disappear from sight, plunging down gorge-like valleys and twisting round blind bends. And I could hardly believe these roads weren't one-way systems, though after a couple of long reversings to a passing place, I gained a little confidence as I found the other car often took the initiative and pulled back first.

We were to cross the river Fal on the King Harry Ferry where I was staggered by the size of the ships tied up in this narrow river. Stunted oak trees clothed the hills on either side, their lower boughs and leaves cut off with geometric precision by the tidal waters. And while waiting in line for the ferry, we saw a couple of herons knee-deep in the green water, standing head-down like a pair of grumpy old men until with a lightning dart, one snatched its prey from the water.

Then it was our turn to board the ferry and still nervous, I edged the car up the ramp. As we reached the other bank after the short, slow crossing, Edith announced I was now in Roseland. As if on cue the sun came out and presently we reached the place where she said we'd be able to park and then walk. From here we could see Nare Head, the precipitous cliffs plunging into water so blue it was like spilled ink and the bay which had become so familiar to me over the past weeks showed me now a different face. No longer wood-clad rounded hills here but the strong sweep of the cliffs and wind-clipped grass. And of course, the sea and an immensity of sky.

There were a few other parked cars and I noticed the seasoned walkers were laden with backpacks. I helped Edith into the wheelchair and stowed our picnic bag and wet weather gear underneath and we set off. I didn't mind pushing the chair - it was quite easy except now and then when we met a stony patch. There was a stiff wind along this exposed coast and I was glad of my weatherproof coat. Edith assured me she wasn't cold, and indeed I'd wrapped her up so snugly that only her nose and eyes could be seen between the brim of her hat and the turned-up collar of her jacket. About fifteen minutes later she told me to turn the chair towards a small cleared space and I parked us both in the shelter of a high bank. I pulled the rug from the bag and sat down and found it was so warm here out of the wind that I could comfortably take off my coat.

We ate our leisurely picnic and I poured out the coffee. And it was then, after we'd eaten, that Edith began to talk. 'That internet thing you've got. You were able to get someone's address on it the other day.' And when I nodded, she went on. 'Could you find a person in Australia, do you think?'

'Well, I should think so. I've never needed to trace someone abroad, but yes, I expect I could.' I waited. Edith had burrowed down in the chair with her beaker clasped in her hands, staring out over the sea as if she was in a trance. But I knew it wasn't the stunning views that held her, but some inward vision of the past. At last she spoke. 'I've never told anyone about this. No one. But if you've got to find this address, I suppose you'll want to know what it's all about.'

I leaned forward and looked up into her face where she sat swaddled in her chair. 'Look, whatever you tell me is between the two of us. One, I don't know anyone to tell, and two, nurses get used to hearing confidences. It goes with the job.'

She nodded and slowly finished her drink and handed me the beaker. ''Twas years ago mind. I don't know if he's still alive even. That's the worst part. Not knowing anything about him after he left.' She closed her eyes and was quiet for such a long time I thought she'd fallen into a doze. I watched a cormorant dive and vanish. I found myself holding my breath and counting, waiting for it to surface but long before the bird popped up, I'd lost count and had to take several breaths myself.

'See,' Edith suddenly went on, 'you have to understand a bit about it all. Me and my husband, we never got on. 'Twas our parents pushed us to marry. His father had that shop at the front of my house, and as you can see, 'tisn't the best vantage place for a business. Now, my father owned a lot of properties, mostly houses, but he also had two good shops along the main street. They more or less arranged it between them. Fred's father, (Fred was my husband's name) he would sell his shop but keep the house at the back for us to live in. Then he would use the money raised to re-stock the new premises he was going to rent from my father. They both knew it would be a good business move. The way my parents saw it was, here was I, nearing thirty, nothing much to look at; about time I was wed. And they knew Fred's father very well. They must have heard the gossip about Fred too, but they turned a blind eye to that. And Bill Rogers, his father, could see he was on to a good thing for his son. Like I said, my father owned a lot of houses as well as the shops. He'd inherited them when his father died and rented out the shops he owned, not wanting to do sales business. He'd been left a tidy sum too and bought up a lot more old houses and did them up. We were able to live quite comfortably on the rents and my father spent his time looking after the properties.' She paused and a little bitterly, added, 'He had a good life, always did exactly what he wanted. Anyway, we got married, Fred and me, and moved into the house. I never liked the place from the beginning but it was convenient for Fred and of course it belonged to him, not to me. That meant a lot to him.

'Our married life is private. But I will say 'twas bad

right from the beginning...' There was another long pause and I could see she had to struggle to go on. 'I'd been used to doing my father's accounts, I'd been to night school to get qualified. So it was natural I did the shop accounts too for Fred's father. We had two good sales assistants. Just as well 'cos Fred was out gallavanting half the time. But our shop did well right from the start. We had a lot of ironmongery and we'd gone into electrical goods. This was in the fifties and television was beginning to catch on in a big way. Fred talked my father into letting him rent the other shop in the main street as well. He said I could run the existing one and he'd start up in the other.

'Well, my father agreed. But that second shop never did much though there was still lot of demand. Then Fred was ill with pleurisy for a couple of weeks and I took over, leaving our good staff in my shop. I soon found out there was nothing wrong with the turnover, it was Fred. He must have been salting away hundreds. After that Fred's father came back into the business. So Fred was able to get away with doing nothing and getting a good income. But his father wouldn't hear a word against him...

'Then one day Charlie Trevelyan came into the shop. It was in the dinner hour and I was alone. It wasn't busy and I used to eat my sandwich behind the counter. Charlie and me, well, we hit it off right from the start. I'd never felt like that about anyone before. Not anyone. He was working at the docks, shift work, so he was able to drop in and see me when it was quiet. I changed. I started getting my hair done regular. Bought some nice clothes at Debenhams. I was a fool, because of course Fred began to get suspicious. Why he should care beats me. He used to have several women on the go at the same time. Pride, I suppose.

'Half day closing was Wednesday and Fred always played golf then. So Charlie and me were able to meet up. He had a little Austin Seven and once he drove us over here and we parked where you did just now. We walked up here. Right here was where we made our plans to go away together. To Australia, said Charlie. I had money of my own from my mother's people, so we would have been alright until Charlie got work.

'Then, like I said, Fred got wind of it. One afternoon, Charlie had come round to the cottage where we used to meet and we were making plans. Then Fred burst in. Shouting like a madman. He snatched a knife from the kitchen drawer and held it at my throat. He told Charlie if he didn't leave Falmouth, my body would be found floating in the harbour. 'I'll make it look like suicide,' he said, 'cos she's not worth swinging for.'

'I was afraid he'd kill Charlie too, and I told him to go. Go right away. He knew what I meant, Australia. And that's what he did. I never saw him before he left; he was too afraid for me. I knew he'd get in touch though so I just waited. But I never heard from him. Not a word. And then, nearly five years later, Fred was drunk one day and he jeered at me. Told me he'd seen

48

Charlie's landlady a month after he'd left and she'd given him a letter addressed to me. "Well," he said, "couldn't turn down a chance like that, now could I? I said I'd pass it on and I gave her a fiver. Lot of money, in her eyes. Told her any more letters, give them to me, yes?"

'You can imagine how I felt when I heard that...' She stopped talking and her throat worked convulsively for a moment. Then she controlled herself and went on speaking in her normal voice. 'He said how did I ever think I'd let that Charlie Trevelyan get the better of him. He put his head back and laughed then, slapping his thighs and stamping the floor like a madman. He had these strong white teeth, like a wolf I always thought. Well. 'twas too late for me to find out where Charlie was. The old landlady had just died, Fred would never have told me else, drunk or no, he wasn't stupid. But no one else knew Charlie's address, he'd no family, see. So I was no better off than before, except I knew now that Charlie had tried. Had written. Only it hurt that he should think it was me who didn't care; that I'd never bothered to answer his letters. And it nearly drove me mad to think *he'd* been reading what Charlie had written just for me...' She fumbled under the rug for her handkerchief and blew her nose.

'So now, if it can be done, I'd like to find out if he's still alive. I want to let him know I would have come to him. That I still feel for him to this day and there's never been another soul in my life since.' Her voice was thick with tears and no one could hear her story without feeling a wrench of sympathy and my own throat ached as I heard her out.

Then I stood up, stiff from sitting on the ground so long. 'Of course I'll try and work it out if I can. Come on, I'll get you back to the car and put the heater on. You look chilled. And tonight I'll see what I can do, but I'm no expert, I might have to ask my friends to steer me in the right direction, but I'm sure it can be done.'

Cold or not, she was much more cheerful on the way back and insisted we stop at a cafe where she knew we could get a cream tea. And by the time we arrived back at the house, the men had gone. We went to inspect the front room balcony and despite the scaffolding set up to reach the floor above, the firm planks felt good beneath my feet and the fresh clean smell of sawdust mingled with the tang of the sea as dusk gathered together the last light of the evening sun and slipped it gently into the quiet harbour.

CHAPTER SEVEN

During the evening Edith said she wanted to watch me work on my laptop but I found her gaze unsettling in its intensity as I hardly knew where to start. The screen kept filling with unwanted messages and I *was* trying to clear them when Edith gave a low moan. I turned quickly and saw her double over in her chair. I went to her and counted her racing pulse as she struggled upright. 'I'll be alright in a minute,' she said. 'Just get me up to bed.' But half an hour later she was still ashen and I told her I was going to send for the doctor. When she actually nodded and said his number was downstairs by the telephone I became even more worried because she'd made no secret of her contempt for the medical profession from the start. And that included me of course. But just as I was about to leave the room I remembered it was Sunday evening. She must have read my mind because she muttered, 'He'll come quick enough, don't worry. I pay him plenty. He's a private doctor.

I found the name, Dr West, and a young woman answered my call. She said she'd fetch her father and when I explained Edith's condition to him, he did indeed say he'd come along right away and twenty minutes later I was letting him in. Dr West was a well groomed and suave man, in his fifties with thick white hair. He asked both of us some searching questions and then examined Edith thoroughly. At last he straightened and said he thought the cramps were probably from a stomach bug. He left some easing medicine, and smiled and soothed her with the most polished bedside manner I'd seen. But despite the smooth surface, I recognised he was an experienced and thorough doctor. In the hall as he was leaving, he turned to me and looked grave. 'Keep an eye on her. I think we may have to get her in for some tests,' and he named the private hospital where he worked. 'Could just be a blip, mind. If she doesn't have a recurrence in the next few days she should be in the clear.' He looked me up and down and I remembered I'd not so much as combed my hair since we'd got back from our trip, what with Edith's insistence that I begin work on my computer as soon as we'd finished our light meal. And then, of course, she'd collapsed. Now he smiled a practised heart-warming smile and told me he could see she was in the best of hands. Would quite like to be there himself he said with a meaning gleam in his eyes. I felt my flesh crawl and breathed a sigh of relief when I'd closed the door behind him. Creep, I thought. And of course it all came back with a rush, all the fear and loss of self worth that I'd suffered at the hands of my tormentor over the last three years.

Edith's bell rang. I was sitting curled in a ball on the stairs and it took a huge effort of willpower to unclench my muscles and haul myself up by the banisters, step by step to the landing. At least Edith was too ill to notice my pale face. I told her the doctor had said she must take one of those sleeping tablets and I would check on her several times in the night. Despite her obvious pain, she gripped my hand, the first voluntary physical contact she'd sought. 'Won't you be able to work on that machine of yours then?'

I shook my head. 'It's getting late now and I won't be able to concentrate, always listening for your bell. Don't worry, we've got all day tomorrow. All the time in the world.'

'That's just it,' she said, 'I've not got all the time in the world. And neither has Charlie, that's if he's still alive.' She suddenly turned her head away from me and. buried her face in the pillow. She waved her hand to send me away and from the doorway as I looked back, I could see her shoulders shaking under a storm of tears. I went downstairs to make myself a cup of tea and found the screen saver on my laptop still whirling its pattern of stars quietly to itself. Like a miniature universe, I thought wryly as I closed down the computer. But when at last I pulled back my bedroom curtains before going to bed, there were no stars at all to be seen in the dark sky, all light blotted out by massed clouds moving steadily in the stiffening wind. I dozed fitfully through the night, getting up several times to see if Edith needed me and I was kept awake by the noise of the wind which was now blowing a gale. Once or twice she turned her strained face towards the door when I came in, but most times she seemed to be in a restless, pain-filled sleep.

As dawn broke I took a quick shower and somewhat refreshed, I dressed and went along to her bedroom once again. This time she was deeply asleep and her face had lost some of the pallor of the night.

I went downstairs and made myself some toast and coffee. Outside I could hear the roar of the wind and looking through the window saw white horses sweeping across the harbour. Curtains of rain whirled past, sometimes revealing sometimes concealing the hills on the farther shore. What a day. And to think only yesterday I'd been sitting in the sun somewhere over there on the other side of the bay. Just then I was startled from my reverie by the ring of the doorbell. Wondering if perhaps the doctor had decided to drop in on his patient, I drew back the bolts and opened the door.

Jack Edwards stood there, water running off his oilskins. He grinned at my surprised face. 'I'm supposed to be building a block wall today. Not a good idea. But I thought seeing the wind is from the southwest I'd be sheltered on the scaffolding. So I can get on with the work on the underside of that balcony of yours.'

'Good lord!' I could hardly believe anyone would be able to work outside on such a day, but I was pleased to see his smiling face and once again I thought what a lucky woman his wife was. Ah well. I asked if he'd like a cup of coffee before he braved the elements and we sat at the kitchen table listening to the wind howling outside.

'You surely never came round in your boat!' I said.

'Nope. No need today, because we stacked all the wood we'd brought over, down in the cellar. I walked down the hill from my house and it's not so bad as it sounds when you're out in it.'

I asked where Wayne was before remembering he was a student. 'Yes, our mate Wayne is over at college organising the revolution, I expect. But what I'll be doing today, fixing new timbers under the balcony is pretty much a one-man job anyway.'

I told him I'd called the doctor out for Edith yesterday and he looked concerned. 'Oh heck, in that case I'd better not start. She can do without all the hammering. Never mind, I've got one or two other small indoor jobs in town I can get round to today.' He slowly finished his coffee and smiled his warm smile, blue eyes crinkling at the corners. 'Pity, but there it is.' As he stood up he turned to me, suddenly serious. 'What do you think of her, Mrs Rogers?'

I paused before answering. Until the confidences I'd heard yesterday I certainly hadn't liked her, though I wouldn't have said so. But now, I felt a protective regard for her so I said I found her very direct and outspoken but I got along with her fine. He nodded his head. 'Glad to hear that. Not everyone can and she's already got through a couple of carers since Mrs Green left.' He was shrugging into his waterproofs as he spoke. 'A woman of mystery, our Mrs Rogers. Everyone thought she'd leave this place when her husband disappeared, but no, she's still here after all these years.'

'Disappeared! I understood he'd drowned?' I frowned my question at him.

'Well, that was the story. Boat found drifting and empty and all that. But they never found a body and it was seven years before he could be declared dead.'

I thought back through the conversations with Edith. 'Yes, she'd mentioned they used to keep the boat moored below the house. 'So no one knows what happened to him?'

Jack gave a somewhat apologetic grin, 'It all happened years ago, over thirty I suppose, but as a kid growing up, me and my mates used to run past the shop if she was inside because everyone thought she'd done him in. But my mother's known her all her life and worked in her shop for a time. She's always had a lot of time for Edith. She said it was common knowledge Fred Rogers was having a fling with a woman across the water at Flushing,' he nodded in the direction of the opposite shore. 'Seems he used to take the boat over of an evening. He'd lost his driving licence see, and he'd messed around in boats all his life. In more ways than one according to my mum.' Again he gave that wry grin. 'Still, although there was a lot of talk, the police found nothing they could pin on her and she carried on with the business as before. Only, when the seven years was up, and he was officially declared dead, she passed over the running of the shops to his two nephews. Anyway, that's all ancient history; water under the bridge. And now I'd better be getting on or there'll be no work at all done today.'

I went with him to the door, chewing over this information. I could understand why people might think Edith capable of such a thing; her frigid manner and air of displeasure took a while to get used to. But now I felt I'd seen something of the woman behind the facade and I didn't dislike what I saw.

At the door Jack suddenly struck his forehead with the palm of his hand. 'Whoops. Nearly forgot. My tools are in the cellar.' He fished in the voluminous pockets and pulled out a heavy key. 'Been down there, have you?' he asked.

'No, I've not. Edith said the steps are unsafe.'

'They certainly are if you don't take care, but it's an interesting place. The tide'll be full this afternoon and by then the floor of the cellar will be under a foot of water, maybe more with the sea so rough today.'

'I'd like to see that, but of course, you've got to take the key with you.'

He nodded. 'Yes, and I wouldn't like to think of you going down there on your own at all. Place still gives me the creeps. Come on down now and see for yourself' He unlocked the door and as it swung open I saw stone steps falling away, steep and narrow into darkness. Jack pressed a switch and dim light appeared below. 'Careful, mind,' he said. 'These steps are very old and worn. Been here much longer than the house. Probably been the base of more than one of the old wooden houses that were built along here in the past.' He held open the door and I gingerly followed him down.

The air was intensely cold; a damp chill that seemed to go straight into my bones. The steps were of some smooth type of stone, slate maybe, and they varied in height and were slippery with the damp. Edith wasn't exaggerating when she'd said they were dangerous. At the bottom we stepped into a long narrow cellar. A striplight was fixed to the low ceiling and the floor looked to be earthen. But it felt firm underfoot and when I remarked on it to Jack, he told me the deposit on the surface was just the silt left by the spring tides.

There were deep shelves along a couple of walls and three or four wooden pallets stacked up in a corner with Jack's bags of cement and sand on top. He nodded towards the pallets. 'Got to keep everything out of reach of the water.' He took down his bag of tools from one of the shelves and pointed to the sea-facing wall. 'See, it's built of unmortared stone so the water can run through. Much less pressure than if the wall is solid. Those old engineers knew a thing or two,' there was admiration in his voice. 'The sea goes right underneath the main street in places. Get a combination of high tide and heavy rain and manhole covers used to start popping up and gushing water all over the place, though it has been sorted out over the years.'

I stood in the centre of the cellar, arms folded and shoulders hunched against the chill, 'It's got to be colder in here than it is outside!' I shivered as I spoke.

'It is. I don't suppose the temperature down here ever changes by more than a degree or two. Come on, you'll get pneumonia.' He took his bag up first and then reached down his hand to help me up those steep steps. His grasp was warm and firm, I could feel the smooth callouses on his palm against my skin as he drew me up. For a moment there in the hall we stood so close it was almost an embrace. His eyes met mine and I stepped jerkily away muttering that I must go up and see Edith (though it could have been only a quarter of an hour since my last check). He nodded, briefly, abruptly, as if he understood, And it was only later that I admitted to myself the disappointment I'd seen in his eyes as I'd turned to go upstairs and perhaps too, a look of sudden hurt.

How could I? How could I let myself think these things. Jack was a married man. He had two children. What on earth would his daughter Katie think if she knew the way my thoughts were drifting...

He called goodbye and when the door had closed behind him, I sat on the stairs much as I had on the previous evening but this time, instead of disgust, I could feel only the beating of my heart and a great surge of desire. The nurse in me told me that maybe this was the beginning of my cure; the first time in years I'd be able to think of a man without that instant rush of revulsion. But not Jack. I couldn't have an affair with Jack, a man who had a family. It sounded foolish even to myself, but I knew I liked him too much to be satisfied with a brief fling. I must just make sure to avoid being alone with him again. Surely that would be easy enough... And I trailed up the stairs to Edith's room with a heavy heart.

CHAPTER EIGHT

She was still asleep when I checked but I was too uneasy to be able to carry on where I'd left off the previous evening in my search on the internet. My son Josh always tells me a good computer is wasted on me; I only use a fraction of the information that's there. So instead of sitting at the laptop I sorted out a couple of the kitchen cupboards and made a list of a few things to buy if I felt confident enough to leave Edith for a short while.

Presently she woke and I made her a drink. She took her medication and agreed with my suggestion to try and sleep some more. Her stomach still pained her, she said, and no, she didn't want that doctor. She was feeling better than she had; must give it time.

I went downstairs and made myself a sandwich and just as I was rinsing my plate, the doorbell rang again. When I opened it a smiling white-haired woman stood on the step. 'Hello,' she said, 'you must be Nurse Sands. Jack phoned just now and told me Edie's poorly and I thought I'd drop in and see her. We're old friends, known each other for years. Oh, I'm Jack's mother by the way,' and she gave me another beaming smile.

I felt my colour rise as she spoke and was glad to hear Edith call from upstairs. Whatever else ailed her, her hearing was remarkable good. 'Come in, of course,' I said. 'That's Edith calling down now, I think she recognised your voice. Go along up and I'll bring you both some tea. She needs plenty of fluids so maybe she'll drink a cup to keep you company.'

By the time I took the tray up to them, Jack's mother had Edith sitting up and she did look quite a lot better, with some colour in her cheeks. They were chatting when I came in and Edith told me to call her friend Maud. 'I believe Nurse Sands likes to be called Lisa, but you can please yourself about that, Maud.'

Maud Edwards laughed. She had the same eyes as her son, a brilliant blue in her fresh complexioned face. 'Lisa'll do very well, Edie. You live in the past, that's your trouble.' And she sipped her tea, quite at ease with my formidable employer. 'In fact,' she went on, 'you might as well go out and get a bit of fresh air my dear. Mind there's plenty of that blowing about outside, you need weights in your pocket on a day like this unless you want to end up in the harbour. But it has stopped raining for the time anyway.'

The thought of a break was tempting and Edith nodded her head. 'Yes, off you go. I'm a lot better. Had plenty of sleep and that old pain's nearly gone now.'

So, without giving them a chance to change their minds, I went downstairs and grabbed my coat and bag and shopping list, and out I went. As Jack's mother had said, the rain had stopped and although it was still blowing hard, the street was comparatively sheltered. It was good to be out of the house and I was walking briskly along when I heard someone shout my name.

'Lisa!'

I turned to see who it was and Katie came skipping across the road, followed by another girl and a couple of boys. 'Hello' says Katie with a beaming smile.

'Well, hello to you. But what are you doing in town today? Bunking off, are you?' And although I smiled, I felt a little uneasy.

Several heads shook, no it was a non-teaching day; an inset day. I recognised one of the boys from the train, Toby perhaps and listening to their chat, found it was so. Katie said, 'We're off to Joseph's dad's cafe for a milkshake.'

'A milkshake' I said, 'On a day like this!" And I laughed as I watched them cross the road, Katie's hair, pony-tailed today, swinging wildly.

I went into a couple of shops and then walked along to watch the sea tossing the boats around even within the shelter of a sea wall. After being blown about for a bit I set off back along the street, thinking I might have a go at searching for Charlie on the net. As I passed Joseph's cafe, Katie and her friends waved cheerily at me from the window where the group sat and I suddenly thought they'd almost certainly be able to help me in my quest. I opened the door and went inside. Apart from Katie's noisy friends the place was empty. They looked a little wary as I crossed the room to them but when I told them I'd like some internet advice, they relaxed, faces alert. Some of their skins were petal smooth, some a rash of teenage acne but in each of them a barely-reined zest for life and eager enquiring eyes looked up at me. There were a few derisory remarks about this being the house of the brain dead, but when I told them I wanted to trace a few old friends in the States and Australia on the net, I got a loud chorus of conflicting advice. Names of search engines and web sites were bandied about and then someone said to ask Joseph, he could nerd for England. Joseph blushed to the tips of his sticking-out ears. 'Easiest way if you've no idea exactly where they are, is call up the phone books.'

I looked blank so he asked me the name of my Internet provider and then told me which search engine I should use. I was impressed; he seemed to be expert on every aspect of computing. 'I'm going to write computer instruction manuals when I leave school,' he said casually.

'Yeah! Write instruction manuals! D'you think you'll be able to stand the excitement, Joseph? Just think, the tension, the drama, all those exciting plots...' They rocked with laughter at their own wit but now that his blush had faded, he just grinned at them and I could see the steady, focused young man he would be. And Katie's friend Stacey gave him such a warm encouraging smile that his ears soon began to redden again.

A vulgar but witty joke changed the subject and as soon as the boys had finished their competition to see who could syphon up the drink in the bottom of their glasses most noisily, I stood up and opened my bag.

'This one's on me. Cheaper than going to a computer professional.' I said. Joseph said no, it was on the house, but his father in the background looked so forbidding that I went across to the counter and paid up with a smile. I waved as I left, feeling it was only a matter of time before they would all be thrown out and after the racket they'd just made, I could hardly blame Joseph's dad if he did shoo them out the minute I left.

But I was glad I'd met them; all the unhappiness and illness I'd left behind in the house was, if not forgotten, at least distanced. It was impossible to be depressed in their lively company. And of course, I'd got those headings Joseph had jotted down for me, safely tucked in my pocket.

CHAPTER NINE

When Maud had gone, I settled myself at the kitchen table with my laptop and took out the piece of paper with Joseph's instructions and found the search engine he'd told me to use. He'd so earnestly explained to me what would happen; no doubt if I'd asked he'd have made me a drawing of those wires and pins that seem to make up the computer's insides. But to me, all this technology is, if not exactly black magic, then a deep midnight blue, perhaps. And his list was certainly a magician's spell, because when I pressed the keys, the search engine's messages hurtled through space and homed in on their distant target, a man-made star, hanging trembling in its place in the unceasing whirl of the firmament. And hey presto! up popped the information on my screen, the way into the Australian phone book.

Diffidently I typed in the name Trevelyan and was told there were eight Trevelyans in Australia. But not a single Charles. So I might still have to go to Joseph's next instructions to find the voters' lists. But first I'd start with these numbers; there might just be a family connection.

I began with Adelaide. Four names and numbers appeared and I saved them before going on. There was one hyphenated name, Trevelyan-Ayrs which I wondered about. I included it and moved on to

Brisbane. It took a while, but presently I sat with the list before me. Eight names and the double-barrelled one.

Just then Edith's bell rang. I quickly saved my work and closed down the machine. She'd just woken up, and felt she'd like to get up for an hour. She didn't want to dress; just put on her dressing gown and go downstairs. Change of scene. She splashed her face with cold water in the bathroom and as I helped her on to the chairlift, I told her I'd just managed to get hold of some telephone numbers in Australia, but that I hadn't yet found Charlie's name.

Her face lit up. 'Then phone them! Phone them all. Someone will know something, there's not that many Trevelyans surely.'

I made her comfortable in the kitchen before pointing out that it would be very late in Australia by now; I didn't think strangers would appreciate getting calls in the small hours. Reluctantly she agreed, but I could see she was bitterly chafing at the delay. She asked to see the names on the screen so I booted up again and showed her what I'd done, letting her call up the search engine herself. She was amazed at the speed of it all and checked carefully that I'd not missed one of the Trevelyans. 'Of course,' she said, 'Charlie may be ex-directory.'

I was tired and felt a spurt of irritation and bit back the remark that Charlie may even be dead. I stood up quickly and made some tea; not that I wanted it, but for something to do. Working as a nurse for so many years I'd never found it particularly hard to cope with difficult patients; there was always the knowledge I'd soon be moving on to the next person and there were other nurses to call on if things got too bad. What I'd not allowed for when I took this post, was the feeling of claustrophobia, of being completely shut into the world of someone so dependent and without the reassurance of another nurse coming on duty in a few hours. Before I'd started I'd been promised there'd be a relief carer for an hour each day, but unless I counted Susan, our silent cleaning woman, I was on my own. If Edith needed the loo while I was out, Susan would certainly be no help. That was why Maud Edward's offer to stay with Edith today so I could have a break had been such an unexpected pleasure. Previously even my briefest sorties at Edith's behest had been guilt-ridden. There, that guilt thing again; I could hear my counsellor's voice telling me I must get rid of my guilt, that most negative of feelings.

Waiting now for the kettle to boil, I did a few exercises, stretching and bending, for once ignoring Edith's sardonic stare. However, by the time I'd set the cups on the table she did make some effort to be more friendly. 'Thank you for finding those names,' she said. She stared into her cup. 'To think, I might have been able to find him years ago. Years ago.'

Talk about negative feelings.

To change the subject I said it was nice of Maud to

call and I'd met her granddaughter in town when I'd gone out. In fact it was one of Katie's friends who'd told me how to find those telephone numbers. She unbent a little more. 'Maud's always been a good friend. Loyal. Not many like that.'

'If you feel well enough tomorrow,' I said, 'we'll go out for a walk. Doesn't do to be indoors all the time and according to the forecast, this wind should die down and the weather is supposed to get better as the week goes on.'

'Well, we've got to make all those phone calls first thing. Outings will have to wait until we've found Charlie.' I crossed my fingers that at least one of our calls would give us some news, otherwise I could see I was going to get very little exercise in the foreseeable future.

I prepared a light meal but Edith didn't want any. She still looked ill but when I tentatively suggested we get the doctor round to have another look at her she practically bit my head off 'First thing he'd be doing is getting me into that hospital of his for tests. Anything to boost up his fees. Nothing wrong with my stomach that won't get better in a day or two.'

I smiled to myself as I remembered those were practically the doctor's own words. But at the same time, it was obvious she was far from well. Maybe it was simply a stomach bug, but her pallor bothered me and I felt sure before long she would have to go in for those tests, in spite of herself. Though how to persuade her would be another story.

But one thing was certain; it wouldn't be until we found Charlie, or news of Charlie. For the rest of the evening Edith sat in her chair in the front room with me and we watched an ancient comedy. At least, we both stared at the screen: I don't know what Edith saw but for my own part I was remembering Katie's bright face across the table from me in the cafe and her grandmother, Maud Edward's blue eyes smiling at me, and wishing I could stop thinking of Jack and the feel of his warm hand grasping mine that morning as he helped me up the cellar steps.

Outside the wind was still blowing hard, booming in the chimney and I was sure I felt the building shudder as the waves hit the basement. 'Tis nothing,' said Edith, I've known much worse,' and she went on to tell some stories of storms much wilder than this.

But presently she asked quietly if I'd take her back upstairs and when I helped her into bed and measured out her medication, she supposed she'd better take another of those sleeping pills; pass the night a bit quicker, she said.

I was in the kitchen an hour later when the phone rang and my spirits lifted when I heard my friend Katherine's voice. But for once, the chat about my old colleagues failed to spark my interest. I told her about the storm we'd been having; and how according to Edith, the spray from the waves sometimes splashed the bedroom windows. However, Katherine was on call and as we spoke her bleep went off and she had to go. I put down the phone, suddenly lonely and missing the pace and demands of hospital work. But then, remembering the terror I'd felt every time I set out for home I knew I wouldn't change places just yet.

I took myself off to bed; I'd had little sleep last night and knew I must make several checks on my patient again tonight so I selected a paper back thriller from the couple I'd brought with me and decided to read until I fell asleep. I drew back my bedroom curtains last thing, and it seemed to me the wind was dying down; perhaps the forecast would be right and we'd have a better day tomorrow.

I slept better than I'd hoped. Twice I woke and listened and once I went along to Edith's room. She was awake but said she was comfortable enough and told me not to bother to come and check again; she'd ring if she wanted anything.

CHAPTER TEN

Next morning I woke to see sunshine polishing the moving water. Yesterday's white horses had galloped away into the night leaving behind a restless swell on which the moored vessels bobbed alarmingly. The air had the clarity that still amazed me and under the golden light of the sun, cows grazing in the fields on the hills across the water stood out like cardboard cut-outs. I opened the window an inch and took lungfuls of the clean air until the stiff breeze I'd let in started to riffle through the clothing laid out on my chair. I closed the window again and found myself laughing with the sheer delight of living.

I stopped abruptly as I remembered the depths of the fear and depression I'd left behind.

I closed my eyes and made a huge effort to recapture my mood of delight. I wasn't going to let those memories keep slamming on the brakes as I fled away. But I was glad when Edith's bell rang and I had other things to think of.

At least she looked a little better. The glitter in her eyes was not down to a fever, unless you could call the desire to hear from Charlie a fever. (Though to that I'd have to answer, yes you could.) She didn't want to waste time having a bath, but I persuaded her she'd feel fresher for a quick shower after having spent most of yesterday in bed. And she did look much better by the time she was dressed and she actually managed to eat a small helping of cereal for her breakfast. She was sipping tea from her beaker with her good hand when the peal of the phone bell startled us both. A man's voice asked if he could speak to Mrs Rogers. 'George Davies here. I'm her agent.'

Edith took the call, said she'd already told him her views of the subject and rang off right away. Poor man! She looked across at me. 'I want you to get started on those calls now, can't be bothered talking to the likes of him. He's my rent collector, not my financial adviser.' She didn't explain what he'd been asking but I could see if he told her he'd just discovered oil under one of her properties she'd still have hung up on him.

I cleared the table carefully to make way for the laptop. Edith wanted to keep a check on those telephone numbers while I started to make the phone calls. Thankfully it was a cordless phone and though it usually stayed firmly fixed to its base on the hall table, at least we could make the calls in the relative comfort of the kitchen.

It would be early evening in Australia now, as good a time to call as any. But the very first Trevelyan I contacted in Adelaide dashed my hopes of a quick result. When I told her I was trying to trace a Charles Trevelyan who'd gone to Australia from Cornwall in the late nineteen seventies, she said, 'Oh, our family's been here since my great grandfather's time. Eighteen sixty-five to be precise.' She was helpful though, because when I mentioned the other Adelaide Trevelyans, she told me they were all members of her family. She wished me luck with her search, said she was interested in all things Cornish and a member of a Cornish migrants society. In fact, she would have kept me talking much longer if Edith hadn't been glaring at me. I thanked her and put the phone down as soon as I could.

'Well, that's the Adelaide ones, apart from the double-barrelled name. Oh dear, I forgot to ask her about that one.'

'Oh, that'll be the same family. Try the Brisbane numbers. I've a feeling Charlie said he liked the sound of Queensland. Try those.'

But there was no reply from any of the numbers. I could hear the familiar burr-burr, burr-burr echo and re-echo in those faraway homes, but no one picked up the receiver. By now I'd exhausted the numbers and told Edith we'd simply have to phone every hour or so until hopefully someone answered. She looked so bitterly disappointed and deflated that I said I would try that hyphenated name anyway.

The phone was answered at the second ring. 'Oh,' said a young woman's voice, 'I thought it was my son ringing.' Quickly I trotted out my prepared spiel and I almost fell backwards with shock when she said, 'Oh, that'll be dad! What a surprise! He's living with my sister and her husband on the station in Queens. Queensland, that is. Look, just give me your number and I'll phone them later, only my son'll do his nut if he can't reach me.' I waited while she got a pen and she repeated our number carefully. 'Lucky for you I kept my maiden name, isn't it? My sister just took her husband's name when they got married. But I like the sound of Trevelyan-Ayrs. And dad likes it too, said it sounds like a Cornish breeze! I expect he'll get in touch though he's been very poorly lately. Sorry, but I must hang up on you now. If dad can't get back to you for any reason I'll call you myself. But don't expect to hear until later, about nine-ish our time. OK? Really must go now. Bye-bye.' And she was gone.

I repeated the conversation to Edith who had been listening avidly and had already grasped that I was speaking to Charlie's daughter. Her eyes glittered with tears. 'So he is alive! I thought it was too much to hope for. What time did she say they would call? Did she mean Charlie would call then or what?'

'I think she was saying she wouldn't have time to phone her dad until later, she was about to go and collect her son or something. She said either Charlie or she herself would phone but it wouldn't be until about our lunchtime. So we've time to go out for a while if you like.'

She took some persuading but as the weather was so much better she did reluctantly agree, 'But not very far, mind,' she said.

I tucked the rug round her and we went out. I'd noticed from our very first walk, that though people would greet her with a nod or brief good-day, no one ever paused beside her chair to speak to her. So today I was surprised when a man crossed the street and came up to Edith who stopped her chair and waited.

'I was just coming round to your place, Mrs Rogers. It's about Mrs Semmens' place. You know, the one her granddaughter would like to buy.'

As they were obviously talking business I excused myself and went along to the baker's. From my place in the queue I could see them engrossed in their talk, Edith's face stern and set, the man emphasising a point with waving hand. With the fresh bread in my bag, I went back to them and this time Edith briefly introduced me. 'This is my rent collector. What they call an agent, these days I b'lieve. George Davies.' We shook hands and I felt sorry for the man as he said he hoped I'd enjoy my time in Falmouth. The thick glasses he wore couldn't hide the worry in his eyes and he quickly turned back to Edith. 'Mrs Rogers, I know it's your decision, but could you at least think it over for another day or two. There's a lot in what the girl says, you know.'

'You're quite right, Mr Davies. It is my decision. So good day to you now, we've other matters to attend to.' And she rolled her chair away from us. The man shot me a look of despair and shook his head but he managed to drag up a smile for me as he turned and walked disconsolately away.

'We'll go down to the chimney,' Edith said abruptly. I

knew the place she meant, the brick stack where customs officers of old had burned contraband tobacco. We went past the chimney and on to the end of the wall which enclosed a small harbour where the water slapped about amongst the collection of boats and dinghies. I sat on a dinghy which lay upturned on the wall alongside a pile of lobster pots, surprised at how quickly yesterday's sea had gone down and I said as much to Edith.

'Not one to hold a grudge, the sea. That's what my dad used to say. Mind, he hardly ever set foot in a boat so he wasn't the one to talk.' Her lips twitched. I decided Edith was making a joke so I smiled. 'That George Davies. Don't know why I got such a softie as him to do my work for me. That girl he was talking about, her grandmother is a tenant of mine, brought the girl up and now she wants to buy the house for the two of them. 'Course, as a sitting tenant, the place'd be cheap. But not as cheap as she wants it. Says she's just qualified as a teacher and wouldn't be able to afford what I'm asking. George Davies says if she can't buy this, she's going to have to take a job up north somewhere, only place she can afford to buy.'

I wasn't sure whether she wanted a comment from me or not, but as the silence stretched I said, 'So Mr Davies thinks you should sell?'

She snorted. 'He said I'd have to live a lot of years to get that amount back in rent. Cheeky beggar! Not a very tactful thing to say to a sick woman, is it?' And as she turned to me I could see she was making another joke. Thoughts of Charlie must indeed be mellowing her. I smiled again.

'You'd agree with him, I suppose.' She shot me a penetrating stare.

The wood of the old boat on which I perched was smooth and warm to the touch and I rubbed my finger along the peeling paint. 'I'm no business woman, so yes, I think in your place I'd let her have it for whatever she offered.'

'You said right there, my girl. You certainly aren't a business woman.'

Stung, I retorted, 'Well, I've got a flat of my own and a couple of tenants too. And that more than covers the mortgage. So I'm not totally stupid.'

She pulled the rug closer to her with her shaking hands. 'Well, stupid or not,' she said, 'we've got to get back before that phone rings.'

Silently I followed her as she drove her chair up the slope to the street. What a rude woman! No wonder the long-suffering Mrs Green had taken her release in both hands when she got the chance. Breaking her hip was a pretty drastic way to resign, but she was certainly making the most of her enforced retirement; another postcard had come yesterday from her son's home in Wales.

But during the silent walk back to the house, Edith must have been thinking. As we turned down the hop-way she said over her shoulder, 'When we get in you can phone that George Davies. Leave the message on the answer phone. The girl can have the place. For what she offered.'

Smiling to myself, I helped her into the kitchen and put the kettle on. Then I went into the hall and found the Davies number in her small book. I reached George Davies' answer-phone and spoke slowly and clearly, 'This message is on behalf of Mrs Rogers. She has decided to take your advice and sell the Semmens place to the girl for what she offered. Thank you.'

When I went into the kitchen I couldn't tell from her face whether she was satisfied or not; her normal expression was never exactly sweetness and light. But while I was making a cup of tea, the phone rang. 'That'll be George Davies, no doubt,' Edith remarked bitterly, 'checking to see if I've gone off my head.'

I went out into the hall and picked up the phone. Far away I distinctly heard the faint echo of my 'hello' and then there was that eerie silence before the caller's words came across the world. 'Charlie Trevelyan here. Can I speak to Edith?'

I turned as I said I'd get her and went back into the kitchen, phone in hand. Edith sat frozen in her chair, eyes wide with disbelief and her face white as parchment as I told her Charlie was on the line and put the phone in her outstretched hand.

Quickly I left the kitchen and went along to the front room to give her privacy. I opened the french window and stepped carefully round the scaffolding to go and lean on the sturdy new railing. But for once I stared unseeingly at the water, thinking only of the man and woman who were speaking now, across space and generations. Poor Edith. I was sorry for my nasty reactions earlier; compared to her, my own life had been blessed; a bed of roses even though it had been a pretty prickly one for the last few years.

I stood in the one small patch of sunshine the jumble of neighbouring buildings allowed, wondering when Jack would be able to fix my bedroom balcony. If he waited until Edith was well enough to stand the noise, I felt it would remain unfixed and unsafe for a long time.

The gentle slapping of the wavelets against the ancient stones of the wall below drew me from my musing. Slap and run, they came and went like playful children, until a bigger swell heaved itself so high towards me I was about to step back until it suddenly dropped teasingly away. From nowhere came the thought, I wonder if the cellar floor is awash, down there in the darkness.

By now my fingers were turning blue in the fresh wind and I went back inside and closed the french window again. I wondered if Edith was still talking and decided to stay out of the way until she rang for me. And another fifteen minutes passed before the door opened and she wheeled herself into the room.

No one could say Edith was a beauty at the best of times, yet now, though her eyes were red and swollen with tears, she was simply radiant. 'I'd like a cup of tea,' she said quietly, 'and then you can go out for a bit. Give me some time to myself'.

So I fetched her the tea and left her to relish and replay over and over the words she and her old lover had exchanged for the first time in so many years.

CHAPTER ELEVEN

The shopping took a matter of minutes so to pass the time I explored two more of the little seaward running alleys I'd so far only glimpsed from the street. At the end of one there was a small pier and I sat on a bollard overlooking the water, sheltered from the breeze and warmed by the pale sunshine. An enormous seagull settled on the railing a few feet away and watched me with its hard golden eyes. I'd never been so close to such a large gull before and for a good five minutes we sized one another up. Eventually it decided I wasn't going to produce a hotdog from my bag and with a great swish of its wings, launched itself into the blue air and was away. I sat there for a while longer, remembering the curve of the great beak, the contrast between its remorseless gaze and the soft whiteness of that downy breast. And the surge in the air as it lifted off and wheeled away into the sky. I wondered idly how many people before me had sat on this same stone bollard, watching the sea and the birds, thinking much the thoughts that were running through my head. And the moment felt like a healing.

It was almost an hour before I went back to the house. Edith wasn't in the kitchen and I went along to the front room to check before going upstairs. To my surprise, there she was, sitting with the window opened, looking out. 'Be nice when this scaffolding's gone,' she said, 'but 'tis a bit too cold for me to sit outside yet.'

I agreed it was and closed the window when she asked and we went back to the kitchen. She seemed to want to talk, but not face to face as it were. So I set about preparing lunch and only turned to glance at her from time to time as she spoke. 'Charlie's wife died years ago,' she said. 'They had two girls, both married now and with children of their own. He still lives on the farm, sheep station he calls it, though he said it took a long time to build it up. The daughter he lives with married one of the hands; the best of fellows, said Charlie, and a couple of years ago he made the place over to them. His other daughter is the one living in Adelaide that you spoke to. She's a lawyer, same as her husband and they're doing very well. Better than the farm, he said, where they're going through the worst drought he's ever known. They got rid of a lot of cattle and sheep in the first months, but scores more have died since then as the bore holes dried up. He said he's sunk plenty of bore holes in his time but on a lot of his land, the water is so far down he could never afford to drill that deep. And now when they need the extra wells so much, the bank won't finance them. No wonder, Charlie said, they're just about on their uppers. His son-in-law has gone to work for a brother in the city and makes enough to keep the place ticking over until the rains come and his daughter works like a man keeping things going there at home.' She paused again as she'd done several times in this recital, not speaking, just

83

staring into space with that small tenderness about her lips, as if recalling his conversation word by word.

At last I asked, 'Did he say anything about not being able to get in touch with you?' She raised her eyes to mine and gave a sad little smile. 'He guessed Fred was the reason I didn't write back. He was so afraid for my safety that after the third letter wasn't answered, he decided he mustn't write any more. If those letters had fallen into the wrong hands, he didn't know what Fred would do to me. So he moved out into the country and found work on a sheep station. Some years later he married one of the daughters and they set up together on a small place. Three hundred acres, he said.' She gave a snort. 'Small place! That'd be a big farm here in Cornwall. And then they gradually built up, buying up a neighbour's place and increasing their stock. Charlie said for years they did well and that's when he sank those wells of his, but he made a big mistake, he said, not sinking deep ones when he had the chance.'

While she was telling me her story, I cooked us both a light lunch, but she hardly touched her poached fish. Over the meal she said she'd told him about her illness. About the wheelchair. 'And you were right,'she said, 'he wants a photo of me. He made me write down that e-mail address to send it to.'

I said I thought I'd better wash and set her hair before I got the camera out. She went along with my suggestion eagerly enough and during the afternoon I took several more pictures before I managed to get one she was reasonably satisfied with. I scanned it into the machine and as she watched, fascinated while I sent it, she regaled me with more of his conversation as she replayed it slowly in her mind.

'Charlie asked what the weather is like here and I told him about the storm yesterday and the water in the harbour white with waves. He misses the sea, he said. He still misses the sea. Although he said the land reminds him of the ocean sometimes, the way it rolls and changes with the light.'

My worries that all this emotional nostalgia might make her more ill, didn't bear fruit. In fact, I thought she looked better than I'd yet seen her. She said she might manage a little of that fish later and sent me out for a particular yoghurt she liked. When I got back she told me George Davies had phoned. She said he couldn't believe his ears when he heard my message on the answer phone and was ringing to find out if she'd changed her mind. 'I told him, no,' she said. 'and he might as well contact the solicitor and get things moving. He jumped at that idea because I'm sure he thinks I'm going off my head and he'd like to get things settled before they cart me off.' Once again there was that twist of her lips; another joke.

Maud Edwards phoned during the afternoon and spoke to Edith. I always left the room when she had a phone call and I used the time today to do some ironing in the linen room, one of those windowless storerooms which led off the passage in the hall. Tall open racks lined the walls, stacked with enough sheets and pillowcases to stock a small hotel. I set up the ironing board, liking the smell of the clean laundry as I did my work. When I went back to the kitchen Edith told me what Maud had called about. She'd suggested Edith spent Saturday at her house so as not to be disturbed by the hammering because Jack was worried about getting the work done, especially that top balcony. 'Maud said you might be glad of a day to yourself though you're more than welcome to stay with us, she said.'

A whole day to myself! But Edith hadn't finished yet. 'I can get a taxi to Maud's place, but if you want to hire that car again, of course you must put it on my account.' Well! Mellowing indeed. I said how nice of Maud that was, and it gave me plenty of time to decide where to go. Part of me would like to stay in the house and make tea for Jack and Wayne and enjoy their cheerful banter. But I already knew that was a choice I must not make.

But later that afternoon Edith flagged; all the colour and brightness left her face and I helped her up to her bedroom and into bed. I bit my lip, wondering whether to risk her wrath and call the doctor but once I'd got her settled she looked a little better again and asked for the TV times. She thought she'd watch something for an hour or two, she said.

I spent an uneasy evening, worrying about my charge. While her multiple sclerosis was not getting any worse at present, those stomach cramps seemed only briefly to improve before coming back again, so fiercely that the colour drained from her face and she doubled up with pain. In the end, I knew I must report her condition to her doctor and I called him at his home. He said unless she herself agreed to have the necessary tests done, it was pointless to irritate her, as he put it. 'She's got more than enough bile as it is,' he jauntily remarked. 'Just keep an eye on her but if she collapses, you must take the bull by the horns and call an ambulance. Only way to get her the treatment that in my opinion she really needs.'

Feeling slightly relieved at having spoken to the doctor (who this time made no personal comments) I settled down to check my own e-mails and contact my friends. I phoned the two nurses who were renting my flat and they told me they'd had another visit from 'you know who.' I felt the familiar twist in my stomach but my voice was quite steady when I told them to call the police if he bothered them. But they insisted he was perfectly polite and calm; just wanted to know where I was and that I was OK. Not to worry, they told me, we didn't tell him anything; said you hadn't left an address; you just wanted to get away from everything for a time. No contact at all, they told him. The two girls didn't in fact know where I was and didn't even have my phone number; calling from Edith's phone (with her permission) I always withheld my number before I dialled. It wasn't that I didn't trust my friends, but I'd experienced too much of my adversary's cunning not to cover my tracks to the best of my ability.

As I put down the phone I realised at least I wasn't reduced to a quivering jelly at the very thought of him. Perhaps Katherine Avery, my wise nursing officer, was right, maybe I would be strong enough to face him one of these days.

But now I went along to the front room and opened the window and stood for a while, listening to the quiet lap of the water below and staring into the gathering darkness. The air was still now, the breeze having gone down as the sun set. A couple of boats were still moving across the harbour, their red and green lights bright and the sound of their engines muffled by the distance. I closed the window and settled down with my book but found it difficult to concentrate. I kept thinking of the wonder in Edith's face as she spoke of Charlie, astonished that the flame between them seemed to have leapt back into life simply by the contact of a phone call. I couldn't doubt the strength of feeling on Edith's part, how much on his side was nostalgia and latent homesickness, only time would tell. And as Edith had so recently reminded me, time was something neither had in abundance. But for the present, their renewed contact seemed wholely positive. And two other people had good reason to be grateful it had happened; George Davies who'd been trying so hard to get Edith's agreement until this morning, and the young teacher who'd just been granted a fair price for the house she wanted to buy. I smiled to myself, if this was day one of Edith's new outlook on life, I wondered what the rest would bring.

But my whimsical imaginings could hardly have been further off the mark. Upstairs, staring unseeingly at the television as she so often did, Edith must already have been working out how to fulfil her dark plans; trying to find ways to free herself from this hated house and the albatross she'd borne for so many years. It was just as well I knew nothing of her thoughts for when at last I closed the front room window and took myself off to bed, I felt more light of heart than for a long time past, and before I slept spent pleasant minutes planning where I should go on my promised day of freedom.

CHAPTER TWELVE

Next day Edith's solicitor breezed in. I'd answered the doorbell and found a tall good-looking man leaning against the wall, fair hair flopping over his forehead. He gave me a thousand watt smile and held out his hand. 'I'm Darren Cornish. I think Mrs Rogers is expecting me. And you?' I told him my name and he grasped my hand and held it much longer than was needed. Another practised ladies man, I thought, but at least there was a mischievous humour about him that was appealing. He was in his early thirties I should think, at least several years younger than me.

In the kitchen he pulled out a chair and sat so he was facing Edith, took both her hands in his and beamed at her. Edith though, was impervious to his charm and shook him off, answering his enquiries about her health impatiently. 'Did George Davies tell you what I want to do, then?' she asked abruptly.

'Yes he did, Mrs Rogers. He's given me all the details of the property and the girl's name. A lucky girl, if I may say so.' But the questioning eyebrow he raised brought no further explanation from Edith.

I excused myself and left them to their business while I slipped out to the shop on the corner for a newspaper, dodging the owner's eighteen year old son Sean who liked to collar customers for one of his long rambling chats. I took my paper along to the front room and presently Edith called and asked if we could all have a cup of coffee. While it was infusing, I checked my e-mails and found one from Australia. Edith's face lit up when I told her and I showed her how to retrieve it and print it if she wished. I let her practise on one of my short messages and at her suggestion took the solicitor and the tray of coffee along to the other room. She would join us soon, she said.

'What's that all about?' Darren Cornish asked. 'I've never seen her so animated. Marble statues generally have the edge on her for warmth and humanity. And this business of selling young Patricia that house way below market value. It's not the Edith I've known of old. What have you been feeding her on?'

I just smiled and said it was nothing to do with me.

'But this Australian stuff, what is it all?'

I was offhand, for this was Edith's business and from the way he blatantly discussed this client and that with her, their foibles and weaknesses, I knew whatever I told him would be grist to his mill. I had seen Edith encouraging his confidences, but I was pretty sure she wouldn't want her own personal affairs bandied about to all and sundry. So, 'Just an old friend she's got in contact with,' I said. 'And now I'd better go and make sure she's OK.' Anything to get away from this inquisition, from the mischievous smiling eyes that implied we were on the same side; that confidences were to be shared between friends.

I put my head round the kitchen door and found Edith

holding a sheet of paper in her hand. She looked up. 'How can I take that off the screen? You don't want my stuff left on it do you?'

I told her how to wipe it and stood back while she did. So this was to be strictly private. I didn't mind, I'd no wish to read her private correspondence and was glad I'd not given in to the solicitor's blandishments and told him about Edith's old flame. She folded her precious piece of paper and held it in her lap as she joined us for coffee. 'Call me Darren,' kept the conversation going in his lively way and I couldn't help laughing at his imitations of his senior partner. Edith too, was amused though a couple of weeks ago I wouldn't have recognised that downward turn of her lips as a sign of mirth.

Presently he collected his briefcase and said he'd pop in again next week with the draft conveyance; the searches shouldn't take long, he'd make sure they were expedited, he said. At Edith's request, I showed him out. 'Well I don't know what's come over her, I'm sure, but she's a different woman to the one I've known all these years.' Once again there was that challenge in his eyes and once again I turned away with an offhand smile. He needn't think he'd made another easy catch today, I thought.

That afternoon I was asked to phone George Davies again and ask him to come and see Edith as soon as possible, bringing the details of all her properties with him. 'I know he's a bit too soft for his own good, but he is thorough, I'll give him that, and he does his best for me too.' Praise indeed from my dour employer.

In the evening I had to show Edith how to send an e-mail and there were no guesses as to its destination. The following day, though, I took a message for her as she was in the bath at the time. It was a phone call from Charlie's daughter Emma to say Charlie had gone down to Brisbane for a new pair of glasses. 'He broke his a while ago and he's been using an old pair. But all this sitting at the computer,' she said with a laugh, 'he decided to get new ones. And a friend was flying his plane down today, so dad decided to hitch a lift. Saves hours of driving.' We chatted a bit more about the distances in Queensland and she asked me to give Edith her best. 'Been a shot in the arm for dad, y'know. Tell her he'll be coming back on our neighbour's plane in a day or two, not sure when. But he'll call her soon as he gets back.' She asked after Edith and I told her she wasn't very well but getting in touch with Charlie had given her a huge boost. She laughed. 'Yeah, love's young dream isn't in it, my word,' and by the time I put the phone down I felt as if we were old friends.

Edith was disappointed not to have spoken to Emma herself, and even more let down that Charlie would be away for a few days. I suggested she might like to send his daughter a thank you e-mail and it bucked her up amazingly. She ate quite well that day and seemed at last free of those sudden worrying bouts of pain. Hopefully the doctor's diagnosis of a stomach bug had been right after all.

After I'd got her dressed and we'd gone downstairs she said she needed to make a couple more phone calls. 'You can go and do your bit of shopping,' she said. 'Susan will be here in a minute and anyway, I shan't need anything done for me for a while yet.' So once again I was being sent out of the way while she made her calls. I didn't mind, her business affairs were no concern of mine and I was beginning to be more relaxed about leaving her for the occasional half hour.

In town I bumped into Maud Edwards, almost literally outside the chemists. 'Are you staying for lunch when you bring Edith up on Saturday, Lisa?' she asked. 'You're more than welcome, but I wouldn't blame you for taking yourself off for the day.' And she smiled her agreement when I said I thought I'd make a day of it since she'd so kindly given me the chance.

On an impulse I suggested we have a coffee in one of the cafes overlooking the harbour and she agreed right away. 'I'm dying to show you my garden,' she said as she dunked a biscuit in her cup. 'Lovely,' she said with a smile, 'I'm afraid of cracking my bridge on one of these hard ginger nuts, so you must forgive me.' As a committed dunker myself, I just laughed and joined her.

'You were telling me about your garden,' I prompted.

'Oh yes. We're at the end of a terrace and there was supposed to be another cottage built there but they never got round to it. So I've got all this extra space. It's on a slope mind, not easy, as my late husband used

94

to complain. But I've always been very keen and over the years, though I say it myself, it's become very nice. Anyway, you'll see it for yourself on Saturday. So tell me, how is Edith?'

'She seems quite a bit better today as a matter of fact. And there's a lot of news though I think I'd better leave it for Edith to tell you herself, I'm sure she'll be disappointed if she finds you already know. But now I really must get back to her. I'll tell her we met, though and I can't wait for Saturday.' And as I stood up to leave I told her I'd decided to take the ferry across to St Mawes on my free day, but of course there'd be plenty of time to look round her garden when I brought Edith to her house on Saturday morning.

CHAPTER THIRTEEN

When Saturday morning dawned a light breeze juggled soft clouds across the pale sky and sunshine spilled as bright as sudden spotlights through the blue gaps. 'Be nice later on today,' pronounced Edith in such a tone of certitude that I guessed the clouds would already be preparing their flight. We heard the putt-putt of the engine of Jack's boat as we were having our leisurely breakfast and when I looked out of the window, he and Wayne were already unloading some more timber. I went out to the town in my now familiar routine of shopping for the two men's lunch, making sure as Edith instructed, to get enough to fatten up that boy a bit. Then I called Stan's taxi and as we waited for him to arrive I went up to my bedroom to collect my jacket and bag. Jack and Wayne were on the scaffolding and I opened the window to tell them we were just off and where the food was; to help themselves as usual. They both gave their cheerful smiles and I was careful not to let my eyes meet Jack's, afraid of what I might read there. Or for that matter, what he might see betrayed in mine. And going downstairs I paused and took a deep breath and gave myself a mental lecture though I knew only too well it was already falling on deaf ears.

I made sure all Edith's various tablets were in her handbag and then the bell rang and helpful Stan was at the door, ready to assist with the wheelchair and we were soon off to Maud's house. The taxi wove its way round the town, losing me along side streets I'd not yet explored despite my growing familiarity with the town, and presently we climbed one of those steep hills that crowd the port and drew up at the end of a terrace. Maud came out to greet us and Stan waved a cheerful goodbye as he drove off. Maud's cottage was surprisingly spacious and Edith was soon ensconced in her chair in the conservatory which had stunning views over the harbour. While she made us a pot of tea Maud suggested I might like to take a look round that garden of hers; she'd join me as soon as she'd given Edith her tea; Edith wasn't one for gardens, never had been.

I went up some granite steps at the back of the house and well might she be proud of her creation. The garden had an almost Mediterranean feel about it, so full was it of colour and light. There were three terraced areas built into the steep slope, and at the back of the uppermost, a pair of dracaena palms leaned towards each other making a bower for the bench beneath; a sun trap already by mid morning. In front was a small level lawn bordered with hebe and hydrangea and a number of other shrubs

I wandered around admiring and examining flowers and shrubs, strangers to my limited knowledge and Maud soon joined me and we strolled about for a while as she told me where this plant and that had come from. 'All my friends know what I'm like. They never throw away a cutting though I can't see where I can put another plant! But come on, we mustn't leave Edith on her own too long. I'm dying to hear her news anyway.'

A pleasant hour or so later I picked up my bag and waved goodbye to the two women and walked away down the hill. And it was with a truly holiday feeling that I bought my ticket on the pier and presently boarded the ferry with the other passengers who'd been cheerfully waiting, leaning on the railings and watching the goings-on between the boats. The water was calm as a lagoon as we moved off and from the deck, across a reach of the harbour I could see Jack and Wayne busy at work on the balcony. I waved foolishly, suddenly disconsolate and lonely, but then I saw Wayne wave and point and Jack too turned and raised his arm in salute. For a moment they stood there and as they turned and went on with their work I found myself smiling. Quickly I composed my mouth and went off to find a place on the top deck where I could make the most of the view. Several of the passengers were below in the covered cabin but a few hardy souls stood near the rails in the bows. The town receded as we forged ahead and the opposite hills grew steadily larger.

The last time I'd been on a boat was four years ago when I'd gone to Venice with Josh, before *that man* moved into my life and turned me into a hunted being, only able to behave with a semblance of normality while working inside my hospital, surrounded by the familiar members of staff. My stomach now lurched but I found with some relief it wasn't from an attack of nerves, but for the more prosaic reason that the boat was suddenly bucking and tossing. One of my fellow passengers, seeing me peer over the side, told me we'd just entered Carrick Roads. 'With several rivers and creeks emptying themselves into the bay here, and with the tide moving in the other direction, you can expect a bit of movement.' He was a pleasant elderly man and chatted interestingly until he excused himself and said he must go downstairs for a drink. Alone again, I watched eagerly as the other shore, crowned with its own small castle, came gradually nearer and twenty minutes or so after boarding we all disembarked on the waterfront at St Mawes.

I walked along the road fronting the beach, heading towards the Percuil River and admiring the expensive houses that stood in manicured lawns overlooking the bay. Very handsome indeed, but not the little fishing village I'd somehow expected to find. There were traces of the past of course, and a number of old cottages now converted into choice homes. I wandered about, glad to be on my own, able to stand and stare at will and I was enchanted by an old well I came upon. I read the notice which told me it was named after the Saint Mawes himself and was reputed to have healing powers. Here the little lanes between the houses were so narrow that you could imagine a laden packhorse, or a woman bearing a yoke across her shoulders with water from the well, would hardly have room to pass along. I've always liked to 'touch history' as Josh used to say, and it was comforting to feel part of something so much bigger than our own lives; it made me appreciate that my own problems were not of such great importance after all.

My stomach rumbled and I looked with surprise at my watch. We'd breakfasted earlier than usual and I went to read a menu board outside the Victory Inn, a very ancient looking pub. The food sounded promising although when I opened the door it took a moment for my eyes to adjust to the gloom of the beamed low-ceilinged room. As it was still fairly early it was only half full and there was no loud music. It would do.

At the bar as I was looking at the menu, a grey-haired woman standing alongside nodded at me. 'If you were about to choose that veggie lasagne, I can recommend it. It's always my first choice.' I smiled my thanks. The man accompanying her nodded cheerfully at me as he collected their drinks and bore them away to a table near the window. I did indeed choose the lasagne and was crossing the room, glass of wine in my hand to find somewhere to sit when I heard my name called. 'Ms Sands! Hello, what a surprise to find you here. Whatever have you done with the dragon? Or are you running away?' Darren Cornish, Edith's solicitor was on his feet, standing alongside the table where the couple who'd just left the bar were sitting. I told him rather coolly that it was my day off and was about to turn away when the grey-headed woman spoke.

'My dear girl, if you're on your own, do join us. Any

friend of Darren's, you know,' and she gave me her quizzical smile. Her husband seconded the invitation and Darren drew out a chair and next minute I was sitting at their table, one of the party. And it felt like a party. The couple were clients of Darren's, Ruth and Ivor Simms and the conversation sparkled like the wine in my glass. The food, when it arrived was every bit as good as Ruth had promised and for over an hour we sat and chatted and laughed. To my surprise, I discovered Darren was something of a local historian as well as the seasoned gossip I'd already become acquainted with, and he told us fascinating tales of the past as well as some tit-bits concerning a prominent Falmouth businessman that had Ruth and Ivor enthralled.

Over our coffee, Darren suddenly glanced guiltily at his watch. 'Damn!' he said. 'I've got to go I'm afraid. Have to be back in Falmouth for an appointment. I can't give you a lift home, I suppose?' he smiled down at me.

I shook my head. 'I've promised myself a visit to the castle and after those stories you've been telling, I'm doubly interested.'

'Fair enough,' he said. 'Another time then.' He bent and kissed Ruth's cheek, looked for a moment as though he might do the same to me but fortunately I was the other side of big Ivor. He left the pub to a chorus of goodbyes, including a rather meaningful one from the pretty barmaid. Ruth laughed fondly as he left saying something about 'incorrigible' though I did think Ivor looked a little disapproving.

The castle was every bit as good as I'd expected. I tagged on to a group of tourists and we were given the tour and more information than I for one could possibly take in. But walking round the ancient building I could almost see the sturdy dark haired soldiers moving up and down the narrow twisting staircases, and feel the tensions of the governor and wily local dignitaries who had to tread that tricky tightrope between state and church.

I spent a happy hour roaming about, relaxed and interested and leaned over the balustrades to take in yet more stunning views from this opposite arm of the bay. But when at last I walked back down the hill and spotted the ferry waiting at the jetty, I started to run afraid of missing it, and I knew only too well why I so suddenly wanted to get back to Edith's house.

CHAPTER FOURTEEN

When I stepped off the ferry on to the pier, I stood for a moment uncertain which way to go. My conscience had nagged me during the whole crossing that the first thing I should do was to fetch Edith. But it was my day off, so I cheerfully turned my back on the call of duty and sped off in the hope I'd see Jack before he left. There'd been no sign of him or Wayne on the scaffolding as the ferry drew in, but just as my heart was sinking with disappointment, I'd spotted his boat tied up below our windows. So my conscience hardly stood a chance.

The door wasn't locked and I scooted upstairs to do my hair after the breezy crossing and then opened my bedroom window and looked out. Jack called up from somewhere below, 'Ah, home is the sailor, home from the sea,' and I smiled and asked if it was safe now to step outside. He climbed up the scaffolding and stepped over the railing and came towards me. 'Yep, all it needs now is the top coat. Undercoat's dried very well. Feels good, doesn't it?' He stamped a foot against the new decking, turned, swung himself over the railing - and vanished.

I gave a cry, so choked in my throat I doubt it could be heard and staggered on failing legs to the balcony, clutched at the rail and leaned over, terrified of what I would see. And there was Jack, lying on the scaffold planks two feet below, grinning up at me. And down on the lower balcony, Wayne was laughing his head off.

I gave another strangled cry and as my legs gave out, collapsed onto my knees, head down, hands outspread on the warm timbers. In an instant Jack was on the balcony beside me. 'Christ! I'm sorry Lisa! I'm a bloody fool. I thought you'd know it was just a stupid joke.'

Wayne joined him, his face long and worried. He read the mixture of horror and relief and anger on mine as I raised my head and quickly leapt to Jack's defence. 'Aw, come on Lisa. That's the sort of thing we do all the time on building sites.'

'Maybe.' I sat back on my heels, heart still hammering away. 'Maybe. But I'm a nurse, not a builder, or perhaps they've not taught you the difference yet at that college of yours.'

Jack reached down and grasped both my wrists. 'Come on. Up you come. And I'll make you a cup of sugary tea. That's right for shock, isn't it.' I could see that despite the laughter in his eyes he was contrite and concerned and if Wayne hadn't been there I felt he might have pulled me into his arms to comfort me and say again he was sorry. But Wayne was there, thank goodness, or so my conscience said, and Jack took refuge in humour and presently we were all three sitting downstairs drinking the promised sedative. I checked the time and smothered an exclamation. 'I must go and collect Edith. Your poor mother will be worn to a frazzle by now.'

'I'll give you a lift back. My van is round at the slipway; we'll take the boat back and it'll only be a few extra minutes.' He grinned. 'You can enjoy another sea voyage, free this time. OK?'

And just then the doorbell chimed and I found Katie there, smiling happily. 'Great, I've caught dad so my poor legs don't have to tackle that hill again.' And when she found we were all to take the boat round to the slipway, she beamed. 'Good, you can show Lisa how to handle the boat, Dad and then in the Easter holidays she can take me and the others across to our beach.'

'Katie! I know you think I'm the cat's whiskers, but not even a genius like me can do all that between here and the slipway. Lisa's in a hurry anyway, she's worried how Gran's coping with Mrs R.'

'Oh, she's fine,' said Katie airily. 'I was up there earlier and Madam was chatting away, really enjoying herself. If that's possible,' she added.

So once again I turned a deaf ear to my inner voice and locked the door behind us all with a light heart. Wayne helped me climb into the swaying boat while Jack lowered the outboard motor and soon we were chugging off up river on the high tide towards Penryn. Katie was sitting beside me, Jack at the tiller and Wayne in the bow. 'He won't let me and my friends take the boat out,' she said, turning to me. 'Says there has to be someone like him with me, some responsible adult.'

'Huh!' I said. 'Responsible adult indeed.'

Jack and Wayne both laughed and Katie said, 'What?' and looked from one to another, bright eyes enquiring. Wayne filled her in on the balcony episode and she thought it was hilarious. All too soon we reached the slipway and transferred the tools and odds and ends to the van. Wayne said he'd walk home, he wanted to call at the shop on the way and I was glad of Katie's presence, glad not to be alone with Jack. Maybe he too felt the same way, though on the face of it at least he was his usual relaxed and affable self. But I was all too aware of Katie's bright eyes that might already have seen more than I would wish, though she was apparently as friendly as ever towards me.

My conscience started yelling 'I told you so!' at me the minute I set foot in the door of Mabel's cottage. Edith was lying on the couch in the sitting room looking quite ghastly. Maud raised her worried face and quickly read the guilt written on mine. 'She's been fine up to half an hour ago, Lisa. Really fine. Then she said she had this pain and I helped her onto the settee. Are you going to call her doctor?'

'No. No doctor.' Edith's voice rasped. 'Just get me home. You know I'll be alright when I get to bed, Nurse Sands.' She spoke through gritted teeth and I quickly fetched her bag while Jack phoned for Stan's taxi. He said he'd be only too glad to take her back himself but could see she needed more comfort than the van would allow but he'd come along with Stan to give us a hand into the house.

A quarter of an hour later the two men were helping me get Edith up the stairs; she hardly able to remain upright on the chair lift. They carried her, unprotesting for once into the bedroom and I told them thank you and I'd manage now and heard the door downstairs close quietly behind them. I undressed her gently and slipped her nightdress over her head and sponged her face. When she curled herself into a foetal ball under the quilt I said I think I must get the doctor but a shrivelled hand shot out and grasped mine with surprising strength. 'No. Not yet. I'm not ready to go into hospital yet. There's things I have to do.' Her voice died away in a gasp of pain and her hand fell from mine and jerked into a fist.

In all my years of hospital work, there was always someone to call on; doctors, consultants and other people with whom to share your worries. And standing in Edith's bedroom that night I felt I was betraying all my training when I just stood and called no one. All my experience cried out she needed more than I could give her. But still I stood, bound by her commands to wait; to do nothing. With hindsight I find it hard to believe I didn't call an ambulance immediately as I felt I should. But it's not so easy to remember now, the strength and power of the woman's personality and the banked rage or hatred that burned in her; that bent you to her will. And of course, even in hospital it's not permitted to go against a patient's expressed wish. So I waited, sponged her face now and then. And waited.

A long hour dragged by; an endless age to the woman silent on the bed. But at last she slowly unclenched her fists and some of the rigidity of her body relaxed. 'Get me a hot drink,' she said.

Quickly I went downstairs and made tea the way she decreed and filled a hot water bottle. When I placed the wrapped bottle on the bed, she reached out her hands and drew it towards her, cradling it for a moment like a baby and then lowering it to her abdomen. 'Leave the tea on the table,' she said, 'and go away now. I'm alright. And if you call that doctor, you can pack your bags.' So I put the beaker of tea with its plastic straw beside the bed and quietly left the room.

Well. She must be feeling a little better to have said all that. But I paced my bedroom floor anxiously for a long time before I felt I could go downstairs again. At last though, I made another cup of tea for myself and ate the solitary bun that Wayne had missed. Then I locked up and went back upstairs and lay on my bed trying to read, but listening all the time for Edith's bell.

Several times I quietly entered her bedroom and stood near the bed, checking on her breathing. Once she turned and asked for a sleeping tablet and I steadied the glass of water as she swallowed it. Soon she slept but I had a troubled night feeling I was worse than useless, unable as I was to persuade my patient where her best interests lay.

At last morning came, and at least she seemed no worse. She agreed with me, to my surprise, that it would be better to stay in bed for a while. The men arrived early to finish off their work and Jack asked how Edith was; his mother was anxious about her but didn't like to phone in case it disturbed her. I told him she seemed a little better and I'd ring Maud myself in a minute.

'Don't worry about making tea and so on, Lisa. We've brought a couple of flasks and sandwiches so as not to trouble you. We won't be long doing the painting anyway, and we'll take the scaffolding down as quietly as we can. Then we'll put the second coat on next weekend and we won't need the scaffolding for that. But we might as well use it today seeing it's there.' He looked at me for a moment and then said, 'You look washed out. If you get the chance, Lisa, go and lie down for an hour.'

I was touched by his genuine concern and felt foolish tears begin to well, so I turned away and said I thought I heard Edith's bell. And later, on my own again and more composed, I phoned his mother and brought her up to date with matters. She agreed with me that it wouldn't do to go against her wishes. 'There's no way you'll get her into hospital, my dear. No way at all. Nothing will prize her away from that horrible dark house. Though I must say opening up those balconies will make it a lot better. You know, in all the years I've known her, I've never seen them in use before.'

The day dragged its feet. I heard the occasional clang as the scaffolding was taken down despite Jack and Wayne's best efforts. And early in the afternoon they tapped on the door to say they were off now. They put the remainder of the paint down in the cellar and handed me the cellar key and asked me to lock the door by the jetty after they'd gone in the boat. I thanked them a little distractedly, tired and worried about my charge.

But by early evening Edith did seem to be much more her old self. That is, rude, bossy and irascible. I was relieved beyond measure. Downstairs I made a large omelette and arranged a small portion of it on a plate for Edith. I took the tray upstairs and perched on the end of her bed while we both ate in a state almost of companionship. 'You were going to phone that doctor last night, weren't you?' she suddenly said. And when I agreed that yes, I almost did, she said 'I meant it, you know. If you get me sent to hospital, you're fired.'

Companionship indeed.

'Alright, if that's what you want, but it's no big deal, you know. Hospital, I mean. And if they can sort out this stomach thing, you'll be grateful.'

She glared at me, her sunken eyes glittering. 'I told you, I've things to do before that happens. Important things. And then, and only then, I'll go along with that doctor's plan for the tests. And much good it will do us all, that I know.'

I shrugged. 'As you said, it's up to you.' And to

change the subject, aware I'd never before spoken so heartlessly to a patient, I added, 'Shouldn't Charlie be back from his trip to Brisbane soon?'

She sat up a little straighter. 'Have you checked those e-mails yet today?' And when I admitted, startled, that I hadn't, I was immediately despatched downstairs. But apart from a brief message from Josh, there was nothing. Her face fell when I told her but then to my surprise, she asked how was my son. Where was his college, would he be able to come and see you over Easter, and so on. Of course, she couldn't have chosen a better subject for me to talk about and it was only as I put out my bedside light that night, that I realised it was her way of making amends; afraid perhaps that her earlier behaviour had caused serious offence. Which it had. But I hadn't realised she cared as much about what I thought.

I was quite wrong, of course; what Edith was afraid of was that if I left, she would have no one else that she could sway to carry out the grim task she must already have been scheming in her mind.

111

CHAPTER FIFTEEN

Next day, despite having agreed at first to stay in bed for an extra hour or so, Edith was soon determined to dress and go downstairs. 'That George Davies will be around dreckly with those papers I asked for. When he comes, we'll work at the kitchen table. You can go out for an hour.' She seemed to be much herself again, not complaining of any pain. Correction: not showing any signs she was in pain; for she never once actually complained.

There was still no e-mail from Charlie and it was a very bad-tempered boss that poor George had to contend with when he arrived. I made them both coffee but decided to have my own in town, since I was being so obviously sent out of the way. I went to Joseph's dad's cafe and spent a pleasant half hour people-watching, as against watching out for people, or rather for one particular person as I'd been doing for the last few years. When I'd recently spoken to Katherine on the phone, she'd told me my tormentor hadn't been bothering my tenants lately and hadn't called at the hospital either. Was it too much to hope that at last he'd got over his obsession? I found I was cautiously optimistic for the first time since he'd begun hounding me.

I saw Jack as I walked back towards the house. He was on a ladder repairing an upper window to a house in a little side street and I went towards him and called "Hello!"

He immediately climbed down and came over to me. 'Well, nice to see you. You're looking a bit better than yesterday too. Does that mean Mrs R has improved?'

'A little. She's busy in conference with George Davies at the moment. I've been told to clear out, more or less, and mind my own business.' I laughed as I spoke, foolishly pleased to be talking to Jack.

Then he took the wind out of my sails. 'Like to come out for a drink with me one evening, would you?' he asked a little diffidently.

'Come for a...' I stuttered. A picture of Katie's happy face sprang to my mind and I stepped back, appalled. 'Of course not. No.' I turned to go. To run. But not before I'd

seen Jack's stricken look and heard him mutter, 'Seems I've been reading the signals all wrong, then. Sorry.'

I didn't wait to hear any more. I hurried along the street, my cheeks burning. It was my fault of course. I had been sending him signals. I'd responded only too well to the attraction I'd felt for him and had seen he felt for me. But somehow I'd not expected him to make a move, knowing that as soon as Edith's work was finished I'd hardly be likely to see him often any more. So maybe I'd enjoyed this unspoken attraction between us too much and had depended too heavily on the knowledge that he was married and had two children. I was expecting him to be the stronger because of that.

I'm not naive; I know only too well how many marriages end up on the rocks, often as a result of some transient affair. But I've seen at first hand how much my friends' children have suffered as a result. And now, to feel I might be the cause of such a break-up...

For the first time I was sorry I'd come to Cornwall, and bitterly regretted my weakness. How on earth would I be able to look Katie in the eye next time we met? Or Maud. And Maud was coming to see Edith today. Oh God.

George and Edith were still engrossed in their business matters when I got back to the house so I went into the front room with the newspaper. But after five minutes staring at the print and taking in not a word, I opened the window and went out onto the balcony. With the scaffolding gone and the fresh new paintwork, it looked much bigger than before. The space was crying out for some potted plants and I decided I'd get a couple for my own balcony upstairs. But that small plan only briefly distracted my thoughts from Jack; from Jack's stricken face as I'd recoiled, crying no, I couldn't possibly go out with him.

George left. I made lunch and Edith ate more than she had of late. At her request I checked my e-mails again. Still nothing from Charlie. Then, just as I was clearing the table the phone rang. Once again I heard the still, echoing silence of space before I heard his voice. 'Is Edith there, my dear?'

'Yes, here she is. I'll hand her over to you,' and as I spoke I went back to the kitchen and gave her the telephone. Her voice shook as she said his name, and I felt that sudden rush of compassion which was the nearest I came to affection for her. Quickly I left the room and went out onto the balcony again, this time feeling a little better. At least someone was happy. And at least no one had got hurt in this attraction between Jack and me. Apart from me. And perhaps, Jack a little. But then, he had his family for comfort...

Maud phoned that afternoon and Edith said not to come today. She's been seeing to some business with that George Davies this morning and later on the solicitor would be coming. Leave it, she said, for a day of two. And I was glad I'd have a little time to compose myself before I met Maud again.

Edith, or course, was enormously boosted by her phone call from Charlie. Not in a seventh heaven exactly, I don't think she'd ever get quite there. Third or fourth, maybe.

'The solicitor' arrived as Edith had predicted and I was glad to see Darren Cornish again. He was so irrepressibly cheerful it was hard not to respond to his happy nature. He mentioned he'd met me over at St Mawes on Saturday and Edith interrupted to say, yes, she'd heard all about that already from me, so we'd better just get on, haven't got all day to waste on chit-chat.

I took my laptop upstairs and sent a few e-mails of my

own. I'd been neglecting my old friends of late, with only Josh getting a regular message from me, either by text or e-mail. And when I'd caught up on my messages, I sat near the window and stared out across the harbour. This afternoon the water was steel grey with a faint sheen on the surface, reflecting the dull sky overhead. A day to match my mood, cheerless and drab. Here and there a boat moved slowly across the bay but even the colours were dimmed, blotted up by the heavy clouds. Oh Jack, how could you? But then I had to remember those mixed messages of mine... How could I?

Edith's bell called me from my wallow of self-recrimination. She wanted coffee and next time Mr Cornish called she'd be needing my signature as a witness so I'd better make sure I didn't go out then. Darren's eyes met mine, his dancing with mischief as he read my face. Then I was told to have my coffee with them, business was finished for today. And Edith actually made us both laugh as she described something that had occurred long years ago to one of the clients Darren had mentioned in his gossip session. She herself didn't laugh and I thought afterwards it was a cruel story she had told. And while we'd laughed in rueful sympathy for the poor chap, the glitter in her eyes had been of glee at his misfortune.

In passing Darren had mentioned one of his lady clerks, a Miss Olga Mundy. 'What, she's still with you? I'd have thought she'd retired years ago,' said Edith with her usual lack of tact.

Darren closed his briefcase. 'Well, she could have done, but she's pretty much indispensable to us, you know. She's coming down to Penzance with me one evening this week to see a client. Not many of the younger ones are prepared to do that, they're all too busy with their families of course.'

But Edith was looking pointedly at her watch. She kept a record of the time he spent to check against his bill, she'd earlier told me. 'You can lock the door when Mr Cornish has gone,' she called over her shoulder as she wheeled herself towards the front room.

As soon as the door had closed behind her, Darren threw back his head and shook with silent laughter. 'What a woman! You must be stacking up a lot of brownie points in heaven, that's all I can say.' And as he went out of the door, he paused. 'Would you like to come with us on that Penzance trip? Our business won't take long and then we can go and have a meal in a nice place I know. How about it? You must be overdue an evening out?'

It was tempting. I remembered the chat and laughter of our lunch at St Mawes. And Miss Mundy would be there too, if in fact one was needed. But I couldn't leave Edith alone for hours in her present tricky state of health. 'I'd love to come,' I said rashly, 'but only if Mrs R is well enough to leave. And she certainly isn't at the moment. When are you going, anyway?'

'Not sure exactly. Olga has a club meeting either on

Wednesday or Thursday. So one or other of those nights. I'll give you a ring tomorrow, OK?' He started to walk away then turned and put a finger to his lips. 'If you can get away, tell Edith you're meeting friends, don't tell her it's me. She'll think I'm mixing business with pleasure and will probably want a ten per cent cut in her bill.' I laughed and agreed and felt a little more human when I went back indoors.

It was a roller coaster of a week. First the plunge into the depths after my confrontation with Jack. Then a series of ups and downs with Edith's bouts of pain. I risked her wrath and told her I couldn't be responsible for her if she didn't allow me to get Doctor West around; at least he might be able to give her something for the pain. Sullenly she agreed to see him; with hindsight I know it was because she was afraid I would leave, I'd been so adamant that he must come. Just as well I didn't flatter myself it was my nursing care she was afraid of losing; she had a lot more than that planned for me. So the doctor duly came and told her he would book her into his hospital for the tests he was sure she needed. To my amazement - and his - she agreed to his suggestion. But first she'd got a few legal matters to get sorted. A week or so, she said. And she wasn't going to stop in the hospital for longer than necessary. Fair enough, he said, a couple of nights at the most would be all that was needed at this stage.

'At this stage,' repeated Edith with a strange look.

118

And, 'We'll see about that when the time comes,' she said again.

Darren didn't phone until Wednesday morning. 'Thought I'd leave it to the last minute, Lisa, to see how madam is. We're going this evening. Any good?' I told him I'd ring back that afternoon and spent the day wrestling once again with that conscience of mine.

I didn't exactly lie to Edith. I just said a couple of friends had asked if I could join them for a meal that evening. How did she feel about me going out? She looked at me with that coldly penetrating stare and then said as long as I 'saw to her' and got her into bed before I left, she'd be fine. 'You can leave your laptop with me and I can take my time over a nice long message to Charlie.' I nodded, because I knew how long it took her to type so painstakingly with her trembling fingers. And I was secretly delighted to have got my way so easily and ran up to my bedroom to call Darren on my mobile.

'Great,' he said. 'If you can be ready seven thirtyish I'll pick you up outside. I can't hang about in the street for long as you know.' Promising I'd be waiting on the pavement, I said goodbye and quickly washed my hair. I hadn't brought many clothes with me so it didn't take long to pick out a pair of dark trousers and a cream silk shirt. It was raining again so my long mac would do quite well.

Most days Edith's main meal was lunch and she ate

119

very little after that. Today was no exception and she was happy with a bowl of vegetable soup and a roll at six o'clock. She told me she'd like to be in bed before seven. She didn't mention my shining hair and careful light makeup but added 'That'll give you time to smarten yourself up a bit,' as she put it. Although how much smartening I could manage in less than half an hour was a moot point. A back-handed compliment perhaps.

I told her I wasn't sure what time I'd get back and suddenly felt on the point of backing out. She could see me dithering and snapped, 'What difference do you think it will make if you're here or not, if I get one of those turns? And I don't need the bathroom until eleven or twelve o'clock and I daresay you'll be back by then?'

So there I was, on the pavement waiting at seven twenty-five, knowing Edith was tucked up safely and already busy with my laptop. A couple of minutes later Darren drew up in a dark blue Mercedes, his single passenger in the back seat. He leaned across and opened the door for me. 'Hop in then, there's a good girl. Nurse Sands, meet Miss Mundy.'

I turned as well as I could as I fastened my seat belt and said hello. Olga Mundy was sitting right behind me and peering round the headrest, I merely got an impression of large spectacles perched on a thin nose and a remote expression. A rather clipped voice wished me good evening and I immediately thought no wonder

Darren had been glad to have someone else along.

'We've just been witnessing the will of an old boy of one hundred and four,' he grinned at me. 'It's his tenth new one in the past couple of years. That right, Miss Mundy?'

'The eleventh, I think, Mr Darren,' she replied in her quiet voice. *Mister* Darren! I could hardly keep my face straight.

Then I asked, 'Why only in the last couple of years?'

Miss Mundy answered. 'He'd never had a penny to his name and was living in a council run old people's home when his only surviving relative died, a cousin who'd made a fortune overseas. So he's inherited a lot of money and keeps changing his mind who's going to get it when he dies.' She sounded amused as she told her story. So I'd been wrong about her, I thought with relief, old fashioned she might be with that feudal mode of addressing her boss, but at least she had a sense of humour. I sank back into the cream leather seat and relaxed as Darren carefully steered the big car along the narrow one-way street and when we reached the by-pass I felt the surge of power in the small of my back as he put his foot down and we flew up the hill. Then, a couple of miles along the road he slowed and turned down a side road and entered a close of small modern houses. He stopped the car and turned to Miss Mundy. 'OK?' he said with that smile in his voice. She murmured something I didn't catch and then they both climbed out of the car. Darren went round the back and picked up a large briefcase and a pilot's bag. 'Won't be a minute. Put the radio on if you like,' he said and followed her up the path to one of the houses.

I was still exploring the dashboard which looked like something from an aircraft flight deck when the car door opened and Darren hopped back in. Before I could turn round to look for Olga, he started the car and drove off 'What...!' I exclaimed.

'Olga has changed her mind about coming all the way down to Penzance. So it's just you and me. Nice one eh?' And he turned to me with a grin on that handsome rakish face as the car swooped off and away.

CHAPTER SIXTEEN

I sat, seething with fury at having fallen into such a neat trap; for he knew quite well I'd not have come with him had I known he'd be alone. I'd made it quite clear already that I wasn't going to be one of his catches. 'So much for having to see a client in Penzance,' I remarked bitterly.

'Oh, but that's true, my dear Lisa. I have to drop some papers off for this old girl. Won't be a jiffy though, and then the night is ours.'

The car was picking up speed now, the engine quieter than the sound of the wind swishing by. I sat in a speechless rage as we flew along the road towards Helston, speed limit signs a blur as we passed. Then, insouciantly ignoring my stiff lipped anger, of all things he began to talk about the siege of Pendennis Castle. 'I'm doing a piece on it for a historical magazine. Fascinating. Did you know the castle was one of the last strongholds for the king during the civil war with Cromwell?' Without waiting for my reply he went on, 'Months, they were stuck there, soldiers, women, children and livestock. Eventually when they had no food left, they finally surrendered and the Roundheads were so impressed by their stoicism they said the soldiers could ride out of the castle on their mounts with dignity, rather than on foot. Thing is, they couldn't. They'd eaten every last animal in the place, dogs, cats, horses, the lot.'

Despite myself, his story disarmed me as I suppose he'd known it would. I couldn't help shuddering at the picture he'd drawn. I'd been up to the castle several times with Edith and I could just picture the granite walls, weathered by centuries of rain and wind, standing above the now grassy moat. Next time I went there, I knew I would re-create the scene Darren was painting so vividly, his enthusiasm palpable. Secretly I thought I'd get hold of a copy of the magazine he was writing for but I'd no intention of letting him know that. I muttered something under my breath which he seemed to take as a sign of encouragement for as we skirted Helston, he gave me a lively history of that town too and told me he'd bring me there one market day to get the feel of the place. I interrupted for long enough to say I doubted that but he only laughed and said he thought I'd change my mind later. The vanity of the man dumbfounded me.

But now, he tells me, we are passing Marazion and he pointed out the castle on St Michael's Mount, a floodlit ghostly shape crowning the island afloat on its inky sea. Despite my stiff-necked mood I couldn't help swivelling round in my seat to drink it in until it disappeared from view. And a few minutes later we drew up in the car park of a hotel. 'Well, here we are. This is where my client is staying. Come in and have a drink while I see her. I won't be long.'

But I had no intention of going into that rather seedy

looking hotel with him. I'd already fallen into one of his traps; he needn't think I'd be caught in another. Fine historian he might be, and a great raconteur he'd already proved himself, but I couldn't trust him as far as I could throw him. 'I'll wait in the car, thanks. And remember Edith can't be left alone too long.'

He pulled a face as he reached over to the back seat for a large envelope. 'Be as quick as I can then,' he said and was gone, walking rapidly towards the hotel entrance.

I sat in the car, my stomach churning. But after the first couple of minutes I recovered myself and sat up straight. I must stop feeling like a victim. After all, I told myself, Darren was not in the least like the man who had driven me to the edge of a breakdown. And also, how would it look if I made a fuss and played the ravished maiden when he hadn't so much as laid a finger on me. No. I'd go along with him to the pub for some food and then insist of going home. In fact I could always get a taxi, though I felt Darren's pride wouldn't let me do that.

But sitting there in the darkness, despite my stern resolutions, memories came flooding back; victim memories I'd been blocking for so long. I could see Giles Christchurch-Smith, tall and elegant in his designer clothes, smiling down at me with that strangely remote look in his eyes that sent shivers of revulsion down my spine. I remembered the times when he'd lain in wait for me outside the hospital and some of the nurses had seen him. 'Wow!' they'd said. 'Just who is that gorgeous hunk, Lisa?' Only one of the junior girls had remarked in her blunt way, 'He may be good looking, but there's something about him that gives me the heeby-jeebies.' I remembered how there would be that sudden touch on my wrist, out of the blue as I took the underground home. Or how a shop door would be opened for me and I'd look up to say thank you and it would be *him* staring down at me with those strange eyes. In the darkness of the car I covered my face with my hands, trying to shut out the scenes my mind was replaying, the weeks and months and years of never knowing when he was going to step out and confront me. And that last ghastly night at my flat...'

The car door opened and I started violently, my hands falling to my lap. 'Here I am again. Oh, did I startle you?' Then thankfully the car door closed and unseen in the darkness I closed my eyes and muttered something inconsequential as we drove off.

I made an effort to respond as Darren slowly drove alongside a harbour gesturing to the moored boats where lights from the town melted and dissolved and blurred in the dark water. At any other time I'd have found these night scenes enchanting but now I was battling against the storm of emotions that had come sweeping out of my recent past. I tried to recollect the calm reassuring words of my counsellor but all I could remember was confusion, disbelief and terror.

Darren was still talking as we drew up on a narrow

quay. I climbed out on my wobbly legs and, playing for time, I leaned against the car and asked questions about the fishing boats moored in the sheltered harbour. Low houses and larger hotels looked across the narrow street over the water and gradually I felt my pulse settling. I straightened up. 'Where's this pub, then?'

And the pub was reassuringly full of people. Normal people, laughing and chatting as they downed their pints. At the bar Darren pointed out the day's specials on the blackboard and said he was having a croque with ham and pineapple. A young assistant passed us carrying a tray and I thought the small mushroom pizza looked fine. I took my glass of wine and Darren his half pint of beer, 'my limit when I'm driving - imagine the glee in town if I lost my driving licence' and we found a table for two. 'Wow! Are you OK, Lisa? You look quite pale.'

I shook my head. 'I'm alright. Been rather a fraught week, one way and another.'

He looked a little rueful and a lot disappointed at my shaky appearance and despite myself I smiled. 'That's better,' he said, 'you should always smile like that.'

I shook my head again at his nonsense and made a deliberate effort to focus on the surroundings; the people sitting near, the bits of driftwood decorating the walls and ceiling of the pub. Gradually the warmth of the room and the friendly atmosphere soothed me. In a brief gap in Darren's chatter I heard one or two snatches of conversation from the next table. What on earth did it mean: 'she was standing on one leg on the banister and I told her going on like that she'd never catch the train...' And 'I take a dose twice a day and it gets me up and going like a long dog.' I looked up and caught Darren's dancing eyes and could see he too was listening and the knots inside me loosened as I smiled back.

The food came and we started to eat. Then Darren leaned across the tiny table and spoke quietly into my ear. There was a burst of laughter from the neighbouring table and I didn't catch what he said, but there was no mistaking the way he drew one finger up the inside of my wrist and the feel of his knee against my thigh. I felt the tidal wave of my recent turmoil sweeping over me and I stood up, rocking the table in my haste and blundered off towards the ladies toilets with my napkin pressed against my mouth.

The young woman standing at the basin touching up her makeup looked up in concern as I burst in and flung back the door to the loo. After a moment, in an uncertain voice she called out to me am I alright, shall she fetch someone. As soon as I could speak I told her No, I'm OK, be fine in a minute and she left double quick. I didn't blame her.

After a bit I came out of the cubicle and saw a white-faced wraith staring back at me from the mirror. Who was I? What sort of woman must I be? I remembered the suggestive manner of Edith's doctor and Darren's persistent approaches. But worst of all was the swamping recollections of the man who'd followed and stalked me for so long, a sort of action replay of those tormented days. Why me? What sensuous messages did I subconsciously transmit so that men for whom I felt nothing at all must pester me with attentions I did not want. The wave of self-loathing that swept me made my knees buckle and I felt my way to a stool against the wall and sank on to it. The walls were lined with mirrors and I looked hard at my reflection. An ordinary woman, almost forty years old. Older than Darren. Very little make-up. Dark hair touching my shoulders, loose tonight but normally caught back in a bunch. Not suggestive, surely. I thought of the young woman who'd been standing here a moment ago. She had bleached hair, dramatic eye shadow and lipstick so thick it was practically three dimensional. If I looked like that...

Then through my hammering blood I seemed to hear my friend Katherine's remembered voice calming me after one particularly grim episode with my tormentor. 'Lisa, just because an inadequate man has fixed his obsession on you, the fault is not yours. You just happened to be in the wrong place at the wrong time. You work with men all the time, with patients and staff and get along fine. For God's sake don't start blaming yourself for other people's weaknesses and in this particular case, for a psychotic illness.'

I closed my eyes and made myself go over her words again and presently splashed some water on my face and dried it with a paper towel. Darren would be wondering what on earth had happened to me. Serve him right, I thought as I shakily pulled myself together. Then I opened the door and stepped back into the noise and bustle of the pub.

Darren had finished his food but I shook my head at what was left on my plate. I said sorry for having to run like that. Tummy upset. Better get back home as soon as possible. I turned down the offer of coffee and a few minutes later, a very chastened Darren escorted me back to his car. I leaned back against the voluptuous upholstery and closed my eyes. As we drove off, I felt his hand touch mine but when I indignantly opened my eyes, I found he was offering me a plastic bag, just in case. From the tangled knot of fears and uncertainties inside me, a strangled giggle broke free. Then I closed my eyes again as the car surged swiftly back to Falmouth and to the strange house I now called home.

CHAPTER SEVENTEEN

Edith's light was still on when I went into the house. I didn't particularly want to see her but after quickly checking my appearance in my bedroom I went along and tapped on her open door. She looked up, peering over the top of her half moon spectacles like the caricature of a stern headmistress. 'Enjoy yourself?' she asked. And instead of making her day by saying no, I'd been gulled, flummoxed and finally sick as a dog, I said, yes thank you. It was all very nice.

But she was obviously not interested and told me she'd sent off a good long e-mail to Charlie so I'd better take the machine away now. The laptop lay on the bed and I put it to one side before making her comfortable for the night. Comfortable: a debatable point of course, she was never very comfortable but it's a handy word in nursing, covering most conditions this side of intensive care.

I spent an hour downstairs in the kitchen, sitting with a cup of tea cradled in my hands, my stomach still playing leapfrog from time to time. Then I trailed up to bed, suddenly very tired and drained. I hoped Edith would have a good night and that I'd be able to take advantage of it too, and not lie tossing and turning hour after hour. As it happened she did sleep well. At least I suppose she did because I went out like a light as soon as my head hit the pillow. But certainly she didn't complain at six o'clock next morning when I went in with her cup of tea and I'm sure I'd have got it in the neck if she had rung in the night and I'd not answered her call.

So we rubbed along in our usual way for the rest of that week. Twice more she suffered those cramping pains but each time she told me to go away and leave her alone. She'd agreed, hadn't she, to go in for those tests soon. So go and find something useful to do. And no doctor, mind.

Maud came one afternoon. Did I imagine a coolness there? I made tea for her and Edith and quickly left them to themselves. I walked fast through the town and across one of the beaches. I toyed with the idea of going up to the castle but didn't want to be reminded of Darren today. He'd phoned the day after our outing, ostensibly to speak to Edith about her instructions, but he'd taken the opportunity to ask me if I was better. When I said I was, he immediately suggested we go out again another evening and seemed surprised when I said no. Edith was out of earshot in the front room so I told him what I thought of him. Serve you right, I told him, tricking me like that. No quick shag in the car on the way home after all. He was affronted. Quick shag, indeed, he said. Certainly not. A nice long shag though, wouldn't have come amiss. Talk about incorrigible...

On Friday evening, Edith said she fancied some strawberry ice cream and I knew there was none in the freezer. 'The supermarket will still be open,' she said and at the royal command I put on my coat and fetched the housekeeping purse. Quite soon after I'd arrived, Edith had been surprised and pleased to find I was using considerably less money for our weekly food supplies than Mrs Green, my predecessor, mainly because they'd had so many pre-packaged meals. So I'd been entrusted with the purse in total, and no longer had to go through the shopping list with her checking item by item while I chewed my bottom lip with frustration and annoyance.

The store was busy as always on a Friday and I had to hunt for a basket. A little girl of five or six, grabbed a trolley alongside and I helped her untangle it from the one in front. She thanked me gravely, bubbly blonde curls framing her face and swung away calling to another smaller child to follow her. 'Come *on,* Rory!' she ordered and the little boy, head tousled with the same fair curls, trotted obediently behind her. I was watching them hurry to catch up with the daddy they were calling to, when the man turned round. It was Darren Cornish.

I stood rooted to the spot. Darren Cornish! He had his back to me and picked up the little boy, gave him a kiss and slotted him into the trolley seat, and all the while the girl tugged at his sweater pleading for some treat or other. And then a woman came round from the next aisle and joined them. There were cries of 'Mummy, pleeese can I have them' and Darren clutched his head in mock despair. I stepped behind the stand and watched them, my cheeks burning with humiliation and anger.

The woman, his wife obviously, was reed slim and elegant in narrow trousers and a loose shirt. Her fair hair fell half-way down her back, shining and straight, an altogether stunningly attractive woman.

So how could he! It had never occurred to me that he was married. Talking to Edith there'd never once been a mention of wife or children and when he'd spoken of Olga Mundy it was to say she was able to work in the evenings unlike other people who had families to think of, never giving a hint of a family of his own.

Anger won in the battle of emotions and I was fiercely glad when it swamped the feeble weakness that had been part of my life for so long. Very deliberately I walked slowly along the aisle, making sure always to keep the Cornish family in view. Now and then I reached something down from a shelf, willing Darren to turn round and spot me. My chance came when the little girl whom I heard him call Gemma, came running back towards where I was standing, pleading for her special cereal. When I saw he was coming towards me as he followed in her wake, I turned to scrutinize the heating instructions on a tin of soup and from the corner of my eye I was aware from his sudden swerve and about turn. Good. He had seen me.

I was still apparently engrossed in my perusal of instructions on the tin when he swiftly collared his daughter, grabbed a packet and hurried away, Gemma protesting vigorously that he'd got the wrong one *again*. I turned cautiously when I was sure they'd moved to the next aisle and then I followed. The back of Darren's neck was dark red and I felt like punching the air and shouting 'yesss!' I could see the way they were heading so I quickly skirted the next aisle and when they came round the corner, I saw Darren glance furtively backwards. When he turned round, of course, there I was, leaning over a frozen food cabinet and although it was the briefest glimpse, the hounded look on his face when he saw me now ahead of him, made it hard not to laugh aloud. I shuffled through boxes of hot dogs and sausages, listening to the children's chatter, as they urged their parents to try this and that. Darren's voice was strained. I heard his wife say 'What's the matter with you for god's sake, I've already put that packet back twice!' I carefully placed another purchase in my basket and turned away, still in the lead.

I was eight feet tall and Darren a little puppet who's strings I tweaked delightedly for the next ten minutes or so. I found an unsuspected talent in split second timing, knowing just when to turn away so as not to confront him face to face, but always staying near enough for him to fear I would. He was the victim now and I revelled in my power and in being in control. I played my game of cat and mouse all round the supermarket, and once I even spoke to the little girl when she came close. At last I decided I'd punished him almost, but not quite, enough. With all the confidence in the world, I swung round and exclaimed, 'Why, Mr Cornish! Well, hello.'

He had gone quite pale and I could see the film of sweat on his suddenly not-so- handsome face. He managed a choked good evening and would have walked on, except I was blocking the way as I turned to speak to his wife. 'Hi,' I said, 'you must be Mrs Cornish. I'm staying at Mrs Rogers' place. I'm her nurse.'

He made a great effort and managed to introduce us though his voice was a little off key as he croaked out my name. She was suspicious, that much I could see from the look she shot at him, the sudden hardening of her eyes. But though he was uncomfortable, I kept my own face bland and friendly, smiling at the children and asking the usual harmless questions about their ages and names. And then, looking at the children's bright faces, I knew my game had gone far enough and I must go. I said, 'Edith will be wondering where I've got to.' And with a final smile, I turned and went on with my shopping.

It was just as well I checked my purchases before I reached the checkout. What would Edith be wanting with fish-shaped fish fingers. Or iced lollies. I did a swift re-run of the aisles, collected the ice cream she liked and was out of the store before the Cornishes had reached the check outs.

All through the evening I kept replaying the incident.

Once Edith asked me what was so funny, I was grinning like a Cheshire cat. I told her some joke of my son's and as I expected she was not amused. But at last I got her to bed and decided on an early night myself.

I lay on my back, staring at the pale oblong of the uncurtained window, so relaxed I felt I was melting. The words of that experienced old counsellor who had tried so hard to help me were suddenly cogent and powerful. I knew now what she meant about losing the victim mentality, for tonight I'd discovered what it was like to be on the other side; to be the tormentor. I knew only too well the torture I'd inflicted on the hapless Darren. The fact that it served him right was beside the point. What I had learned in that cat and mouse pursuit through the store was all about power and the sheer enjoyment and relish of using that power to dominate and command. So this was what Giles Christchuch-Smith had felt when he'd shadowed me, this was what undoubtedly 'turned him on,' in the words of my counsellor. I had acted primarily out of anger and pique at being duped by Darren Cornish. I'd wanted to tease and punish him. But having achieved that with no small success, I hadn't wished to prolong the torture. My 'accidental' meeting and brief conversation with his wife and children were my signal of reassurance that I wouldn't betray him, for their sakes, not his, and I thought by now he'd have worked that out for himself.

What I'd not expected as a result of my action, was the sense of equilibrium which still remained hours later. I no longer felt like a victim, nor did I intend to feel that way again. If and when Giles Christchurch-Smith renewed his pursuit, he'd get no more pleasure from the chase, for I was no longer afraid of him. I could hardly believe how simple it now was to put together the pieces of the jigsaw of recovery. The professionals had tried so hard to help me; they had told me exactly what the problem was, but paralysed with fear, I could only suffer. But no more. If and when he came after me again, I'd leave it to the police. The fact that he could afford to employ the best legal brains in the business didn't matter any more because I would no longer be a jelly in their hands, but a calm and rational woman with right on my side.

I woke next morning to find sunlight streaming through the window and I stood on the balcony and stretched, drinking in the salty air and revelling in my feeling of total wellbeing. Only now did I realise how much I'd been changed by my victimisation. I'd become a frightened rabbit, capable of periods of normality and then retreating into frozen terror. I wondered how on earth my son and my friends had put up with me for all that time and was more than ever grateful for their unswerving loyalty and generous support.

Although it was still very early a number of boats ploughed their way over the pale dawn waters of the harbour. I wondered wistfully if Jack's boat was one of them as he liked to go fishing on Saturdays if he could get away. I thought of him sadly but without the familiar wild rush of condemnation. I faced the fact we'd both responded to a powerful attraction. There had been that almost instant rapport between us, an easy friendship that had deepened so swiftly it had taken us both, I think, by surprise. Jack wasn't the first married man to be tempted to stray. But my own feelings about his family remained; there was no way I would be responsible for making Katie's bright eyes lose their laughter or for Maud to look at me with shock and disappointment.

So I stopped searching for Jack's boat and turned away from the window bolstered by my calm new confidence. I dressed quickly and ten minutes later I was taking Edith her early morning cup of tea.

CHAPTER EIGHTEEN

Edith looked rested and comparatively well. As I was getting her bathed and dressed, she told me she wanted some photos of the harbour taken from the front room balcony. 'I've told Charlie all about the repairs we've had done and he said he'd like to see it. And I thought you could take some pictures of the boats and the water for him. Show him what we can see when we're sitting outside. And next time you're out that way, you can take some pictures of the docks. Bit different from when he used to work there.' Suddenly she looked uncharacteristically diffident. 'And he says he'd like some more pictures of me.'

Charlie's own photos now had pride of place on the sideboard in the front room. One was an enlargement of the only snap she had of him, a young man seated on a chair, long legs crossed and smiling shyly for the camera. The other was the one I'd downloaded from the computer; the same man, skin now deeply lined and furrowed by years beneath the relentless sun, his body much shrunken but with the same sweet smile in his gentle eyes. We'd sent him the best one I'd taken of Edith and I hoped he would think the bitterness etched on her tense mouth was from her illness and pain or even, more romantically, caused by her thwarted love for him. But when she'd taken out that snap of Charlie from an old album, I'd seen some photographs of her which she said were taken before and during the early years of her marriage, and I couldn't help but recognise my cold aloof patient in the face of the younger woman on the faded prints. Unfortunately there were no photos of Edith during the time of her affair with Charlie; photos that might have shown the transformed woman Maud had spoken of so wistfully. I was prepared though, to believe how much he'd changed her in those days after seeing for myself what a difference finding him again had made to her now, even though her better humour never lasted very long.

While we were having our breakfast, the noise of a powerful motor boat charging to and fro irritated her. 'Go and see who that is,' she told me, as if I would possibly know. But it was unusual to have a boat so close to the house and I too was curious so I went over to the window and looked out.

The boat, a powerful motor launch was turning as I opened the window, sitting back in its wake and puddling all the smoothly radiating patterns on the surface of the water. I'm no nautical expert but even to my eyes the gleaming chrome and polished wood spoke money. There were two men on board, one controlling the great engine and as I looked out, the other man was pointing a pair of binoculars straight at our kitchen window.

My first thought was that Giles had tracked me down but I could see immediately that neither man in the least resembled him. But what on earth did they think they were doing' I smothered an exclamation and ran into the front room and snatched up the ancient pair of glasses Edith kept there with which I often looked over the big tankers lying far out in the bay. I went over to the window and concealed myself behind the curtain where they would be unlikely to see me, and watched the watchers.

The boat was idling now and the owner of the glasses was slowly raking the faces of the buildings which fronted the water. He seemed to be taking a particular interest in our small jetty and then turned his head as if to examine the house once more.

I quickly put the glasses down, opened the window and stepped out onto the balcony. With studied indifference to the men in the boat I strolled slowly to the rail and looked across to the hills opposite and then up to the sky. When I allowed my gaze to fall on them, both men were staring up at me, the boat rising and falling on the gentle swell.

The tide was low and they were as close to our wall as they could come without churning up the mud. I stared back at them coldly, not liking this close inspection. Then the one with the glasses hanging round his neck, a heavy thickset man, said something to the other, the engine growled deep in its throat and the boat spun round again and surged away. I watched until it disappeared between the yachts moored out in the harbour before I finally turned back into the house and went along to the kitchen.

Edith was sitting at the table, anxious and worried. 'Who was it?' she asked, leaning forward, her hands gripping the sides of her chair. And when I described the boat and the men and the inspection of the waterfront buildings, her normally pale face became even more ashen. 'What was he looking at? Was it this house? How close did they come?' She sounded so anxious that I wished I'd not said anything about the men. Then she spoke again, her voice thick with worry, 'Do you think they were police?'

'Police!' I echoed. 'Good lord no. And it was certainly not the harbour launch. Just a couple of blokes fooling round in their posh new boat I suppose.' I remembered the close examination of our jetty. 'Maybe they were looking for somewhere to come ashore this end of the town.' She nodded slowly and her hands unclenched. But what on earth was that about the police, I thought. Then I remembered her husband, missing for so many years. Perhaps to this day she expected his body to come to light. Perhaps any unusual happening in the harbour made her think this was the day it would happen. And I shivered a little in the warm kitchen.

'Come on,' I said, 'the sun is shining. 'A good day to take those photos for Charlie.' But for once his name didn't lighten her mood. She said she needed another cup of tea first. And perhaps one of those tablets to settle her stomach. But I felt her sudden ailment owed more to the mysterious boat and its occupants than to her illness.

But later she came agreeably enough to the front room and let me arrange her chair on the balcony so I could pose her with a glimpse of the distant hills across the water behind her shoulder. It was strangely intrusive today looking at Edith through the eyes of the camera. In the other photos I'd taken she was self-conscious and self-aware and neither of us was pleased with the result. But today, she saw neither me nor the camera; she was gazing straight into the eyes of her Charlie. I used the zoom for a close-up and knew she would want this picture. Gone was the closed bitter face of the sick and ailing woman. Now the dark eyes were liquid and so full of a deep sadness and yearning it made me feel like a voyeur peering into that old romance. I took several photos and then handed her the camera for her to scroll back and see for herself. She said nothing, but I saw a solitary tear trickle silently down her cheeks. I retrieved the camera, muttering something about taking those pictures of the boats for Charlie and as I focused, there was that mysterious craft again, heading this way. I zoomed in and took a couple of shots and then as the boat came closer I quickly said I thought it was a bit cold out here and she agreed absent-mindedly, too much involved with her own feelings to be aware of the approaching vessel.

Back in the kitchen, Edith wanted the photos e-mailed straight away. We were soon in contact with her old lover and I left them to their electronic courtship and went back to the balcony to see what that boat was up to.

Once more it was idling along close to the buildings but this time when the men saw me come out onto the balcony, they edged closer and the one with the binoculars called up to me, 'Who's the owner of this house?' No smile or greeting softened the arrogant tone of his enquiry. He was almost as offensively rude as Edith herself and I felt it must be catching as I myself gave him a snooty stare and turned away to go back indoors without so much as a word. Thick-skinned, he called after me, 'I need to speak to the owner. Now.'

I was taken aback and hesitated, then made a meaningless gesture with my hands, went inside and deliberately closed the french windows. Again I hid behind the curtains and watched as they slowly circled and several times used their glasses to examine the waterfront. For a long five minutes they hung about outside until with a sudden burst of power, they roared away.

Edith was still on line to Charlie so I made some coffee and while it was infusing, slipped out to get the newspaper from the shop at the head of the alley-way. But I found myself unable to concentrate on world news; the purpose of the two men in that boat kept intruding. What on earth did they want and should I tell Edith they wanted to speak to the 'owner of the house.' After seeing how shaken she was earlier, I wondered if I should keep it to myself. But I had a feeling they'd be back and it was only fair to prepare her.

Having made up my mind, I settled down with the paper and was well into the supplements before Edith finally came back to earth. She didn't want to talk to me, that I could see from the inward-looking gaze and the almost-smiling mouth. But she drank her coffee and at last I told her about the men in the boat and the strange question they'd asked.

She dropped her beaker abruptly. I stood up and fetched a cloth to mop it up. She refused another cup and then asked me again, 'Are you sure they weren't police?'

I said what I thought. 'Certainly not police. Quite the opposite I should think. Not ordinary people, certainly. Ordinary people go to estate agents if they're looking for a place. Ask the neighbours, maybe. But this pair... There was something about them. They seemed in a terrific hurry. And they came as close to your jetty as they could without grounding, two or three times. I'm going to check that door down the alley is still locked.'

Edith said nothing for a while, then suddenly decided she would have that other cup of coffee after all. And she seemed less worried now. I mentally shook my head; there was no understanding this woman. Half an hour later she told me she was going to take her e-mails from Charlie into the front room for a bit. I might as well go out and do a bit of shopping.

I smiled to myself, remembering the bit of shopping I'd done last night, but went out cheerfully all the same, ready to enjoy the sunshine and the busy Saturday morning feel of the town.

CHAPTER NINETEEN

Halfway along the main street I saw Katie's fair hair, dreadlocked today. She was pushing a child's buggy; her little brother Sammy, no doubt. This was the first time I'd seen her since I'd so abruptly fled from Jack. That was only on Monday but it seemed a much longer time with all the things that had happened during this strange up and down week. Maybe she too, would be cool, but I'd made up my mind I was no longer going to run away from anything, so I caught her up. 'Hi, Katie,' I said, 'how's things?'

She spun round and beamed. 'Lisa! I was going to drop in and see you, show you my little bruv. Come on Sammy boy, say hello to Lisa.'

The little boy in the pushchair grinned up at me, chubby legs kicking at the footplate. He was a sturdy little chap, not at all like his blonde sister with his dark straight hair and enormous heart-melting brown eyes. 'Isn't he sweet?' says Katie. And I had to agree that he was very sweet indeed. And then, 'Hi, mum. Look, here's Lisa.'

I straightened and found myself face to face with Jack's wife. She too was smiling. 'Well, nice to meet you at last. I've heard such a lot about you. I'm Helen, by the way,' she said with a laugh as if of course I would know that, and held out her slim hand. She was not at all what I'd imagined. Fair hair cut in the latest

148

style and wearing her casual clothes with panache. She gazed at me from a pair of intelligent grey eyes, friendly and enquiring.

I'm always at a loss when someone says they've heard a lot about you. What should you do, puff out your chest with satisfaction or cringe with embarrassment? I did neither, but sidestepped the remark by saying what a gorgeous child her Sammy was. 'Oh yes. He's going to be a heartbreaker, alright.' And we both stooped over the pushchair again. Sammy beamed and held out his arms to his mother and she crouched down and smothered his face with kisses while I tried to smile and ignore the ache in my heart. The child pushed his mother away after a bit and stared enquiringly at me with those great dark eyes. 'Look at him!' she laughed, 'what a little Cassinova. He's his daddy's boy alright. We're waiting for him now. Oh, look, here he comes.'

I turned, schooling my face to meet Jack but coming towards us smiling at Katie and her mother was a man I'd never seen before. 'Gavin, meet Lisa, you know, old Mrs Rogers' new nurse.' And I found myself shaking hands again, trying to hide my confusion. Helen's husband! But... He and Katie's mother made a strikingly good looking couple, he as dark as she was fair. I could see now where the little boy's almost Mediterranean looks came from and as we chatted for a few more minutes I could feel a cloud of butterflies performing weird stunts in my stomach.

We smiled our goodbyes and I walked on. So Jack

was free after all! Had been free from long before we ever met. If only I had known. But I supposed both Katie and Maud assumed I did know. That's if they were conscious of our mutual interest. My thoughts whirled in confusion. But out of the disarray came the imperative that I must get in touch with Jack. I had to tell him I was sorry. He might not want anything more to do with me of course, but I owed him a profound apology and would have to come clean about why I'd turned down his invitation. And then, if he should...

My arm was suddenly grabbed and I turned to find Katie had caught me up. 'Hey! You didn't know mum and dad were divorced, did you?' she was grinning at me in a rather pointed way. I felt colour rise in my cheeks and she didn't wait for me to answer. 'Got your mobile on you, have you?' she asked and I smiled back and took it out of my bag asking if she'd run out of credit on hers again, glad of the change of subject.

But she shook her head as she tapped the keys. 'There you are,' she said, handing the phone back to me. 'That's his mobile number. Go on, give him a ring, he's been like a bear with a sore head all the week. Maybe a call from you will soften him up a bit. I need to ask him for some extra cash later on.' And off she breezed without waiting for me to catch my breath and reply.

I stared at the number. Call? the little screen asked. I was near one of the narrow streets leading down to the water and walked slowly away from the busy shoppers, down to where the water sparkled and a few people strolled along the jetty, watching the boatmen busy about their craft. I sat down on a stone seat warmed by the sunshine and stared again at the printed number. It was all very well for Katie, but I must have hurt Jack deeply by my refusal. And if I told him why I'd turned down his invitation, I would hurt him again by implying I'd thought him the type of man to two-time his wife and family.

Then I remembered my brave new persona who was never going to run away from anything any more. I took a deep breath and pressed the call button. The ringing went on and on and I felt the decision had been taken from my hands and only then did I realise the depth of my disappointment. And then 'Hello'. His voice was abrupt and a little breathless as if he'd left the mobile somewhere and had to hurry to find it. My own voice sounded strange when I spoke and he asked, still terse, who was this?

I took a deep breath and started again. 'It's me, Lisa. Jack, I just want to say how sorry I am. About not going out for that drink with you. Thing is, I've just met your wife and Gavin. Only she's not your wife.'

There was such a long silence I thought he'd rung off. Then I heard him exhale. 'Whew! Would you like to say that all again. Only a bit slower.'

I was holding the phone against my ear as if it was Jack's hand, my knees weak with relief and happiness. 'Oh, Jack,' was all I could say. And once again there was a silence before he spoke again as if he too, was suddenly lost for words.

'Well, well,' his voice smiled. 'Shall I ask you again, then?'

I shook my head as though he could see me. 'Nope. I'm asking you this time. Jack, will you come out for a drink with me? Or something?'

There was another long pause before he spoke. 'I think from the sound of it I'd prefer the "something". This evening suit you will it? Or what about now? Where are you?'

And that's how Jack arrived on the jetty twenty minutes later and came striding over to where I walked to and fro, unable to be still. We stood a foot apart, suddenly shy and we said nothing but I knew that everything that was important between us, was there to be read in our eyes.

CHAPTER TWENTY

We walked to the end of the jetty and sat down, looking out over the waters of the harbour, our heads close together, hands clasped like teenage lovers. Presently I must go back to Edith, but it was enough for the moment to be together, even though in such a public place.

Jack released my hand and wrapped his arm round me, holding me close to him and sighing, 'I've wanted to do this from the first time we met. Sounds daft, doesn't it? But you looked so lost and alone, I just wanted to put my arms round you and tell you it'll be fine, not to worry.'

I reached for his free hand and raised it to my lips. 'I felt that way about you, right from the beginning. That I'd be safe with you.' I looked at the hand I held, the blunt fingers, work hardened, his nails neatly trimmed and I traced the lines across his palm with a fingertip.

'Christ, Lisa. Don't do that. Safe, she says. You won't stay safe if you carry on like that, my girl, and I don't care if half Falmouth is watching.'

I laughed. I couldn't remember ever being so overwhelmed by happiness; this great tidal wave of ecstasy. And as Jack turned to look at me, I could see he felt the same. I don't know how long we sat there, close together, murmuring the universal little nothings that are the vocabulary of lovers the world over. But at last I remembered Edith and said I must go, though I made no move to leave my place of sanctuary at his side just yet. But at last I relinquished his hand and reluctantly his arm fell from my waist.

'I'll go back with you,' he said and walking along the main street we managed to stay a foot or so apart most of the time. I wondered if we'd see Katie on the way and said as much to Jack. 'Even if we don't bump into her, what's the betting she's goggling at us from one of the shops. Our Katie doesn't miss much.'

I laughed and told him how she'd punched his phone number into my mobile, 'You're right,' I said, 'she doesn't miss much. And here was I thinking I'd pulled the wool over her eyes.'

Edith looked up as we entered the house together. 'You've been a long time,' she said, but no, she didn't want anything. 'Just as well, with you out gallivanting round the town.' She stared at Jack. 'You've come to be paid, I suppose.' She told me to fetch the box where she kept her bills and fished out his statement and making a great to-do about it, wrote her cheque and handed it to him. But as he carefully receipted the bill I could see she didn't for one moment believe that was what had brought Jack along. When I'd hung up my coat and glanced in the mirror I hardly recognised the woman who glowed back at me. I wondered for a moment with that old feeling of guilt how to hide my joy and then remembered there was no need to be furtive for we were both free, weren't we? And I could hardly contain my happiness at the thought. I made coffee and Jack sat at the table with us for a while until Edith abruptly said this won't do. I want to go down the town for a bit. Buy a few things. But she didn't get rid of him quite so easily as he stayed to help manoeuvre her chair down over the ramps and along the street. Then, with obvious reluctance, he touched my hand and said he'd see me later, nodded to Edith and stood and watched as we turned the chair to go into one of the shops. Through the window I saw him standing for a while then I had to give my attention to Edith who was impatiently telling me she couldn't reach the jumpers she wanted to inspect.

We made our slow way along the road, going into stores in which she'd never before shown the slightest interest. I was finding it increasingly hard to concentrate, wanting to go home where I could think of Jack without all these stupid interruptions. But Edith then decided she wanted to go on down to Custom House quay where the contraband smokestack stood, as she fancied an ice cream. And just as I handed over her cone, my mobile rang. My heart lifted when I heard Jack's voice. 'Where are you?' he asked. 'I've not seen you for over three quarters of an hour. Any more of these long separations and I can't swear I'll stay faithful, you know.'

I walked a little way off, cradling the phone tenderly as I told him not to keep calling like this, my sailor friend doesn't like it. A bit more foolishness and then I looked up and saw Edith staring at me, her lip curling with undisguised contempt. I choked back a laugh and casually asked Edith would it be OK if a friend called to see me this evening. Only after she's been settled for the night, she said and I guessed she'd be pretty late going to bed for once. I passed on the spoken message and reluctantly rang off. Edith ate her ice cream in silence and I strode to the end of the pier to watch the boats, hardly able to stop myself from skipping.

The harbour was busy on this sunny Saturday with a number of small yachts tacking to and fro to catch the breeze. A motor boat came roaring in amongst them causing one of the boats to tip over on its side, its sails trailing in the water. I heard the yell of rage from the startled yachtsman and at the same moment noticed the guilty motor boat was the very one which had been so carefully inspecting Edith's house and jetty earlier. I watched to see where it was going and wasn't surprised to see it swerve round the ferry pier and head again towards our place.

Edith had finished her cone and the seagull which had hung about waiting for a scrap of biscuit flew off in disgust as we set off for home. When we entered our alley-way and Edith slowly trundled down the cobbles, I went on ahead and tested the door at the end. It was still firmly locked and I didn't bother to answer the question in Edith's eyes. But later, as I scrolled through the photos I'd taken that day, I was pleased to see that when I'd zoomed in on the mysterious boat, the photos

I'd taken of its occupants were sharp and clear. I loaded them into the computer and printed out an enlargement showing just the men's faces. And it was only as I put the print safely amongst my papers that I acknowledged to myself how suspicious I was of their actions. It wouldn't hurt to keep that photo safe, just in case.

The rest of the day flew by and at long last, later than usual as I had anticipated, Edith was finally settled in her bed. 'When this "friend" of yours comes, tell him I don't like late hours,' was her goodnight greeting as I switched off her top light. I supposed I must be grateful she'd actually allowed me to invite him round. But now with hindsight, I know the only reason she did permit "my friend" to visit was she knew quite well who it was and she was already aware he might be useful to her later.

He didn't use the doorbell when he came but gave the little tap-tap I'd come to recognise when he called. I opened the door and he stepped into the hallway. The lighting was very dim, Edith's trademark meanness with electricty, but it was light enough to show me Jack's face and the tender passion in his eyes. I walked into his arms and into the embrace that until today I'd only dreamed of. At last we broke apart and I led him along the passage to the front room.

'Let's go outside, I can't stand this house,' Jack said and strode over to open the french windows. I fetched my coat and we took one of the armchairs out onto the deck and cuddled up together. There was no wind and we were content in our nest, though I doubt we'd have felt the cold if a blizzard was raging round our ears. Now and then I was aware of the red and green lights of boats passing by out on the harbour, and Jack pointed out the great moon which sailed from behind a cloud. 'Full moon, spring tide. Your cellar will be awash right now.' But we had other and better things to think of and the thought of water swirling in the darkness down below failed for once to give me that familiar shudder.

Twice Edith rang. 'Making sure there's no hanky panky,' grinned Jack and from the sharp looks I got each time I went to her, I could see he was right about that.

After the second summons I agreed that hanky panky must wait. But not too long. I told him Edith was soon to go into hospital for a couple of nights for tests and his face lit up. 'She told me I must find a bed and breakfast as she doesn't want to leave me alone here. Anywhere you can recommend?' I asked. And he told me he'd got just the place. Nice comfortable double bed. Sea views, the lot.

Presently, the roar of a powerful engine reminded me of our strange visitors today and I told Jack about their examination of the house and jetty. He agreed with me they sounded a fishy pair. 'Place like this, of course, with its own mooring and right in the heart of the town, would be pretty handy for a bit of smuggling.' He warmed to the theme. 'Call it a holiday let, different people coming and going, hard to keep tabs on. And those storerooms off the passage. Easy to put in false walls, you could hide a lot there. Drugs, people, whatever.' And when I said surely it would be safer to find a secluded spot, he disagreed. 'Unusual activity up one of the creeks, say, would be a lot easier to spot. Our coastguard system is pretty sophisticated, you'd be surprised how much they know. But a motor boat going out for a spot of fishing, perfectly normal. They wouldn't even have to meet up with a larger incoming vessel, who's to say what they pull in when they're out fishing? After all, there's marker buoys and floats all over the place and the fishermen are only interested in their own. Yep, this place would make a great base. But they're up against the immoveable object in Edith. She'll never sell. She could have moved times over, but no, this is her home, she says and she'll only go out in her box. So your house hunters are out of luck here.' But then he said what are we wasting time talking about them for and suddenly it was late, much later than Edith would approve of.

I went with him to the door and oh, the reluctant parting. But I was smiling as I locked the door behind him and walked slowly up the stairs. I opened the window and looked out at the moon which hung like a Chinese lantern over the water and wondered if Jack was looking at it too as he walked up the hill to his home, a home that I was soon to see. A home that perhaps might soon be mine to share.

CHAPTER TWENTY ONE

I was up with the lark next morning and found myself singing in the shower, something I'd not done for years, albeit quietly because of Edith. Morning showers in the past had been rushed affairs, with breakfast to get, my son's lunch box to prepare and all the other things to be done by a busy working mum, because even though Josh's grandmother lived with us, I didn't expect or indeed want her to get up early to see us off. So today I washed my hair in the pleasant bathroom and beamed at my reflection in the steamy mirror.

I took Edith her cup of tea with my head wrapped turbanwise in a towel. She made no comment about my visitor last night, but I mentioned his name casually so she would know I wasn't hiding anything.

After breakfast I slipped out to the newsagents next door and as I was paying for my paper, Iris the shop owner beckoned me over to where she was busily sorting out the magazine shelf. 'Did they two men catch you yesterday then?' she asked. And seeing my puzzled face she went on. 'Two blokes came in here wanting to know who owns Mrs Rogers' place. I wouldn't have told them, but my boy Sean id'n the brightest and 'course he went and told them her name, how she's in a wheelchair and all the rest of it. And then he told them he'd seen the pair of you going out shopping not long before.' Worriedly I asked her what they looked like and when she described them, I knew it was the two mystery boatmen. 'They told Sean they had business to do with Mrs Rogers and they'd be back today.' She sniffed. 'Fancy coming round to do business on a Sunday.' And she went on stacking her shelves busily, work that was obviously quite a different matter from 'business'.

I picked up my paper and went back indoors, uneasy at the thought of a visit from those men. I'd have to tell Edith, of course. I needn't have worried about her reaction to the news though for she took it very much in her stride. For the hundredth time I thought what a strangely unpredictable woman she was. But when I said would she like Jack to be here when they called, she turned on me furiously. 'Just because you need a man around, you needn't think I do. I've looked after myself all these years. I'm not starting to have a man poking his nose into my business now and you needn't think I am.'

Stung, I responded in kind. 'It was just a suggestion. Actually I doubt he'd come, I doubt he'd bother to give up a free Sunday to do you a favour even if I asked him.' And I bounced away up the stairs. But before I'd reached my room, her bell peeled insistently.

I took a deep breath, pressed my hands against my burning cheeks and went slowly back down the stairs. Edith was holding out her beaker. 'If there's another cup in the pot, I'll have it. And then you can take me along as far as Greenbank. I don't want to go far in case these men come, whoever they are.' Words failed me. I poured her tea and sat down and read the paper in silence until she said she was ready to go.

It was only a short and fairly level walk along the road towards the point where she was heading and most of the way we had a fine view of the harbour on this sunny spring morning. I looked for the powerful motor boat but there was no sign of it among the other craft out on the water today.

I wondered where they were staying and why I had such a negative feeling about them. Edith interrupted my thoughts by suddenly saying she wanted to go back now because there was nothing worth looking at anyway.

But on the way back I found my tongue. I'd been walking alongside her chair but now I put out my hand to stop her. 'Look, Mrs Rogers, I'm not talking nonsense whatever you may think. We don't know who these men are. But they do know you are an invalid and that there's only you and me in the house. And there are two of them. Now I've been on the receiving end of an attack, and believe me, it's not something you get over in ten minutes and I don't feel I can stay in the house alone with you if they come, but I can't leave you either.'

She gave in straight away, taking the wind out of my sails as she usually did. 'Alright, I'll ask Sean to come in when he sees them. He spends half his time standing in the shop doorway anyway so Iris won't miss him. I'll

162

tell him we'll give him a ring and he can come straight along. Though the chances are he'll see them first.'

Sean! Mr Universe himself with his scrawny frame and thick glasses. Still, better than nothing I supposed. I went into the shop and told Iris what Edith wanted. 'Huh!' she said, 'we shall have rain, Edith Rogers asking for a bit of neighbourly help.' But I could see she was pleased and Sean beamed with delight at the idea of suddenly becoming a bodyguard. I could see what Edith meant about him standing around doing nothing. Perhaps he shared his mother's reluctance to working on a Sunday, though in his case it seemed to include the rest of the week as well.

I'd left my mobile on the kitchen table and when we went indoors I saw there was a message waiting. I read Jack's text trying to keep stony-faced before Edith's gimlet gaze and then I ran upstairs and called him. We talked our sweet nothings and I made sure not to mention Edith's prospective callers. I knew he and Katie were having lunch at Maud's today but he hoped I might be free later. I said I'd call him as soon as I knew. He asked where I was and I told him I was in the bedroom, lying down looking at the ceiling and he was just saying... when I heard the strident peal of the doorbell. He heard it too and knew I must go so we rang off, and I at least, was aglow.

I hurried down the stairs as Edith called that she was phoning the shop. Slowly I released the lock and opened the door a few inches. Instead of the two sinister strangers, Sean's face beamed at me. I opened the door wider and told him to come in. He said in a stage whisper, 'They're in the shop. Came in for cigarettes. Forty Marlborough. King size.'

I was about to follow him into the front room when, right on cue, the doorbell rang again. As soon as I opened the door I saw that it was, of course, the men we'd seen 'casing the joint' as I'd described it to myself. They told me they wanted a word with Mrs Rogers and reluctantly I stood aside and waved them along the passage to the front room. Sean stood up as we came in and greeted them like long lost friends. Wonderful.

They introduced themselves to Edith politely enough and then said with a pointed look at Sean and me that they'd like a word in private. I surprised myself by saying we'd no intention of leaving Mrs Rogers on her own but we had work to do and they could speak as privately as they chose. As I spoke I opened my laptop and called Sean over to the side table where it lay. He immediately asked what games I had and asked me to show him how to play patience.

Edith moved her chair over to the french windows and they joined her at the far end of the room away from where my eager pupil and I sat. Even if I'd wanted to eavesdrop, Sean made sure I heard not a word as he hummed and gasped his way through a couple of games. Then Edith broke in and said the gentlemen would like a look round the house. I was to take them. I gave Sean a meaning look to come along with us but had to put it into words before he stood up and followed us importantly.

I'd noticed the only thing in the front room which interested them was the balcony where they spent some minutes looking down at the jetty and the remains of the wooden walk-way. It was the same in the kitchen, no interest apart from that quick look out of the window. But they went inside the walk-in larder and tapped the walls and did the same in the laundry and the huge linen room. I remembered Jack's words about false walls and hiding places. The warmth of the enclosed space brought out the full strength of the men's aftershave and I quickly backed out into the passage, the pungent smells catching my throat. Sean was now in estate agent mode, tapping floorboards, admiring the downstairs cloakroom and following at my heels like an eager puppy as we went upstairs. Here again, the men showed little interest in the two bedrooms though they followed Sean out onto my balcony when he opened the glass door. They merely glanced into the bathrooms and then we were downstairs again. 'You'd better show them the cellar,' said Edith somewhat grimly as she handed me the key. But Sean was the only one interested, despite cracking his head soundly on the low beam at the bottom of the steps. Under the dim light, the cellar looked the same as ever, the long narrow space with the rough wall at the end and the fresh deposit of silt on the floor from the last high tide. 'Cold,' was the only remark the men made though Sean reckoned it was really cool.

Upstairs again, I gave Edith back the key and she sent me into the kitchen to make tea. Sean was about to go with me but I told him to stay in the front room and he said great, he'd have another go at that game. When I brought in the tray Edith was looking at a sheet of paper and amending some figures. She turned it face down as I passed her the beaker and I coloured angrily. As if I cared what she was doing. She was an obnoxious spiteful woman and probably always had been. I'd try the agency again tomorrow. There were plenty of other openings for me; the trouble was finding a replacement to look after Edith.

The two men drank their tea in silence and then stood up. One went to look out of the window again, came back and gave a quick nod to the other. And then they said they must be off. 'Two weeks, you said?' the short one addressed Edith.

She nodded. 'I'll let you know one way or the other in two weeks.'

They seemed disappointed but even in this brief time they'd seen enough of Edith to realise she couldn't be pressured. The place still reeked of their body sprays and I couldn't wait to get out into the fresh air. And to contact Jack of course. Sean was reluctant to leave. 'Anytime you want my help again, you know where I am,' he said importantly while casting a longing glance at my laptop. Edith handed him a five pound note and at last he bounced out of the house and back to his mother's shop with a fine tale ready to tell.

CHAPTER TWENTY TWO

When he'd gone, Edith said 'I suppose you want to know what that was all about.' But when I snapped back that no, I wasn't in the least interested she told me anyway. The two men wanted to buy the place. 'Cash, they said. I've been thinking about it ever since you said they might be looking for a mooring so I asked a silly figure, not caring whether they said yes or no. But in the end they came up to it and I can see it's the position makes it worth it to them, with the twenty-four hour mooring. But then they said they wanted to be in here within six weeks so I said it'll cost them extra and they never quibbled. You heard me tell them I'll let them know within a fortnight.'

I shook my head. 'And here was I believing you'd never leave this place.'

'I know what I'm doing my girl. But first I've got to get those tests done. It all hinges on that. One way or another, it comes down to what they find out about me in that hospital.'

We ate our lunch in silence; strained on my part, thoughtful on hers. I wondered what was going on in her secretive mind. Why the quick decision to sell, and to this pair of shady characters? She suddenly looked up and said she'd like to lie down for a couple of hours and then I could go out if I liked.

If I liked!

As soon as she was settled I called Jack. I could hear voices in the background as we spoke and realised he was still with Maud and Katie. He told me to hold on a minute and when he spoke again he said he was in the garden and they'd been asking him to take them for a drive. 'It's not what I want, Lisa, but I can't suddenly dump them, can I? Or can I?'

'Of course not,' I laughed. 'But can I come along too. Madame's asleep, or at least in bed for a couple of hours.'

'Be there in ten minutes,' he said and I quickly got my coat and went out to wait on the pavement, wondering how we could all pack into the van. But a few minutes later he drove up in a fine old Rover. He leapt out and came round the car to me. 'Mum's in front, she doesn't travel very well.' And then, under his breath, 'God, Lisa, this is no way to carry on. But I promise you won't have mother-in-law and step-daughter along on our honeymoon.'

'I can't wait,' I laughed and he opened the back door and I climbed in beside Katie. The old car smelt of leather and polish and Maud told me how Jack had found it in someone's old shed and resurrected it. 'Taken him a couple of years to do it up, mind, but we like our little jaunts on a Sunday.' At this rate that honeymoon he'd spoken of would be the first time we'd be alone together, but I found it was enough at the moment to sit and look at the back of his head and listen to the easy talk between the three of them.

Because Maud was such an old and trusted friend of Edith's, I told them about the morning's visitors. I said it seemed they were interested in buying the house and Maud laughed and said that'd be the day. 'She'll tell you all about it, I expect,' I said, not wanting to say too much, knowing Edith's passion for privacy. But I did say I thought they were a very suspicious pair and told Jack how they'd shown such an interest in the storerooms I felt he might be right; they were looking at possible hiding places.

Jack was angry to hear Edith had let in a pair of strangers though Katie hooted with mirth when I said we'd had Sean as our protector. There was a lot of talk about it all and Maud said whatever was Edith thinking of, and her so sick and all.

But I was diverted from the subject by the countryside we were passing through. We pulled into a little car park and walked down through woods to a tiny hamlet on the edge of a river. Maud sat down on the edge of the granite slipway and Katie ran off to find shells and as Jack and I walked along the water's edge, he took my hand in his. 'I've told them I'm seeing you,' he grinned at me, 'and I think they've got the message. They both like you, so that's alright. OK?'

'Very OK,' I said. 'Except I'd rather like to kiss you right now. But not in front of the children, right?'

He blew out his cheeks. 'You and me both. I'll be round again this evening though, after the old dragon is in bed. And don't say you'll have to ask her first. You never get time off so what the hell can she expect.'

But when he spoke I remembered my evening out with Darren Cornish. I must tell Jack before he heard some garbled version from someone else; I was learning about the powerful bush telegraph that operated in the town. But more seriously, I knew I must tell him all about Giles Christchurch-Smith. Because I knew that sooner or later he'd turn up again, and we had to decide what to do about it.

Despite our mutual reservations about the family outing, we all enjoyed ourselves. Maud was pleased to see me so enraptured by the scenery and Katie pulled me aside and told me she was dead glad dad had found someone at last. When I told her to hang on a bit, don't go rushing things, she dismissed me with an airy wave of her hand. And when Jack and Maud turned and waited for us to catch up, I knew he was as impatient as I was for us to be properly together at last.

Only first we'd have to do something about Edith. But little did either of us guess the boot was on the other foot and right at that moment she was busy making her own plans for us.

CHAPTER TWENTY THREE

The next few days kept me on my toes. Jack and I snatched whatever short time we could to spend together, but with the working week, both of us were committed and had to make do with those brief meetings. Our phones were busy though.

First thing on Monday morning, Edith told me Darren Cornish was coming to go over some business matters with her. I was not to go out as my signature would be needed. I smiled to myself at the thought of Darren coming. How would he handle meeting me after that encounter in the supermarket? But remembering his blithe self regard, I doubted he would behave much differently. However, when the bell rang spot on time for the ten o'clock appointment and I opened the door, it wasn't Darren standing there, but an earnest looking very young man who blushed as he spoke. 'I'm Liam Blight,' he said. 'Mr Cornish is rather tied up this morning so he's asked me to come.' I was about to ask who'd got him tied up, some blonde or was it her husband but one look at Liam's sober face told me he wouldn't appreciate the remark. Probably wouldn't understand it, come to that.

I led him into the kitchen and introduced him to Edith who was seated at the table with a stack of papers before her, all prepared. She dipped her chin to peer in her characteristic way over the top of her glasses, glared briefly and then said, 'Go back and tell Mr Cornish I want the organ grinder, not the monkey.' And she turned her head away and began to read one of the papers in front of her.

Biting my lip I led the pale and affronted young man to the door. As I showed him out, his face drawn with worry and confusion, trying no doubt to re-phrase Edith's command in a way acceptable to his boss, I took pity on him and asked for Darren's office number. My mobile phone was in my pocket and I gave my name and said I wanted to speak to Mr Cornish. When I was put through, I thought he sounded rather subdued and wary. I told him I had a message for him and baldly repeated Edith's words while Liam's eyes bulged with horror. There was a short pause and then Darren laughed. 'I wondered who that tin of Chappie in your Tesco basket was for. Now I can see it was for Edith. I should have known it wasn't for you, shouldn't I?'

'Yes you should, you, you...' I tried to find a word which wouldn't shock Liam, 'you turd. You'd better get down here double quick though or I won't answer for what Edith might do.' I pocketed the phone and smiled at Liam who was now red-faced with embarrassment. 'Darren says you'd better go back to the office, Liam. Mr Cornish seems to have got himself untied rather more quickly than he expected. He's on his way down here right now.'

After he arrived it was a good half an hour before Edith unbent enough to be reasonably civil to him.

Darren had created a fairly creditable death-bed emergency to excuse the fact he hadn't been able to get here earlier. 'I know how you value punctuality, Mrs Rogers, so I thought Mr West could hold the fort until I arrived.' Then he looked up and caught my cynical gaze and quickly looked away.

I made myself scarce until Edith rang for me to come. 'Go and get Iris from the shop. She can be the other witness. And don't bring Sean, we've had enough pantomime for one day.'

We signed a number of documents and as Sean's mother left she said, 'First time I've ever set foot in this place you know, and I've lived over the shop next door for twenty-eight years. Sean said 'tis lovely upstairs though he never got much chance to look round, he said, having to keep a close eye on those upcountry chaps all the time.' She was angling to be shown round herself, of course, but Edith's mood today wasn't to be trifled with so I just shook my head in her direction and Iris nodded sympathetically and walked away up the alley.

While I was folding up the papers for Edith, Darren hung over my shoulder a bit too closely and I dug my elbow sharply into his side. He disguised a gasp of pain with a cough, but when I went to the door with him, I let him know I didn't think him so funny any more. With no young clerk listening, I told him, 'You're a shit, you know Darren. A real lump of shit. You don't deserve that gorgeous wife of yours, or those lovely children. Willing to give them up are you? Just to prove you've got bigger balls than most?' I shook my head and glared at him.

His face reddened but Darren to the last, he began to bluster. 'Really, Lisa, you don't have to be so coarse. Nurses! I should have known better than try and tangle with a nurse.'

'Yes you should,' I snapped. 'And next time your hands wander in this nurse's direction, she'll see you get a six inch hypodermic needle shoved up your arse pronto.' I went inside and closed the door firmly, my cheeks hot and as I did I remembered Edith's acute sense of hearing. Had I raised my voice? Probably. But when I entered the kitchen, Edith had set aside the documents and was engrossed in the daily paper. It was only as I cleared the coffee cups that I noticed the page she'd been staring at so intently was an advert for cut-price MOT inspections.

After all the business, as she said, she wanted to go and lie down again that afternoon and since Jack was working, I took myself off for a brisk walk, thinking over how my life had changed since coming to Cornwall. Even before I'd met Jack, I'd fallen in love with the harbour and the town and the surrounding countryside. I'd already felt I didn't want to return to my old way of life. And now I hugged myself when I looked ahead, hardly daring to believe the undreamed of happiness that had come my way.

But when I got back to the house, I found Edith in

pain again. She told me to go away, she'd be alright again soon. And by evening once more, she seemed much better. No chance of seeing Jack tonight, though; for she sat in the front room and watched a film with apparent enjoyment until eleven. My own eyes were heavy by the time I'd got her into bed and I had to content myself with a quick call to Jack to say goodnight.

Next day I broached the matter of her going into hospital for those tests. Edith snapped at me that she would say when she was ready to go, and it was not yet, so kindly keep my opinions to myself. I'd got quite good at mentally shrugging by now and did so again. But now my reason for wanting her admitted was due to more than concern for my patient's health, for as soon as I was relieved of my responsibility, I'd be able to escape to Jack. So who could blame me for watching my patient ultra carefully each passing day and while not exactly wishing it upon her, hoping that sooner rather than later she would make up her mind to go into hospital for those much postponed tests.

Halfway through the week I nonchalantly answered the door to find with a shock, one of Edith's visitors, 'the boat men' as I called them, standing on the step. It was the larger of the pair, the one I'd mentally labelled Mr Big. He was carrying a strangely shaped package. 'I want to see Mrs Rogers,' he said, treating me with the disdain due to a menial. I was reluctant to admit him and asked him to wait while I found out if she was well enough to see him. But she impatiently told me to let him in for goodness sake, what was I thinking of, keeping the man waiting outside. Another shrug. When he went in to the kitchen, he greeted her with a degree of deference he was plainly uncomfortable with but seemed to think was necessary to flatter Edith. 'I've just bought this little table for my wife,' he said, 'and I don't want to take it back to my hotel. I wondered if I could leave it with you for a day or two. Just until Friday, I'm going back up to town then.' He drew back the brown paper and showed us a small occasional table with a pedestal and a highly polished mahogany top. Edith looked at it for a bit and then, 'Don't think you can stampede me into making up my mind by moving your things in here bit by bit. I told you I'll let you know in a fortnight whether or not I'll sell. I don't want the place filled up with your furniture by then.'

'Oh no, I wouldn't dream of it,' he replied quite unperturbed. 'I'll take it with me if it'll be in your way. It's just that when I bought it in the shop just up the road, I suddenly thought of you and wondered if I could store it with you just until the end of the week.'

Edith came to a decision. 'Well, if you must. Put it in the front room, out of my way. I'm going for my nap.'

He quickly picked up the table as if he were afraid she'd change her mind, and I followed him along the passage, still not prepared to let him out of my sight. He ignored me completely, went over and looked out of the window and then put the table down. A quick goodbye to Edith and he was gone.

But as I was taking her upstairs, she turned to me. 'While I'm sleeping I want you to go to those second hand furniture shops up the road and ask if they've just sold that table. There's two or three places you could try. Call themselves antique dealers. Junk shops, more like. But I want to know where he bought it. If he bought it.' So, Edith was as suspicious of the men's motives as I was. But why on earth then was she thinking of doing business with them? Still, there was usually method in her madness so I held my peace and said OK I'd go and find out.

Stretching the point a bit, I included a charity shop and went much farther along the street than could be called 'near' by any stretch of the imagination. Each time I told the assistant that a friend of mine had just bought a pretty little antique table which I described to them. But no, no one had sold a table like that. Not today or in the past week come to that. But two of them would like to buy one if I came across any. Back at the house I looked the table over, feeling a little foolish as I ran my fingers over the wood looking for a secret compartment. Nothing, of course. But all the same, what was going on? When Edith woke up she merely nodded her head when I told her the result of my enquiries in the shops but made no comment.

I told Jack about the incident when he phoned at tea time and he said he was coming to see me that evening,

Edith or no Edith. I was beginning to feel a bit that way myself and was very glad when she decided to have an early night once more.

After he arrived, it was quite a while before we bothered about the table, but eventually Jack asked to take a look at it. As a carpenter, the construction of the table was no mystery to him but he said the pedestal was thicker than it should be. 'Spoils the proportions, see?' he said. 'Nice piece of wood too, but the stand is much newer than the top. It's no antique but it is made of old wood.' He looked at it for a bit longer and then turned to me. 'It's a puzzle alright. I don't like the sound of that pair at all. You can tell Edith that tomorrow I'm coming round to put a spy hole in your door. You need to know who's outside. Then you can call me anytime you get unwelcome visitors.' He was frowning and his voice was grim. 'Can you give me a good description of these blokes? Only I've got a pal who works for the Customs and Excise, he might be glad to hear if there's something brewing.'

'I can do better than that,' I said and went and fetched the print I'd taken of the men in their speed boat as they circled near our jetty.

'Good girl,' he said, 'I knew you were more than just a pretty face.' He went to put the photo in the pocket of his jacket in the hall and came back and put his arms round me. 'Much more than just a pretty face. There's this, and this...'

'Stop' I squealed, 'you're tickling.' And then we sank

179

down on the couch and the sinister men and their mysterious table were quite forgotten.

When I told Edith next day that Jack was going to fit a spy hole in the door, she asked how much he was going to charge seeing as how she never asked for it to be done. But when he'd finished fitting it, without asking, she gave him some cash and said to make sure he wasn't out of pocket. And I was very relieved at last to be able to see whoever it might be standing outside our door.

That evening I heard Jack's familiar tap and I looked through to make sure it was him as he'd said I must. I could see someone else was with him and when I opened the door there was a short, heavily built man beside him, holding a spaniel on a lead. Puzzled I let them in. Edith was watching a soap on the big set in the front room and didn't appreciate the interruption but Jack said it would only take a minute The man, whom he simply introduced as Simon, released the dog's lead and it immediately headed for the little table and sniffed and barked excitedly with his nose against the wood.

Simon soothed the dog and refastened its lead. 'What are the names of these two men, Mrs Rogers?' he asked.

'Mr Jones and Mr Smith,' she announced with some irony.

'Ah well. Makes a change from Smith and Jones,

anyway,' he said. Then, 'Can we borrow your kitchen for ten minutes? We won't make a mess, I promise you.'

'Do what you like,' she said abruptly and turned back to the television set. Simon picked up the table and they went out of the room. I started to follow them but Jack shook his head and reluctantly I sat down, wondering what on earth they were about. They were a little longer than ten minutes but when they brought the table back it looked no different from before. Simon thanked her and said not to worry but if anything odd happened to call this number and he handed her his card. 'Better call me rather than the police, right? Not that I think you will need to call anyone mind.'

Edith took the card and looked at it. 'I don't know what you're up to, and come to that I don't know what those men are up to. But if it suits me to do business with them, I shall do. Selling a house isn't illegal.'

Simon mollified her by agreeing that it was a free country and of course she could do what she liked. He was only giving her his number in case of some unlooked for development. But now he must go and give his dog some exercise. Jack went with him to the door and they spoke quietly for a few minutes. Then Jack turned to me and asked what time Madam would be off to bed. I said I'd phone the minute I was free and he promised to come round.

But once more Edith stayed up late and once again we had to make do with a long goodnight phone call. But I

181

was smiling to myself when finally I put out the light for surely it wouldn't be long now before we could properly be together.

CHAPTER TWENTY FOUR

Next morning Edith said for goodness sake stop fussing about the place and sit down. I looked at her in surprise because I was simply clearing the breakfast things. We were later than usual as she had slept heavily for once and I'd been careful not to disturb her. Now, in obedience to her command, I pulled out a chair and joined her at the table. She had one of yesterday's fat documents in her hand. 'I want you to take a look at this,' she said. 'It's my will. It's alright,' she went on when she could see I was reluctant to read the paper, 'you're not mentioned in it.'

'I know that,' I retorted angrily. 'I'm not quite such a fool as you think. I witnessed the blessed thing, didn't I, so obviously I couldn't benefit from it. In any case,' I stood up as if to leave the table, 'I've only been here five minutes. What do you take me for? Or perhaps you'd better not answer that.' I was nearer to telling her what she could do with her job than I'd ever been. How dare she treat me with such contempt!

'Alright, alright. Sit down. I shouldn't have said that. I don't always mean what I say.' This was a fulsome apology on Edith's part and she was looking at me anxiously, aware she'd gone too far, her hands shaking more than usual. Once again the nurse in me took over; she was a sick woman and it was second nature now to humour her. But still I had to prowl round the room for a bit until I felt calm enough to go back to the table and sit down. And after all, it would be interesting to discover the final arrangements this strange woman had made.

She put the document carefully in front of me and I was conscious of her eyes watching me as I read. When I'd finished, I raised my head and found myself smiling at her. 'Well,' I said, 'there are going to be some very happy people when...' I caught myself, aware of what I was about to say. But this time there was no doubt about it, Edith herself was smiling, a strange lopsided grin.

'I know. A lot of people will be glad when I'm gone. Won't bother me though, will it. But do you think it's a good will? Young Darren Cornish couldn't find any fault with it, but then I don't care for his opinion.'

Despite my earlier exasperation I couldn't help but be pleased with the implication that she did care about my opinion. 'I think it's quite wonderful.' I meant it, full of surprise that this weird woman could come up with such pleasant and imaginative proposals.

'Put it over there in my box. And then we'll have a cup of tea and I want to tell you something in confidence. Alright, alright,' she said again, impatiently repeating herself, 'I know. You said that once before, that you don't tell secrets.'

I made tea for Edith, coffee for me and we went along to the front room to settle down with our cups. The sun was shining again and when she was sitting in the sunny patch on the balcony, she told me something of what was on her mind.

'These men. Jones and Smith or whatever they're really called. You said you thought they were a bit iffy and as soon as I set eyes on them I could see what you meant. Pair of crooks if ever I saw them.' I was about to interrupt, to ask what on earth she was thinking of doing business with them if that was her view, but she forestalled me. 'I told them I would let them know in a couple of weeks about selling this house. It all depends on what results I get from those hospital tests. If they're clear, I'll sell to them regardless. Their money's as good as anyone else's. And then I'd like to take a trip out to Australia and I'd like you to come with me.' Again she held up her hand when I would have spoken. 'Hear me out before you say anything.' She stared out over the water for a while as if uncertain how to go on. 'If the results are not good, then I shan't go. I don't want to die away from Cornwall. I've never been away before and just thinking about it these last few weeks has made me see how deep my roots go. 'Twould be a wrench leaving even for a short time, and I wouldn't like to think it'd be for ever. I believe Charlie feels a bit that way, that he'd like to come back home when 'tis his time to rest.

'But if the news is bad, and I can't go, I won't be able to sell up either. I can't explain why at the moment. But when that time comes I shall be asking for your help.

185

And I'm hoping you'll be able to persuade Jack to help too. I know he doesn't like me.' Once again she waved aside my protest. 'He thinks I put upon his mother. And I suppose I do. I've got used to her, see. I've known her all my life. She's younger than me and I've always been able to make her do what I want. Mind, I gave her a good job in my shops and she'll tell you I was always fair. But as I said, Jack doesn't like me and he won't put himself out on my behalf. Not unless you manage to persuade him.'

My head was spinning with all these alternatives, but what was bothering me most was the thought of going off to Australia. The thought of leaving Jack. I said slowly, going to the heart of the matter for me, 'It's a very long flight to Australia. Do you think you're up to it? And, forgive me, but by the time you get there, you probably wouldn't be in very good shape to meet Charlie.'

'I don't plan to meet Charlie. I don't want him to see me like this. Old and sick and helpless. But I would like to see a bit of the country where he lives. The outback. We were talking on the phone the other morning. Well, it was morning here and I was looking across the water like I'm doing now and it was already evening there. He said he was sitting on his verandah too, looking across the parched land to the hills far away and blue with the distance. I would like to see that for myself, with my own eyes.' We were both silent for a while and presently I blew my nose.

186

'I'm going to make us some lunch,' I said. 'You've given me a lot to think about. I need a bit of time.'

She nodded her head. 'No hurry. And like I said, it all depends on what those doctors find. No point making decisions yet.'

But she had at least made one important decision. She asked me to ring that smarmy doctor of hers, (her words) and then give her the phone. She waved an irritated hand at me when I would have left the room and beckoned me to stay and listen while she spoke. From the one-sided conversation I gathered he would have to arrange things at the hospital and call back. And when the phone rang soon afterwards, I was again told to stay and listen. It seemed Dr West would be able to admit her the next Monday morning. 'Not till then!' she exclaimed. 'I thought with all it's costing me you'd be sending a helicopter to pick me up in ten minutes.' I heard his embarrassed and uncomfortable laugh, unsure whether or not she was serious. Then he explained that the consultant he most wanted her to see was on holiday but would be back at work next week. He would send a car to collect her.

'Well,' she said as she put the phone down on the table, 'that's that.' She pushed the handset across the table towards me. 'Phone that Tom Pooley at the garage and see if he can let us have a car this afternoon. I feel like a bit of a drive out in the country. And we can pick up Maud. She'll want to hear about all my doings

187

lately.'

I thought it was a bit short notice, but once again Tom came up trumps. 'Only a small Volvo, but there's room enough in the boot for the chair. After lunch, you said. I'll bring the car round at half past one, OK?'

Maud sounded pleased when I phoned with Edith's invitation and laughed with surprise when I told her we were going to Truro. 'Truro! The things she used to say about Truro when she was in business. Her biggest rivals were there, of course.'

I'd not been to Truro before and I quite enjoyed driving this smaller car. When we parked, Maud insisted that I go off on my own, saying she could supervise the chair though Edith hardly needed much help. So I strolled off and wandered round the streets, losing myself a couple of times in the narrow lanes and alleys that criss-crossed the small city. An hour wasn't long enough to do much, but I admired the domes of the attractive law courts and spent a while inside the cathedral. There was an aerial map of Cornwall there that intrigued me, giving the best overall view of the wildly indented coast and the river estuaries I'd seen; I was almost able to orientate myself at last. But a glance at my watch made me tear myself away and I reached our meeting place only a couple of minutes before Maud and Edith turned up.

'We've had a very successful shopping spree,' Maud announced and I was surprised to see the large bags crammed into the wheelchair storage carrier. But later, back at the house I was shown their purchases. I should have guessed of course; several new nightdresses, a lightweight dressing gown and a whole range of expensive toiletries. I must have shown my surprise at the amount of shopping because Edith said, 'I might be needing a few new things if I'm to go off travelling, apart from the hospital of course.'

Maud nodded her head and smiled. So Edith had confided in her. Good, it made our chats easier if I didn't have to watch what I was saying for fear of betraying my employer's confidences.

Jack came to collect Maud and followed me in his van to Tom Pooley's garage when I returned the car. So I had a few unexpected minutes with him as he drove me back to Edith's. And after Jack and Maud left, I asked Edith if I could tell Jack about her plans, seeing she'd already told his mother.

'Yes,' she said, 'he'll have to know. And you're going to have to soften him up a bit on my behalf'. I said I'd do my best and then I put the new garments away in a drawer. She told me there was a small suitcase somewhere and I found it on a top shelf. 'Bring it here,' she said. It was an overnight bag, blue and with a designer label. 'Mrs Green gave that to me for Christmas three or four years ago. Always hoping she'd get me into hospital, she was. Bought the case specially.' I laughed but then, remembering the handsome legacy Edith had planned for this much disparaged lady, I felt a glow of pleasure. The poor woman had certainly earned it, though I very much doubted she expected more than a nominal bequest, or anything at all for that matter.

Jack came and once more we sat, swathed in rugs, out on the balcony. Only once did her bell disturb us and we talked seriously about Edith's plans. 'Australia! God, Lisa, do you have to go?'

'I haven't agreed to anything yet. Fact is, Jack, I don't think she'll be going anywhere. Dr West is pretty sure they're going to find a nasty problem when they do those tests. And she's definitely gone down hill in the last week or two. I just feel I must keep up her spirits as best I can and if that means talking about this trip of hers, then I have to.' But snuggled against him under the rug, I felt it would be the hardest decision in my life to get on that plane without Jack.

But while Edith was in hospital there'd be at least one night for us to have together. A whole long night. I locked my fingers behind Jack's head and drew him towards me. Speaking against my lips he said, 'I'm taking Monday off. And Tuesday.' I freed myself and beamed at him.

'How d'you manage that?' I asked. 'What did your client say?'

'She said she never expected I'd be there on Monday anyway. She knows what these tradesmen are like.' He nuzzled my neck. 'Do you know what these tradesmen are like?'

I shook my head. 'No,' I said, 'but I'm perfectly

willing to learn.'

CHAPTER TWENTY FIVE

Mr Big, or Mr Jones according to his claim to Edith, did not come back to collect his table on Friday as he'd promised. Instead there was a phone call from him in the middle of the morning when he insisted on speaking to the lady of the house personally. She told me he said he'd been unavoidably called back to London and hadn't had time to pick up the table. He hoped it wasn't in her way and he'd collect it next Friday. And had she seen the solicitor about the searches yet? I couldn't help hearing her side of the conversation when she snapped back she'd already told him she'd take a fortnight to decide and she wasn't going to be pushed around by him or the king of Siam and if he didn't come for his table next Friday it would be put outside in the alley. Then she switched off.

For the rest of the day and over the weekend Edith's mood went up and down like mercury, sensitive to every smallest variation in the atmosphere. And despite my awareness of her fragile state of health, there were plenty of moments when I was hard put to rally an iota of sympathy for her. She was even more venomous than usual, and despite my pretended indifference, her comments hurt. Later though, when the sting had worn off, I would recall her words and wonder if she hadn't meant them to be taken quite so seriously. Often there was an element of black humour in her remarks.

Perhaps she could have been a nice person if the potentially cheerful bubble somewhere inside her hadn't been so roughly burst by the circumstances of her life.

But Monday morning came at last and by the time the doorbell rang to announce Dr West's transport had arrived, I think I was feeling at least as jumpy as Edith, though apart from the merest flicker of apprehension which crossed her face when the bell rang, she showed nothing of her emotions. Standing alongside the driver in the alley was a very superior young woman, who introduced herself as the doctor's daughter. We knew she had just qualified as a nurse and she said she'd come along to look after Edith on her trip to the hospital as if this was a great privilege. Edith said nothing with considerable effect.

I was soon locking the door behind us as they conveyed Edith to the car and settled her in the back seat. She'd already given me orders not to go back to the house until I heard when she would be arriving home, and then I was to switch on the heating. She looked so shrunken and forlorn sitting in the car that I reached in, wanting to drop a kiss on her cheek. But the look in the gimlet eyes forbade any such liberty and I patted her hand instead. And as the car drove off, she made no response to my goodbye wave and the pity I felt for her at times came rushing back, poor woman, enclosed in such an unbreachable shell.

I stood on the pavement watching the car drive off

with a heavy heart. But then Jack arrived and my depression vanished like the spring showers we'd been having these last few days. He was driving his lovely old Rover but there was no time for more than a brief hello as, goaded by the impatient tooting of a couple of cars already waiting behind us in the narrow street, I slung my holdall on the back seat and jumped into the car.

Jack's house was on the edge of the town near the top of one of the many hills. He'd explained already how the place had had a closing order on it when he bought it, and over the years, whenever there was a slack period in his work, he'd put some time to renovating it. 'Rebuilding, in fact,' he said. 'Helen used to moan about it, and about the fact I'd increased our mortgage to buy it in the first place, but when she took up with Gavin it was a godsend in more ways than one and my share of the divorce settlement helped me finish doing it up.' He hardly ever spoke of the divorce and seemed to be on good terms with Helen but from a certain strain in his voice when he did mention it, I guessed how much he'd been shattered by the break-up of his family.

The cottage stood on its own in the middle of a walled garden, mostly lawn with a few young trees. We parked on the short driveway and he told me the stone front of the house was original, but almost everything else was new. 'Won't take long to show you my castle,' he smiled, 'three rooms down and three up.' He opened the front door and waved me ahead. 'Come and have a look round'.

I don't know what I expected or why I should be so surprised, but the cottage was a dream. The large kitchen had an ancient dresser and a porcelain sink with wooden draining boards and a plate rack above. 'Found the sink and those things all about to go into a skip,' he grinned as I admired them. There were two windows, one overlooking the garden at the side and the other faced seawards; not with the view of the harbour that I was used to, but giving a panoramic view of the outer bay, a great sweep of sea and sky, wonderfully liberating after Edith's claustrophobic house.

The sitting room had a low, beamed ceiling and a wood-burning stove stood on the wide hearth. 'I made the room bigger by moving the stairs out to the back hall,' Jack explained when I commented on its size. A door at the far end led into a small office, bare apart from the computer on its desk, a couple of chairs and some shelves with file boxes neatly stacked and a collection of books and paper backs.

Upstairs there was Katie's room, a riot of clothes tumbled across the bed and the walls were covered by vivid posters. She lived with her mother during the school week and spent weekends mostly with Jack. I crossed to the window of the small bathroom and looked down into the garden. 'No need for frosted glass in here,' Jack grinned, 'I don't even bother to draw the curtains. It's nice being able to look out at the sky when you're taking a shower.' Next door there was a tiny room with a single bed 'for when Katie brings a friend along.' And then Jack's bedroom, large and sparingly furnished with an old limed oak wardrobe and chest and the bed, the comfortable double bed he'd spoken of, where an Indian bedspread brought a bright splash of colour into the room.

He put down my holdall. 'And now,' he said, 'before I take you off on that mystery tour of the county I promised you, would you like a cup of tea or coffee or something?'

I looked round the pleasant room tucked under the eaves of the house. And then I turned to Jack, standing so close beside me. 'I think it's high time we tried that "or something", don't you?' I said. And so it was a good hour before we came down for that proferred cup of coffee. A very good hour as a matter of fact.

Later as we wandered, arms enfolded, round his small garden, Jack smiled his pleasure at my delight in his cottage. It looked out to the sea over the top of a copse which was in the garden of a house down the hill. I knew there were other houses too nearby, but they were out of sight beyond the high wall and I revelled in this feeling of being completely alone with Jack. I felt I could stay there forever looking out at the ships dotted across the great bay under the canopy of the blue sky, with its scatter of high fluffy clouds. But Jack wanted to use his day off to show me some more of his home county. 'Unless, of course...' he smiled. But I shook my head reminding him we'd still got the coming night for ourselves.

So off we went in the car. 'If you think of this bottom bit of Cornwall as an old boot,' he said, 'Falmouth is just above the heel and we're going to cut across to the instep, along Mount's Bay and then down to the toe at Land's End. Then up the front of the boot, that's the north coast, for a while, depending how we go for time. Get the general picture?' And I said I expect it will all become clear as we go.

Both of us were in such a state of euphoria that the Russian steppes in the depths of winter would have seemed exotic. But with the sun shining and the hedgerows bright with wildflowers, we were often lost for words as we drove along. Several times we stopped, once to walk down a bumpy lane to a small cove. 'A smuggling king once lived here,' said Jack. 'I wonder if he looked anything like your Mr Big.' And suddenly smuggling didn't seem quite so romantic.

'By the way,' he went on, 'that photo of yours was a great help. The excise boys know who your men are and they're keeping an eye on them. And they want to know where that table goes. They'd already sussed there's a racket in fake antiques being set up but now there's this drug connection too. I don't like it one bit, and I wish they'd just catch those guys and lock them up. But they said they need to catch the big boys first and that'll take time and patience. Just you make sure you use that spy-hole and never let them in.' But I was in no mood to worry about that unpleasant pair and in the warn sunshine, Jack soon let the subject drop.

As we drove past St Michael's Mount, I told him of my jaunt with Darren Cornish. He shot me a quizzical look but I was glad that apart from muttering under his breath something about that randy bastard, he seemed quite unfazed by my story and laughed when I described my meeting his family in the supermarket. We lunched in the same pub in Mousehole but this time I thoroughly enjoyed the food. Then we went on towards Land's End. As we headed for Zennor, the sun drifted behind a bank of cloud and we reached the Atlantic coast under a heavy shower. The sudden gloom and thundery light only served to emphasise the splendour of the scenery, the most dramatic I had yet seen. The road switchbacked and twisted between ancient stone hedges, with tiny fields falling from the steep hills to the sea. Jack told me those little meadows, dotted here and there with great grey rocks, were some of the earliest enclosures in the country. The rain stopped. We stopped. And walked up one of the hills and as we reached the crest, the clouds parted and the land was suddenly bathed in golden sunshine. We were silent. It was enough, the primeval rocky hills, the fields, the backdrop of sea and sky. Jack's hand found mine and we walked slowly back to the car.

'Anything else after this would be anti-climax,' I said as we drove on and Jack agreed to leave the rest of the scenic route he'd planned for another day. 'Tell you what,' he said, 'how about an ice-cream in St Ives? It's a great place, you'll love it. And then if you're really hell-bent on visiting Edith, we can go straight on up to Truro.'

He was right, I did love the place. I spotted a nice little bookcase in one of Edith's 'junk shops' and bought it. 'Souvenir of St Ives for your cottage,' I said and pressed my fingers against his protesting lips. Then he led me over to a cabinet and pointed out a gold Victorian ring set with small rubies. 'Do you like it?' he asked and when I nodded, he asked the assistant if I could try it for size and the next moment the ring was mine. He smiled at me, 'Another souvenir of St Ives. I'll get you a proper ring when we've more time to choose.' But I knew that this was the one I wanted, discovered so unexpectedly on such a fantastic day.

Jack carried the bookcase up the hill to the car park, easier than bringing the traffic to a stop in the narrow lane, he said, adding, 'Pity you didn't get me a pair of cuff links or a couple of collar studs. Still, better than that grandfather clock you were eyeing up, I suppose.' Then, with a last fond look over the exquisite little port spread out down below, we set off for our next destination, the small private hospital where Edith lay.

Jack waited outside the little room I was shown into. Edith lay in the bed looking very white and drawn. She hadn't expected a visitor and despite herself, her face brightened when I came in. She told me they'd taken about a bucket of blood out of her during the day and she'd no idea what they were getting up to tomorrow. She hoped they'd give her something to help her sleep; the noise was terrible, building work going on right outside her window. And the nurses were that sharp with her, you wouldn't believe. 'Calling me Edith, too. The cheek.' She asked me to help her sit up a bit and how did I get here anyway.

I told her Jack had brought me and she asked where he was and said tell him to come in. I knew he had a thing about hospitals, even though this one more resembled a good hotel.

But he came in when I asked him, and took up a position standing awkwardly midway between the bed and the door. He was wearing casual clothes and his fair hair had lightened from working in the sun and his face and arms were tanned already. He stood, hands thrust in pockets, shoulders hunched. He looked fit and strong. And physical. I wondered what Edith saw as she stared at him.

'Did she tell you I might need your help, the pair of you?' Edith asked with her usual lack of finesse. And when he said yes, Lisa had mentioned something, she said, 'But will you do it? Help me if I ask?'

Jack's face was grave. He spoke quietly and without a smile. 'I don't sign blank cheques any more than you do, Mrs Rogers.' But when she closed her eyes and shook her head despairingly, his face slowly softened.

'But if I can, yes, I will give you a hand,' he said.

Her eyes flew open and her breath came in a gasp. 'Well. That's something I suppose. You better go now, both of you. I expect they'll let me go home tomorrow.' And she turned her face to one side. I said goodbye but she made no acknowledgment she'd heard and in the corridor outside her room Jack blew out his cheeks and shook his head. What a woman she was, he said as we returned to the car.

Back at the cottage Jack set the bookcase beneath a window in the sitting room and filled it from the shelves in his office. It immediately looked at home and Jack's smiling eyes were thanks enough. We bickered amicably over who was to cook our meal, Jack claiming he was a master chef. But I wanted to play housewife so in the end he uncorked the wine and sat at the table while I prepared the meal. Several times I had to escape his clutches as I moved round the kitchen, but finally we took our plates into the sitting room. He'd already lit the fire, not because we were cold but because I'd said I like to watch real flames. And after we'd cleared away the plates I sat on the rug and leaned back against his legs as he lounged in the big armchair. His fingers played with my hair and I turned my hand and let the firelight gleam on the rubies in my ring.

Edith's problems, Mr Big and his sinister friends, Giles Christchurch-Smith, all were forgotten. There was only this room, this warm fire, and the touch of his hands. Only tonight. The rest could wait.

CHAPTER TWENTY SIX

Jack had set the alarm for six thirty. I said I thought we'd be able to have a lazy morning as he'd taken the day off and he replied there's nothing like the pleasure of turning off the alarm and knowing you can go back to sleep again. Or whatever.

Later on I slipped out of bed and brought us both a cup of tea and then, lying in the crook of his arm, I told him what had driven me from my home.

My first contact with Giles Christchurch-Smith had been in the hospital where I worked. He had a badly broken leg and was a patient for several weeks and though I treated him no differently from anyone else, he became infatuated with me. He found out where I lived from casual chats with other nurses who were unaware of his growing obsession. And as soon as he was discharged from the hospital, it began. Flowers first, huge bunches of flowers were delivered to my door which I promptly lugged straight along to the hospital. Then it was the occasional encounter, 'Oh hello, Lisa. Lovely to see you. How about dinner?' And a complete disregard of my refusal, my obvious wish to have nothing to do with him. At first I'd been too embarrassed and uncomfortable to be downright rude to him - I felt he was a rather sick and disturbed man who needed to be treated with some care. But it got worse and worse. He turned up everywhere. Waiting at the tube station, I would look round and he would be there beside me, smiling that strange cold smile that never touched his pale eyes. Or I would at last reach my flat, jumpy from a journey full of apprehension but relieved to be home at last, and there he would be, standing just inside the open stairwell. When I told him I was not about to invite him in, he would nod his head gravely and go quietly away. But I never knew how far off he went, and if Josh was out, I worried that Giles might way-lay him as well. Katherine, my senior nurse advised me to get a restraining order taken out. But Giles came round to the hospital full of consternation; declaring he only came to see me when I invited him, how could I think he would want to upset me. And which weekend was it we planned our trip to Paris? All this in front of the eagerly listening receptionists. Apart from Katherine, everyone thought I was making a fuss about nothing. He never hurts you, they said, never says anything nasty, gorgeous to look at and rich. What more do I want? They didn't have a notion how my flesh crawled each time he came near me. Then the silent phone calls started in the small hours. And when I rang to check the number, the impersonal voice was telling me the caller had withheld their number. Packages arrived from expensive stores which I promptly sent unopened to that grand address of his that he'd quoted to me so often. Sometimes a week would go by with no contact from him and I would begin to think it was over. Then he'd turn up again, often as much as two or three times in a day. It became almost a relief when I did see him; at least the nervous anticipation was over. The police spoke to him again but he was easily able to convince them I was a foolish and neurotic woman. And so it went on. One year. Two years and then three. I lost weight. Couldn't sleep. Only my work kept me from a complete breakdown. Giles, of course, with his private income, had no need to work and was free to shadow me as often as he chose.

Then, a few months ago, one evening after work, I'd negotiated the tube and the walk from the station, glancing round constantly as had now become my habit. No Giles. I looked tentatively inside. No Giles. I climbed the two flights to my flat and let myself in, safe and able to relax at last. Josh was away at college and my flat mate was on night duty. I made myself something to eat, watched the box for an hour and then had a long soak in the bath. And then, as I pulled on my dressing gown and walked into the bedroom, Giles stepped out from behind the door. He gave that little laugh of his. 'You've been waiting for this, haven't you?' he said. Then he raped me.

Jack's arm tightened round me and he half sat up. 'Don't,' I said, 'let me finish. I need to get it off my chest.' And he lay back, his head turned on the pillow to watch me as I spoke.

I'd fallen backwards across the bed, fiercely struggling, and then he'd struck me hard across the face. I was wearing a thick towelling gown and he flung it up over my head and pressed his arm across my throat. I couldn't breathe. I thought I was going to die, and can only remember that terrible struggle for air. It must all have been over in a couple of minutes. The police told me later I'd have died of suffocation if it had gone on for much longer. But I couldn't tell them how long it had gone on for as I'd passed out and when I came round he'd gone. I lay there for a while in a daze and then phoned Katherine. She came. Sent for the police. It's still a bit hazy to remember but I know the police woman was good. Very stern but sympathetic. They had to treat the matter seriously because of my obvious injuries, bruises on my face and throat and the burst blood vessels in my eyes that showed how nearly I had suffocated.

It was Katherine who saw to it I was given the morning after pill. And strong drugs in case he was HIV positive. They did blood tests and the first ones were encouraging but I had to wait five days for the final all clear. And it was Katherine again who suggested they contact Giles and tell him I'd been stabbed by a drug addict's needle and was under investigation for Aids. I was glad to hear it simply terrified him but when we learned through the grape vine that his tests too were clear, it was a great relief.

Then the woman PC came round to advise me not to pursue the case in court. 'I'm on your side, Lisa, one hundred per cent,' she'd said. 'But I heard his tape of the account and believe me he's pretty persuasive. He's certainly convinced the chaps who interviewed him that it had been a kinky sex thing with your agreement which went a bit too far. His only remorse, he said, was that he'd run away when he was scared you had died during the encounter.' The policewoman said she wouldn't want to see his clever barristers tear me apart in the witness box. And she had only to be with me for a few minutes to realise how quickly I'd fall to pieces in their hands.

'So here I am, Jack. No longer a mouse, though. And if he turns up again, as I'm sure he will, I'll tell him to expect an arrest. The charge is still on file, all the samples were taken. And I know I could stand up to any inquisition from those lawyers now, because I know what really happened and I'm strong enough to face them at last.'

Jack was silent for a long while, his body tense as he held me. Then he said, 'I'll kill the bastard if I lay eyes on him.' And coming from my gentle lover the words, spoken in a fierce low voice, held a deadly promise that chilled my blood and I felt I must never let the two come face to face.

We got dressed and went downstairs but my story had left Jack deeply troubled and though we lazed about the house and garden, yesterday's carefree delight had vanished. I phoned the hospital and was told the doctor hadn't yet decided whether to keep Mrs Rogers in for another night. I was to ring at five. I decided I'd better switch on the heating in any case and Jack said he'd drop me in town and then take the materials he needed next day along to the customer's house in readiness. The place was halfway to town, so I opted to walk from there and we arranged to meet later for tea in one of the cafes. We parted more cheerfully and I was in much better spirits by the time I reached Edith's door. There was a card sellotaped to the doorjamb, a florist's note saying no one was in when they called and please phone this number. I wondered if Charlie had sent flowers and was smiling when I stepped into the hall.

It was much colder than I expected because the heating had only been off for a day. The same chill penetrated my bones that I'd felt that day down in the cellar. I picked up a couple of letters which lay on the mat, both addressed to Edith, and put them on the table. I'd never been alone in the house before and the silence was uncanny. There was of course the muffled rumble of the traffic in the street at the end of the alley, and I thought I could hear the slap of the water against the outer walls. But here in the dark hall there was no sound, just a feeling of drawn breath and waiting. I shivered and recalled a couple of lines from an old prayer I'd seen in one of the tourist shops, 'from ghoulies and ghosties and long-leggetty beasties, and things that go bump in the night, good Lord deliver us.' I added a silent amen. Then I forced myself to step into the laundry room where the boiler stood and switched on the heating. The boiler came to life with a roar that made me jump back. I had planned to re-make Edith's bed but I felt so nervous all alone in the house that instead, I turned tail and sped out from the hall, my heart beating wildly as I locked the door behind me.

Out in the alley, I puffed out my cheeks with a sigh of relief and then realised I still held the florist's card clenched in my hand. I'd no intention of going inside again to make the call and used my own phone to call the shop. When they answered, standing there in the alley, I gave them Edith's name. They said they had no record of flowers for her, but when I repeated the address, the girl on the line said, 'Oh yes. I remember now. The flowers are for a Ms Sands.'

My heart, still unsteady from my self-inflicted imaginings, fluttered. I asked what the sender's card said and was told, 'Love, as always. Giles.' I was silent so long the girl asked again when can they deliver the flowers and at last I pulled myself together. 'Just drop them off at the local hospital, would you?' and yes, I was quite sure thank you.

I stood there, wondering how the hell he'd discovered where I was. I realised with grim satisfaction that my immediate reaction had been anger. Not fear but anger. However I still wanted to know what he'd been up to lately. I rang Katherine's flat on the off-chance it was a rest day. But there was only the answer-phone, so I briefly stated that Giles had found my address and asked her to call my mobile when she could as I didn't know where I'd be for the rest of the day.

Because I'd done nothing inside the house, I was early for my meeting with Jack and I went to the entrance to the alley and waited on the pavement. A minute later, Sean appeared. 'I saw you come,' he said and then began to prattle his Sean-talk.

Preoccupied I murmured yes and no for a bit until he suddenly said, 'Lisa. You're not listening. One of those men came back yesterday, with another guy, who looked like a bouncer. It wasn't long after you'd gone off. I heard them ringing your doorbell and then knocking. And then they came into the shop and asked me where you were. So I told them all about Mrs Rogers having to go in to hospital for tests but they weren't interested, I could tell. All they wanted to know was when would you be back and they weren't very pleased when I said not for a day or two I think.'

While he was telling me his tale, Jack turned up and Sean was delighted to have a listener who did give his story the attention he felt it deserved. Jack thanked him and as we walked off, he turned back and pulled out his wallet. He handed Sean a note and asked him to keep an eye out for the men and to ring him right away if he spotted them again. Sean scribbled down Jack's number and fervently promised he'd keep watch and then went back into the shop visibly inflated.

Jack wanted to phone Simon immediately with the news but neither of us had his number with us. 'We'll ring soon as we get home,' Jack said, frowning with concern. But as we sat outside one of the cafes in the sunshine drinking our tea, his mood lightened and he agreed with me that Sean was a somewhat original sleuth. I didn't want to spoil things again by telling him about the flowers from Giles so I said nothing, though I was very conscious of the florist's card in my bag.

But just as we went inside the cottage, my mobile rang. It was Katherine Avery. 'I was in the bath when your message came, Lisa and I've just called the hospital and spoken to that secretary of mine. She's the only one who has access to my organiser where I'd written your address. And this is what the fool of a woman told me. Giles had been in a time or two. Given her chocolates. Buttered her up. Then he told her he didn't want to know where you were, but it's your birthday and he would like to send you flowers. He left her the addresses of three florists to choose from and asked her to send you the biggest arrangement possible and he used his credit card to pay the bill. He told her he'd thought out this way to get flowers to you without himself discovering your address. Then he went away. Well, when she told me that, I phoned the shop she'd chosen and they said, yes, a Mr Christchurch-Smith had rung back to check that his secretary had given them the right address. The lady had just moved house you see. So of course they told him exactly where they'd sent the flowers. So now he knows where you are, Lisa and I could wring that stupid woman's neck.'

I told her it didn't matter. I was no longer scared of him and I told her of my game with Darren and how it had opened my eyes to the feeling of power which Giles so obviously needed. 'Anyway, Katherine, I've much more important things to think of. You must come soon and meet the most important one of all. He's called Jack.' Thankfully he'd been out of earshot for most of this conversation but he heard the last part and grinned as I mentioned his name. Just as I was saying goodbye, Jack's own telephone rang. He spoke for a while and then handed me the receiver with a smile.

'Its Katie,' he said. 'She wants a word with you.' Katie was just in from school and wanted to know where we'd been yesterday and I was glad she couldn't see the blush I felt as I chatted to her. Jack didn't help matters by nibbling my ear but I turned the tables on him by saying, oops, I think your dad has something to tell you and handed the phone quickly back to him, calling my goodbyes to Katie as I did.

At precisely five o'clock, with Jack anxiously listening, I phoned Edith's hospital and a nurse told me the doctor was keeping her in for another night. 'She's very weak and tired,' the nurse elaborated 'and Doctor West thinks she'd be better without visitors this evening. But she should be able to go home tomorrow. If you ring about ten in the morning we'll be better able to tell you when to pick her up.'

I put down the phone and turned to Jack with a wide smile. 'You've got your lodger for another night. Edith's not coming home until tomorrow.' And in our delight we quite forgot to phone his friend Simon and tell him about the two men who had called at the house, very anxious apparently to collect that little antique table.

CHAPTER TWENTY SEVEN

It was raining heavily next morning and as Jack's proposed job was to paint the outside of a house, he called the customer and said he'd be round that afternoon if it cleared up. The owner replied that he might as well write off the rest of the day, the forecast is terrible and Jack put down the phone with a grin.

We ate our breakfast in front of the woodburner whose bright flames cheered the dismal day. Not that we two needed cheering as it meant Jack could now drive me up to Truro to collect Edith, another trip together we hadn't expected. My secret guilty wish that they'd keep her in a little longer, however, didn't come true. When I phoned, they told us we should pick her up that afternoon after the consultant had spoken to her.

But even Jack later admitted he was shocked to see how ill Edith looked when we went into her room. She had been dressed and settled in her wheelchair but she seemed visibly shrunken and barely greeted us when we came in and we were all three quiet on the drive back. Jack drew up on the pavement and dropped our bags outside the door in the alley and then came back to help Edith into her chair. 'I'll park the car up the road. Back in a couple of minutes. Alright?'

I was glad he wasn't working today; because after the break from Edith I knew I was going to find it difficult to adjust and any few extra minutes with Jack must surely help. Edith gave a great sigh as she waited in the alley for me to unlock the door. 'First time I've been away from this place since Fred died,' she said.

I opened the door and pulled the chair up the ramp into the hall. It was still cold but Edith headed her chair for the kitchen and there at least the heating had done its job and the room was warm enough for the returning patient. She wanly wondered if she could manage a cup of tea and I put the kettle on. Then she asked if I'd brought my laptop back with me and I told her yes, it was in Jack's car, he hadn't wanted to leave it outside the door with our cases. Just then he came in and put it on the table and went outside to fetch our bags.

We drank our tea in the stiff silence that Edith seemed to command. Then she spoke. 'That doctor is coming round this evening to explain about the tests. He said he'd be needing to speak to you as well,' she looked at me as she spoke. And this time the fear in her eyes was plain to see. She shivered despite the warmth of the kitchen and I went along to the front room to fetch her wrap.

At the door I came to an abrupt halt and let out a low cry that brought Jack hurrying to my side. The room had been ransacked. A big armchair lay on its back, its underside slashed. The doors to the sideboard were hanging open, the contents spilled, and overturned drawers lay on the floor amid a pile of scattered papers. And as we looked the papers stirred in the wind from the open french doors which swung to and fro on their hinges above a heap of broken glass.

After a moment's stunned silence, I reached into my pocket for my mobile. But Jack put out his hand. 'Before we ring the police, I think I'd better contact Simon. Look, that table of theirs has gone. You go and keep Edith company and I'll check over the rest of the house.'

I went slowly back to the kitchen. Edith's sharp ears had told her something was wrong and with some return of her old fire she demanded to know what had happened. As I was explaining, Jack came back. 'All the rest of the rooms are OK, Mrs Rogers. The bedrooms are fine. It seems they only bothered with that one room.'

'Is the cellar door still locked?' asked Edith, her eyes glaring, and she relaxed visibly against the chair when Jack said yes, the lock hadn't been touched. For the next half hour, we spoke to each other now and then, but most of the time was passed in awkward silence waiting for Simon to arrive.

When he came he had a glazier in tow. The two men and Jack were rather a long time in
the front room and then he came and asked Edith if she could come along and say what was missing.

I was surprised how orderly everything was again; the men had certainly been busy. The new pane of glass in the window showed up because of the absence of blown salt on its surface, the white film I was constantly having to clean off. 'We put the papers back in the drawers,' said Simon, 'but I'm afraid you'll need to sort them out. And we've put a few stitches in that chair base to keep it tidy for the time. I'll send someone along to make it good as soon as I can. Now, Mrs Rogers, what is missing?'

Edith's sunken eyes roamed round the room. 'That table's gone. But you already knew that or you wouldn't be here. Good riddance.' Her eyes examined the sideboard. 'There was a big canteen of cutlery in there. A wedding present. Never been used. So that's no loss. And there was a couple of silver candlesticks. They've gone too. And the mantle clock.'

'Did you have any important papers in those drawers?' Simon asked in his quietly persistent way.

She shook her head. 'Only electric bills, rates. Stuff like that. No loss if they took the lot of it. No money or share certificates. I don't keep valuables in the house.'

'Sensible woman. Now look, we've done what we can and I'm sure you don't want the police tramping all round the place as well as us. I'll be in touch with someone though, about that canteen and the other stuff and maybe they'll turn up. But now, the other thing is this. That lock on the window has been broken and it'll take a little while to get a matching replacement. We can secure it roughly but if you feel nervous, we'll put a man in here for the night.'

'No need,' said Jack. 'I'll be staying. I've been eyeing that big couch, that'll do me until the window is fixed.'

I expected a burst of outrage from Edith but she surprised me once again. 'Yes,' she said, 'you'll be alright sleeping on that. The arm at the end goes down. It's quite comfortable. I've had many a nap on it.'

The men went off together, though Jack only went as far as the alley, their heads bent in earnest conversation and when he came back he found a moment when we were alone to tell me they'd already known the table had gone. 'I helped Simon hide a tracer thing beneath it that first time he came. And he said it started to travel on Monday night. They're still tracking it. What we've got here, Simon said, is a clumsy pretence at a robbery when the only thing they really wanted was that table. He thinks the other things will be dumped nearby. He's set some of his boys to try and track them down as he doesn't want the local police involved. He says they're getting too close to their target for their work to be messed up now by getting the coppers involved as well.'

I shook my head. 'Surely it'd be a lot simpler if they all worked together.'

'Not always easy,' said Jack. 'And if too many people know about an operation, there's a bigger chance of a leak.'

I kept Edith company in the kitchen while Jack worked on the window. The hinges too had been damaged but presently he came and told us they would at least close properly again. 'Bit of string round the handles will have to do for tonight,' he remarked cheerfully.

I went with him, ostensibly to inspect his work, actually to tell him he needn't rough it on the couch, mine was a double bed. But he shook his head. 'I don't think for one minute they'll be back. But you never know. I'd better stay down here. Look,' he said, 'come and see how they got in.' He opened the windows again and showed me the score marks on the balcony rail. 'Came in close in their boat and slung a grapnel up over the railing. Piece of cake for an agile bloke to shin up the rope.'

'Then it certainly wasn't our two chaps. Neither of them could be called agile.'

'This is what's bothering Simon. Possibly a rival bunch moving in. But time will tell. Come on, let's go and put some food on. I'm starving.'

Edith ate nothing. She kept looking at the clock. 'That doctor should be here any minute,' she said. But before he turned up I told her it was time she was in bed, she was looking very tired. Without protest - a bad sign in itself - she let me take her upstairs. I re-made her bed while she watched from the chair and presently she was settled between the crisp linen sheets. 'You go down and wait,' she said. 'You can bring him up when he arrives.' And when I went out of the room she was switching channels on her television set to try and find something to watch.

Dr West arrived at seven thirty full of apologies for being so late. 'Emergency, I'm afraid. Emergency.

Now let's go up and see Mrs Rogers. She won't appreciate it if I talk to you first.'

She'd heard the doorbell of course and had switched off the set by the time we reached her room. Dr West sat down on the chair beside the bed. He reached out as if to take her hand but the look in her eye changed his mind. He cleared his throat. 'I'm afraid the tests have given us some rather bad news,' he said slowly.

Diffident about going on, he was prompted by Edith's, 'Well? What is it then? Cancer?'

He nodded his head gravely. 'I know you want the whole truth. So I have to tell you that we've found your pancreas is badly affected.'

She nodded. 'I thought it must be something bad. I've felt it for some while.' She looked up at him, her dark eyes burning. 'How long have I got? It's important that I know.'

Again he hesitated. 'Never easy to predict these things. But,' he paused, 'weeks rather than months.'

'Weeks. Huh. How many? Two? Four? Ten? You lot won't commit yourself will you. Still, a few more weeks should be enough.' She fell silent. Her colour hadn't changed when the doctor made his pronouncement and now she looked more preoccupied than upset.

He turned to me and gave me instructions about her medication. 'You're in good hands, Mrs Rogers,' he said looking back at her. 'Nurse Sands will take good care of you. Later, of course, you may wish to go into one of our hospices. But that might not be necessary.' After a few more comments, he wished her a goodnight though Edith barely acknowledged him, dismissing him with a curt wave of her hand.

In the hall downstairs he shook his head. 'I can never read that woman. But for the moment I meant what I said about you looking after her. She may even be well enough to go out for a little trip if she wishes. But a couple of weeks down the line, however, it may become a different matter. I'll drop in whenever I'm in the town anyway and you know I'm always on call.' I was glad to see he made no suggestive comments this evening, whether out of deference to the seriousness of his visit or because Jack was in the kitchen was anyone's guess.

Although I'd more than half expected what the news would be, both Jack and I were shaken by the short time the doctor suggested Edith had left to live. She would certainly not be able to make that trip to Australia, to see with her own eyes the landscape of Charlie's new homeland and I wondered whether she would tell him how ill she was in her next conversation with him.

Jack slipped out for a few minutes to buy himself a razor. 'Can't start work tomorrow looking like I've slept in my clothes even if I have,' he grinned. When he came back we passed the evening uncomfortably aware of Edith lying in her lonely bed upstairs and sat together on the sofa, hand in hand, each lost in our own thoughts.

It was late when we went to bed, Jack to his comfortable nest of blankets on the couch, myself wistfully alone to my own bed which already felt unfamiliar after my short spell away. Once in the middle of the night after seeing to Edith, I slipped quietly down the stairs to check on Jack. He opened a sleepy eye as the hall light spilled into the room. 'Come to ravish me, have you?' he asked. And when I told him that no, I just wanted to make sure he was warm enough, he grinned. 'Warm as toast,' he said. He sat up. 'You look cold though, come in here with me a minute,' and he drew me down among the warm blankets. I huddled beside him until my shivering stopped.

Then, remembering he had to be up early to start work, I freed myself from his embrace. He said he always sees his girls home and got up and walked with me to the bottom of the stairs. From the landing I looked down and he blew me a kiss. I turned away with a smile,

took one last look in on Edith and went back to bed, thinking of Jack, and warm and comforted, I quickly fell asleep.

CHAPTER TWENTY EIGHT

The weather had cleared in the night and Jack set off for work after our early breakfast. Although he was still worried at the thought of the break-in, our fears seemed a little unreal in the morning's sunshine but he still made me promise to call him immediately if anything should happen and at the last minute he was reluctant to leave.

I pushed him away. 'Go on, now. You'll be late and giving the British workman a bad name.' And just then the ping of Edith's bell recalled us both to our respective duties and he gave me the grin that never failed to melt my heart as he turned and walked off up the alley.

Edith was still woozy from her drug-induced sleep but said she felt better after being washed and dressed. She insisted on going downstairs. She wanted to send Charlie an e-mail. I was surprised because she generally preferred to use the phone, no longer bothered about the size of the bill she would receive. When she once complained to me that Charlie hardly ever phoned her, just used that e-mail thing, I pointed out that if they were going through hard times, they would be watching their pennies. But today she said she wasn't ready to speak to him just yet on the phone, in person~ she'd wait until she was a bit stronger. She would use the e-mail if I would just start it up for her.

The phone rang just then; it was Simon who told me a man would come to fix the lock on the window that afternoon. He gave me the man's name and said I was to ask for his identification and check it out before I let him in. I shivered a little and then my heart sank. No more excuse for Jack to stay once the lock was fixed. And I had to admit to myself the break-in had unsettled me. I kept remembering how scared I'd been when I'd come back to switch on the heating and that was before I knew anything had happened. With hindsight my sensible self told me the chill that afternoon was obviously due to the broken window, but the atmosphere of the house seemed somehow charged. I knew I didn't want to be alone and with Edith so ill, to all intents and purposes, I was very much on my own.

However, I forgot my problems to some extent as I helped Edith get started on her e-mail and then she turned to me in her old way and told me to go out and get a bit of shopping. When she saw I was about to protest at leaving her alone, she said Susan would soon be here for what that was worth and anyway if she was going to drop dead, my being here wouldn't make much difference. Another mental shrug from me as I pulled on my coat.

The air was warm and balmy, Easter was on the way and already there were a number of tourists about and the shops were busier than before. I thought how good it would be to walk up to the castle and enjoy the view but thrust the thought away and finished my shopping quickly and hurried back, knowing that despite her orders, Edith shouldn't be alone for long.

In the kitchen Susan was standing red-faced as Edith told her she wouldn't be needed much longer. 'Why, aren't I no good?' she spluttered, the longest sentence I'd ever heard from her lips.

Edith shook her head. 'Nothing wrong with you, my dear. 'tis me. I'm going.' And when Susan stared, still mystified, she shook her head in irritation. 'Dying. I'm dying, woman. That's why you won't be needed much longer.'

Susan's trade mark speechlessness became suddenly imbued with an awed and respectful dignity. Her eyes filled with tears and then she bent her head in a slow bow, as if paying homage in the presence of death. She looked so stricken I made both women a cup of tea and told Susan she needn't bother with the vacuuming, there was hardly anything to be done since the house had been empty these last couple of days.

Edith had a look of some satisfaction on her face at the reaction to her dramatic announcement. She was also buoyed up by having contacted Charlie and 'had a good long chat, though 'tis slow with these fingers of mine.'

The locksmith came and I dutifully checked through the spy-hole before opening the door and checking his photo on his pass as instructed. He worked quickly. The new handles were very similar to the damaged ones and the key clicked firmly in the lock when he tested it.

Then, turning down the offer of a cup of tea, he collected his things and left.

The hours had dragged themselves slowly by and I hoped Jack's day was not as tedious as mine. But just after the locksmith left, Edith said I'd better phone Jack and tell him he might as well stay for a night or two longer. Until she's sorted out her plans with those two men. And the stout one was supposed to be coming tomorrow to collect that table and goodness knows what he'll have to say about that. I quickly called Jack's mobile and after a bit of humming and hawing and saying he suffers badly from homesickness but he supposes he'll have to grin and bear it, he said he'd call at the cottage and pick up some clothes after work. Be a bit late. Don't burn the dinner, woman.

More cheerfully now I set about making a pie for the two of us, Edith being restricted to a largely fat-free diet. She asked peevishly why she couldn't eat whatever she fancied, too late for all this wishy-washy stuff now. I reminded her the doctor had said she could avoid a lot of pain and sickness by watching what she ate. But she was a little consoled when I said I'd make her favourite vegetable soup. She asked to have her tea early, she's not hanging round 'til he gets back from work. But after a couple of mouthfuls she pushed aside her dish and said it's time she was in bed. It was a quarter to five and she was deeply asleep within minutes of being settled on her pillows.

I watched the clock eagerly for Jack's return and when

he gave his familiar tap on the door I ran to greet him like dutiful wives were expected to do in the twenties, scented and groomed and with the table set with candles and wine. He laughed. I laughed. And it was enough just to stand in that hall, the ghosties and things that go bump in the night all banished to their icy realm by the warmth of our embrace.

The doctor phoned in the morning and said he'd drop in later to see how Edith was coping with her new medication. Expect him elevenish, he said. Edith told me she didn't care how often he came now, the payment for his bill would come out of her estate, and that meant those two nephews of Fred's would be stumping up. From the way she always spoke of them I was surprised she'd named them in her will but I knew how much store she put on convention and guessed she would be afraid people might think the worse of her if she didn't see they got Fred's share at least of her fortune. They certainly did nothing to earn it; the couple I'd met the night of my arrival had called only once since then, and the other brother contented himself with a weekly duty phone call.

Edith remained in her bed until ten and then ate a little porridge for breakfast and said she felt better after her long rest. She read the paper in the kitchen but said she would go along to the front room as soon as Susan and her red eyes had finished in there. And ten minutes later as Susan emerged hauling the vacuum cleaner behind her like a reluctant dog, the doorbell rang. 'Well go and let the doctor in,' snapped Edith, 'and you'd better come along with him,' and she trundled her chair independently along the passage.

I opened the door hurriedly, forgetting Jack's imperative that I must always check first. And found myself face to face with Mr Big. 'Mrs Rogers is expecting me,' he said eyes fixed on some spot somewhere to the left of my head and the door was pushed from my hand as he mounted the step and walked into the hall. I looked hastily up and down the alley. No one else in sight. I couldn't use the phone with him standing there and neither did I want to leave him alone with Edith, so I gestured to the door at the end of the hallway and followed him along to the front room.

Edith looked up and if she was surprised to see him instead of her doctor, she gave no sign. 'Come for your table, have you?' she said as he looked round the room with growing anxiety. 'Been stolen, it has. Couldn't let you know because I never had your number.'

The man stood opened mouthed with horror. I was watching his reaction closely but his shock was genuine, his face blanched and he collapsed rather than sat down onto the sofa. 'Stolen!' came his harsh whisper. 'Who... when...?'

Edith waved her hand at the window and told him in a few terse sentences what had happened. As she spoke he started to rise as if to go and look over the balcony but it seemed his knees wouldn't carry him for he flopped down again with a sheen of sweat on his ashen face. 'The police,' he croaked. 'Did you get the police?'

Quickly forestalling Edith's reply, I said, 'Of course we got the police. This room was a mess, broken glass and furniture. Mrs Rogers' possessions were

stolen. We only noticed your table was missing later.'

'What did they say, about the table?'

Edith spoke. 'What d'you mean, what did they say? They asked for a list of what was taken and I told them. Everything I could remember anyway. I've thought of a couple more things since then that are gone. My crystal bowl and the glasses.' She looked at him. 'Anyway, your table was on the list.' And she anwered the question in his eyes. 'I never said whose it was. Just an occasional table.'

He was silent, leaning forward, elbows on knees and head propped on hands. A partial recovery position. And after a few minutes he seemed to feel better. He sat back. 'They went all over this place, I suppose. Upstairs, downstairs, everywhere, the police?'

Edith shook her head. 'There was no need. We told them this was the only room messed up. We found it out when we got back. Been away, see. Anyway, the police didn't bother much, they could see the way the thieves came in. I don't think they cared one way or the other, not much taken. I doubt we'll be seeing our things again.' I was pleased Edith had so quickly taken my cue not to let this man know the customs and excise men were involved. And I could see the man himself seemed to be a little reassured by the casual way the break-in had been handled. But when Edith asked if he was still interested in buying the place, first his eyes widened and glittered with triumph but then he bit his lip and his gaze slid away. 'I will have to discuss that with my partner. Yes, I'd very much like to buy it but things have changed. I shall have to let you know.'

'Well, don't leave it too late,' said Edith with unwonted cheeriness. 'I'm a very sick woman. I won't be here much longer.'

But she'd met her match for once and the man responded with an indifferent shrug of the shoulders. 'That might delay the sale,' he said. He stared into space for a couple of
minutes, the silence in the room broken by the hoot of a boat's strident warning signal somewhere out on the harbour. Then he stood up. 'I'll let you know,' he said.

Edith replied, 'Well, like I said, don't leave it too long. I shall expect to hear from you before the weekend is over. If not I shall go ahead with my other plans.' He nodded and turned to leave. I followed him to the door and he went out without a glance in my direction, but I could see the perspiration still forming drops on his forehead and I had the fanciful thought that under the wave of body spray there would be the strong smell of fear.

Jack had put Simon's number on my mobile and

before Mr Big was at the end of the alley, I was ringing him. He immediately asked did the man realise who had been involved and he was pleased when I told him no, we'd let him assume it was the local police. A few more questions and then he asked if Jack would be there if he called round this evening and when I told him yes, he thanked me and quickly rang off. Susan was just coming down the stairs with her basket of cleaning things and I put the kettle on for her before going back to Edith who seemed pleased with the encounter with her Mr Jones. I thought she'd planned to sell to him only if her test results were clear but here she was, promising to sell right away. But there, I should know better by now than to try and fathom Edith's thinking.

But just then the doorbell rang and this time I made sure to check who was there before releasing the catch. It was the doctor, of course, and I let him in and as we stood in the hall he asked some probing questions about Edith's reaction to her drugs. We spoke quietly but I nodded towards the front room door to let him know she was there, and probably listening so he inclined his head and followed me along the passage. Edith was watching the television and seemed annoyed at the interruption. However she did switch off the sound and let him take her pulse without comment. He kept his fingers on her wrist much longer than was needed as he sat alongside her and I suddenly realised it was his way of giving the sick woman the comfort of another person's caring touch, something she would not normally accept and I warmed to him. She nodded gravely as he spoke to her and he looked startled and pleased when she asked him to leave some details about those hospice places.

As he left he paused at the door and asked if I was coping, do I need a relief nurse and to let him know the minute things got too much. 'I'm amazed she's even considering the hospice,' he said, 'but it will certainly be better for you. Far too much for one person I always feel, nursing a terminal patient.' I thanked him for his promise of help, genuinely glad of his support and went to see if Edith needed anything and ask her what she'd like for her lunch.

An hour later as I was washing our few dishes, the doorbell rang again and this time it was Maud, standing smiling on the step. She gave me a little hug when I let her in which filled me with pleasure. Edith too was pleased to see her old friend and immediately told me to go out and get some fresh air for goodness sake, you look like a sick hen. At Maud's discreet nod, I fetched a light jacket and went out, closing the door behind me with a sigh of relief at being in the open air.

As I walked along the street I thought of buying some flowers for Edith but decided she'd only make some comment about it not being her funeral yet. Instead I bought her a bar of the luxury soap I treated myself to from time to time and a couple of pretty face flannels.

I came out of the shop, glanced to my right before

crossing the road and came to an abrupt halt. For there, ten yards away from me, stood Giles.

CHAPTER TWENTY NINE

As I stood stock still outside the shop, Giles vanished round the corner. I felt a wave of fury sweep over me. I'd been expecting him to put in an appearance ever since the arrival of the flowers, knowing he'd discovered my address. And now, I charged angrily along the street to confront him.

But when I reached the corner there was no sign of him. There was a hotel doorway nearby and I was tempted to walk inside to see if that was where he'd hidden. Giles and his little games! I wondered if he was watching me, measuring the success of his presence in unsettling me. Terrifying me. And suddenly I threw back my head and laughed. Go on, Giles, I thought. Make what you will of that, of the totally different woman you're trailing today.

I turned and continued my interrupted walk along the street as far as the maritime museum and stood admiring the attractive building and some yachts for a while. Once or twice as I'd been coming along, I'd paused to look in shop windows and turned to check. Oh yes. He was following me; just a second's glimpse before he darted out of sight. I decided to stop for a coffee on my way back home and was soon sitting at the café's pavement table with an unobstructed view of the street in both directions. No sign of Giles now. I took a while over my coffee, chatting with a couple of tourists at the next table and presently I picked up my bag and left, in no doubt he'd soon be behind me.

And so we played a grim little game of grandmother's footsteps for the length of the street. Several times I spotted him in shop window reflections but each time when I spun round he'd vanished. I could hardly credit my determination to catch him out and confront him and it gave me a lot of satisfaction to think he too must be surprised and unsettled by my change of attitude and bearing, no longer the terrified victim he had tormented for so many months and years.

By the time I reached the entrance to the alley he had still not stepped out to greet me as he used to do. I stood there on the pavement for a moment then gave an irritated shrug of my shoulders and went down the cobbles to Edith's door. Giles could wait. I must go and relieve Maud.

But when I went in she scolded me for not taking a longer break. Edith was napping in her chair, she said.

I nodded. 'The tablets she's taking make her very sleepy but most of the time she won't go and lie down. She says it's better dozing in the chair than being hauled in and out of bed a dozen times a day. And she's not staying up in that bedroom all the time and I needn't think she is.'

Maud smiled. 'She's not an easy woman and I think you do a wonderful job, Lisa. Not many would stand for it.'

I smiled back. 'Well, I've found a good reason to stick

around the place as you may have noticed. I've just been buying some chops for his tea.'

Edith was in the front room and as we spoke her bell rang and we both went along to keep her company. Maud said Katie was going to pop in for ten minutes. And when the young girl came, hair in two bunches now, she said she hoped Edith would soon be feeling better, with a sweet gravity that touched me. Soon, at a nod from Maud, I bore her away to the kitchen for some lemonade and biscuits. I put her unusual quietness down to her concern over Edith but I soon found that wasn't the case.

'Lisa there's a man outside on the street. He called after me when he saw me turn down the ope.' She looked at me, suddenly guarded and suspicious. 'He said if I was going to see Lisa would I give her a message from him. He said tell her the divorce is off and he wants you back. He said tell you it's Giles.'

My jaw dropped. 'Divorce! My God!' I blew out my cheeks. 'Katie, my love, he's the man I've been trying to run away from; the reason I left home. But believe me, I wouldn't have married him if he was the last man on earth. He's a stalker.' I could see the doubt in her eyes and remembered how cogent and plausible Giles's stories were. 'Ask your dad, Katie. He knows all about it. So do the police, come to that.' Then I bit my lip. 'Trouble is,' I said slowly, 'I'm afraid of Jack meeting him, he's so angry I'm worried what he'll do.' I looked at her steadily. 'Giles is a very disturbed man but I've at last cottoned on to what the psychiatrists told me from the beginning; that he gets his satisfaction from reducing me to terror. But now I'm no longer afraid. I want to meet him face to face. He was following me today but he kept dodging me. It's his trademark behaviour.'

She still looked troubled. 'But will he hurt you? Especially if he sees you with dad?' This was a question that had raised its head with me too, and I knew she could sense my uncertainty.

'I shall call the police, Katie, if I feel there's the slightest danger. But in the past he's never tried to hurt me physically. Except once and that was unintentional.' I'd no intention of telling her about the rape. 'I truly think that when he sees I'm no longer afraid of him, he'll lose interest in the game. Because that's what it is to him.' I told her a little more, that he'd been a patient at my hospital. About his obsession.

She nibbled a biscuit, thinking this over. Then she looked up with her old grin, friendly and open once more. 'When I saw him first I thought he was drop-dead gorgeous and I thought poor dad, he doesn't stand a chance. And I felt really upset. But then when he put his hand on my shoulder it gave me the creeps.'

Maud came along to the kitchen just then. 'Stan's taxi will be here in a minute, Katie. Better go and say goodbye to Edith.' She turned to me. 'I can't stay until Jack gets in from work, Lisa, I'm going out with some friends this evening, and I've got to water my greenhouse first. Give him my love.'

When the taxi arrived I walked up the cobbles with them. Stan gave me a friendly grin. Since that first evening when he'd brought me to the house, he'd always given me his cheery wave as his taxi passed me in the street. 'Never thought you'd last this long, me dear,' he said now. 'And here you are, looking like you've had a holiday. Thrive on trouble, you must.' He opened the rear passenger door for Maud and Katie. He'd parked on the pavement and had to come close to where I stood in order to squeeze round the front wing to his own door and as he did, he said quietly, 'Chap asking for you just now. I told him I never heard of you. I thought he seemed a bit funny like. Just so you know'

I nodded and rolled my eyes. 'Thanks. I know who it is. I shall get the police on to him if he hangs around. But thanks again.'

He went round to his door and saluted the driver of a Range Rover who'd just appeared and was frustrated at not being able to pass instantly and I waved to Katie and Maud as they drove off.

Blast Giles! I remembered Katie's clouded gaze when she'd thought Jack was going to be upset again and I looked angrily up and down the road but either Giles was not there or he'd hidden himself away once more.

Edith wanted to go to bed when I went back indoors and I gave her a bath before settling her down. She would probably ring for attention a couple of times during the evening, but generally speaking Jack and I had the front room to ourselves. We watched television or chatted but both of us found it impossible to relax in the companionable way we did at his cottage. This evening Jack sighed. 'How long is this going on, Lisa? How long before she takes the plunge and goes into that hospice?'

I frowned. 'She's still on about selling up to that pair Simon is so interested in. But she's told them if she doesn't hear over the weekend, she'll make other arrangements.' I was sitting beside him on the couch and took his hand in mine. 'If it's too much for you, Jack, if you want to go home, I do understand.' But before I could go on he interrupted me and told me he'd no intention of leaving until he could take me with him.

My eyes welled with gratitude for I knew how he hated being in this house and his long-standing aversion to Edith. I leaned against his shoulder. 'I don't think it'll be for much longer. Two weeks at the outside. Can you stay away from your place that long?'

He nodded. 'Yep. I can drop back and water the plants and pick up the post. It's just, these nice light evenings, I'd like to be going for a walk with you. Or a drive. So many places I want to take you to. Instead, here we are in this place. Waiting. Waiting for something to happen.' He waved his hand. 'I don't mean waiting for her to die, it's something I can't explain. Those men, perhaps. But there's no way I'll let you stay here overnight without me. I feel bad enough about you being here in the daytime.' I laughed and told him we'd hardly had five minutes to ourselves today, so many visitors we'd hardly been alone at all. And he was pleased when I told him I'd called Simon to bring him up to date about Mr Big and I passed on Simon's message that he'd be contacting Jack shortly.

We went to bed fairly early, by common consent Jack to his couch and I to my bed. Edith's presence loomed and we would have been uneasy in my bedroom. 'Besides,' said Jack, 'until I hear from Simon what the score is, I think I'd better stay downstairs. You never know.'

On Saturday, Dr West called again just as I was in the hall answering the phone - to a double glazing salesman. I let the doctor in and by the time I went upstairs, he and Edith were earnestly talking. Dr West looked up as I entered the room. 'I was just telling Mrs Rogers about Nurse Meadows whom she knows. Mrs Meadows worked in my surgery for years. She's retired now but stands in as a relief from time to time. We've agreed that it might be a good idea if she gives you a break now and then. She can come this afternoon for four hours. That alright with you?'

My heart lifted, but aware of Edith's scrutiny of my face, I tried not to show how pleased I was. 'Thanks very much,' I said to them both. 'That'll be very nice.'

I thanked Doctor West when I saw him out. 'No problem,' he said. 'Nurse Meadows doesn't mind doing a few hours now and then. So make the most of your afternoon off'.

As soon as he'd gone I called Jack's mobile and told him the good news. 'Great' he said. 'I'll be finished here by noon. See you then sweetheart.'

And the afternoon was all we could have wished for. When he asked where I wanted to go, I didn't hesitate. 'To your place,' I said. 'You can cut the grass and I'll do a bit of weeding. Does that sound exciting enough for you?' I didn't tell him I had an added reason for keeping a low profile – that I didn't want him coming face to face with Giles.

So we pottered about his cottage for a while. Then he said his back is giving him hell. He thinks it must be from sleeping on that sofa but an hour in his own bed should put things right again. What did I think?

I said 'I think I'll race you to the top of the stairs.'

CHAPTER THIRTY

And the next morning Maud phoned 'I'm coming down to see Edith this afternoon, Lisa,' she said. 'Give you two a chance to go out again.'

'Oh Maud,' I said with a groan. 'That'd be wonderful. But Edith was sick a lot last night. I think I'll have to see how she goes this morning before making any plans. I might be needed here.' But she insisted she'd ring again later. And after all, she said, after three children and five grandchildren a bit of sickness doesn't add up to much.

Jack had gone out to meet Simon who'd phoned the previous evening and when he came back he told me they'd tracked that table to a warehouse in Kent. And although Jack said Simon had been pretty cagey, it seemed there'd been some inter-gang trouble and they'd found out it was a rival group who'd broken in and stolen the table. In the midst of the in-fighting, Simon's people had been able to slip one of their men amongst them to keep tabs on things. And, said Jack, 'Simon was very grateful for our help. He wants us to go out for a drink with him one evening when we're all free. How is she now, by the way?'

I shook my head. 'She's sleeping. Poor woman.' I told him about his mother's offer and he held up his hand and crossed his fingers fervently.

Once during the previous night Jack had come upstairs

241

when he'd heard my movements as I saw to Edith. I was aware of him standing outside her bedroom door and after I'd got her settled I went out to him. 'Anything I can do?' he asked. 'Cup of tea?' as he put his arms round me.

I shook my head. 'I'm hoping she'll go to sleep now. You go back to bed.' But I briefly laid my cheek on his bare shoulder, breathing in the familiar smell of his skin and he held me for a long comforting moment. Then I freed myself and went back to sit beside Edith and he turned slowly away and went downstairs.

But during the morning Edith perked up in her indomitable manner. She knew Maud had promised to come and insisted I ring and confirm it. 'I'm better now,' she said. 'Tell Maud to come down right after lunch.'

Tell. Not ask. Typical Edith.

So that afternoon Jack and I had the chance to go out after all. I was still uneasy about Edith, however and Jack agreed with me it wasn't fair to leave his mother very long in case Edith had one of her violent bouts of sickness. We told Maud we'd go for a short walk and then come back and we could sit out on the balcony in the pale sunshine. There were few people around this Sunday afternoon and I quickly checked for Giles and thankfully saw no sign of him. Not that that proved anything.

As we walked along the street a big middle-aged man in a baggy sweater hailed Jack by name. He crossed the road smiling and asked to be introduced to the young lady. 'William's a policeman,' grinned Jack. 'Don't see many of those around these days. Rare as a cuckoo in winter,' he said and asked William what crime wave had brought him out in such force.

William tapped his nose. 'You mind what you're saying,' he said. 'I'll be up your place checking on your car before you know it.' And they both chuckled at some shared memory and then William nodded his head and ambled off across the road.

We strolled down to my favourite little inner harbour and stood looking down at the moored boats bobbing on the half tide. Just then someone else called Jack's name and he muttered under his breath that it was a customer, be back in a minute and he went across to a couple who sat in their parked car eating ice creams.

I turned my face to the sunlight and wriggled my shoulders, aware how tense I was after Edith's troubled night, and glad to be out in the warm sunshine with the musical tinkling from the yachts in the marina carried on the breeze across the moving water. I must remember to ask Jack what makes that pleasant sound. Then I walked slowly along the harbour wall pausing now and then to read the names of the boats and wondering about the people who owned them. I was stooping to read the half obscured name on a battered old wooden dinghy when a hand grasped my shoulder and I turned with a smile of pleasure for Jack.

But it was Giles who stood there, staring down at me

with that pale unblinking gaze, his lips curved in the smile that never reached his eyes. I flung off his hand with a shudder of revulsion and the banked rage within me flared.

'Get lost, Giles,' I said furiously. 'Can't you get it into that thick head of yours that I don't want you. Never have. Never will.' And I swung round angrily to walk away, hoping Jack still had his back to us as he chatted to his customers through the car window. This was certainly not the time for the confrontation with Giles that I'd been seeking only a couple of days before.

But Jack had seen. He strode quickly across the quay towards me. 'Is this the bastard?' his grim voice asked before he reached my side. I didn't reply but my silence was answer enough and his hand shot out and grasped a fistful of Giles' silk polo shirt. Giles let out a strangled yelp of protest and I was forced back as the two men struggled to and fro, dangerously close to the harbour wall's edge. Giles was half a head taller than Jack and very fit from the daily workouts at his exclusive gym and I teetered about on the edges of the skirmish ready to leap to Jack's defence if I got the chance. But Jack too was fit and strong and he was fired with protective anger on my behalf. I could see he was gradually forcing Giles backwards along the wall in a sort of slow dance, feet shuffling as first one then the other struggled to keep their balance. Then Jack's left foot hooked Giles' leg and at the same time he barged into his chest with his shoulder. And Giles went backwards over the edge of the wall into the water several feet below. Jack himself stumbled on to his knees on the granite stone of the wall, breathing deeply.

I gave a cry of terror. There were boats down there. If Giles got hurt, Jack could go to prison. Terrified I ran to the edge of the harbour wall and looked down. Thank God there were no boats moored in this section and Giles was thrashing wildly about in the patch of open water. Jack was already on his feet and he slung himself over the edge and on to one of the narrow iron ladders set into the harbour wall. He scrambled down towards the water and harshly called to Giles and held out a hand to grab him, first by the hair and then that shirt again. And as he was hauling him up the ladder, with Giles coughing and gasping for breath, the policeman William appeared at my side.

'Stand back my lover,' he said to me with an unmistakeable wink, and then, 'Come on lads, out you come,' and as Jack reached the top of the ladder he motioned him aside and bent down to haul Giles on to the wall himself, all the time keeping up a soothing prattle. 'I've called the boys up,' he said to the breathless and shivering Giles. 'The car'll be here in a minute and we'll have you home and dry in no time. Just you sit down for a bit and get your breath back. Now, where you staying then, my handsome?' he asked with his open friendly smile.

But Giles ignored his question. 'Arrest that man, officer,' he gasped. 'He tried to kill me.'

'Tried to kill you did he sir? Well, from what I saw he was doing his best to save you; pull you out of the water after you tripped up like that.'

Giles was sitting on the stones of the quay his legs stretched out, his wet trousers clinging to his legs and the water from his expensive loafers forming a puddle round his feet. No wonder he'd floundered about so wildly in the water and made such heavy weather of climbing the ladder up the wall. His normally expensively styled and blow-dried hair lay flattened on his scalp and thin threads of seaweed trailed across his pale face. He raised a hand and pulled a strand of bladderwrack off his ear. 'He pushed me, you bloody fool. Are you blind or something?'

'Why no, sir. Had my eye-test only last month as a matter of fact. No, I saw with my own eyes how you tripped up and went over backwards. And Jack there was quick as lightning going down the ladder for you. Not everyone can manage those ladders you know.'

I looked round for Jack and saw him standing a little to one side, his face grim and unsmiling and I went over and stood beside him while the shaking Giles continued his tirade against the policeman. 'Those other people, that couple in the car, they'd have seen what he did,' raged Giles and I turned apprehensively because of course they would have seen everything. But the car had mysteriously disappeared.

'Why, what car was that, my bird?' asked William and Giles made a strangled noise in his throat. But just then a police car drove down on to the quay and William turned to speak to the young copper who climbed out. 'Got a blanket for this poor chap, have you Tommy? Fell right in, he did. And he's shaking with the cold.' He turned back to Giles. 'Where did you say you're staying then, my dear,' he asked tenderly and I could feel the helpless fury raging from the bedraggled figure on the stones.

'I'll be writing to the chief superintendent about this, you oaf. You can bank on it.' Giles' teeth were chattering so much by now it wasn't easy to make out what he was saying and William kindly asked him what was that again.

And then he said, 'You do that my lad. My Super dearly likes getting letters. He's always got a stack about a foot high on his desk.'

The young policeman by now had pulled a blanket from the boot of the car and came over to help Giles to his feet and wrap the rug round him. With an involuntary shiver sending his face into spasm and his jaws working like a pair of castanets, the drop-dead gorgeous image Giles was so vain about, lay somewhere in the murky water down below the wall.

William spoke to Jack loudly enough for Giles to hear as he was ushered into the car, 'I'm sure the gentleman will be wanting to thank you for what you did, Jack. He's feeling a bit shaky just now. Stands to reason, cold and wet and that. But on his behalf, I'll be saying well done, pard.' Again he winked and slowly lowered his bulk into the car and waved again as they drove off

We were holding hands. I looked at Jack and at last he turned to me and the cold rage on his face thawed and his mouth curved in a wry grin. 'OK?' was all he said and we walked slowly back along the street.

Half way home, I said, 'I thought he'd fall on one of those boats and break his neck and they'd put you in prison.' My voice was tight with tension.

He put his arm round me. 'I made sure I didn't tip him in until I saw a clear patch. I'm not daft you know.' Then he added, 'Have I made things worse, do you think, or will he leave you alone now? Because I can't tell what I'll do if he turns up again.'

I gave his arm a reassuring squeeze. 'I don't think we'll see him again. I'll tell him if he does turn up, that I'll bring that rape charge against him. And I mean it Jack. And I don't think he'd risk it now, the scandal and raised eyebrows of his society friends. He puts a lot of store by all that. No, I think what you did will draw a line under it and I can never thank you enough.'

'Is that so?' he said turning to me with his old relaxed smile. 'Will you put that in writing. Give me a blank cheque? And then, next time we go home, I can ask for the first instalment.'

'No,' I said. 'Because you owe me too. Giving me heart failure like that. I shall tell your mother how you chucked a bloke in the harbour just because he spoke to me.' And in the same vein, our shared laughter was a release from the tension of the recent drama as we strolled back and soon left the sunny street into the gloom of the cobbled alley.

CHAPTER THIRTY ONE

Back at the house Maud and Edith were having a quiet cup of tea and I had to make a huge effort to stop thinking about what had just happened and make the usual sort of small talk. Jack too was uncharacteristically quiet and tense, a fact Maud instantly picked up. 'Whatever's the matter with you, Jack?' she asked with concern.

'Me? Why nothing.' I could almost see him shuffling through his mind to come up with a valid reason for his silence and he quickly did. 'Met Bert and Lucy Matthews down at the quay. They want me to start on their extension soon as I can. Like last week. I'm trying to work things out.' He gave the two women his normal wide smile. 'Sorry ladies, if I was rude.'

We all went out on to the balcony for a while but as soon as the sunlight moved away it became chilly and Edith said she wants to go back to bed, all very well having company but a sick woman needs a bit of peace. Maud's eyes met mine but she made sure the laughter I saw there didn't quite escape her lips.

'Jack, I'll get Mrs Rogers ready for bed while you take your mother home.' I said and I thanked Maud again for her kindness, though words weren't needed for her to see what these unlooked for moments of freedom meant to me. And I told her also that Nurse Meadows had arranged to call every other afternoon of the coming week, so I'd get plenty of time to go out. Maud looked surprised at the news while Edith scowled, angry no doubt at not being able to have her old friend at her constant beck and call.

But just then the doorbell rang and Jack answered it. From the front room we could hear the murmur of men's voices and Edith stiffened. 'That'll be Mr Jones,' she said with grim satisfaction. But when Jack came back, he was alone and said it was a message for him from a friend. From William, he added meeting my eyes with the glint of a smile in his.

While Maud was saying goodbye to Edith, Jack quietly told me the police car had taken Giles to his hotel and there he'd asked for his bill. He was leaving as soon as he changed.

The receptionist had pointed out he'd be better catching the next London train from Truro and our taxi driver friend Stan was to take him there right away.

Jack said that after he dropped his mother off, he'd arranged to meet his policeman pal to hear what was happening about the affair and I nodded my agreement. 'Don't forget to thank William for me, Jack. And don't hurry back. I'll be a while settling Edith down and then there's the Sunday papers to wade through. So take your time.' Naturally, these remarks were not made within her earshot; she still expected to be addressed as Mrs Rogers by me just as she still called me Nurse Sands. That is, whenever she used my name at all. More often it was just a bald command.

251

I set about getting her ready for bed. But though she'd asked to go upstairs, when she was at last freshly bathed and lying between her clean sheets, Edith looked wide awake once more. 'Bring the phone up,' she said. 'I'm expecting a call from that Mr Jones.' She frowned. 'He should have rung by now. He needn't think he can string me along. In business you have to keep your word. Trust is everything.'

I fetched the phone and put it within her reach. She was staring into space. Then she turned her head and looked up at me. 'Can I trust you?' she asked.

I was taken aback. 'I should think so. What have I done to make you think you can't?' I said, bridling despite my resolution to ignore her jibes and remember her terminal illness.

But she shook her head. 'If he buys this place, that man, it won't be necessary.' And with that enigmatic remark she told me to go downstairs and get the meal for that man of yours.

Jack brought a bottle of champagne with him when he came. 'Time for a little celebration,' he said and as we sat in the front room with our glasses, he told me what he'd learned. 'It was no coincidence the police being on the spot this afternoon,' he said. 'Your friend, Katherine something, had got on to the woman detective who handled your case and told her Giles knew where you were. She was concerned enough to get our boys to keep an eye out for him. They traced him to the hotel yesterday and found he was already following you so they've been watching him. And when he gets back to London he's to be given warning that the rape charge will be brought against him if there's a single complaint of harassment from you. But they think today's episode will mark the end of it. Bullies don't like being on the receiving end. And that's what stalkers are, in your policewoman's book. Bullies.' I said nothing, but the huge relief I felt that it was all over at last, welled inside me and tears of relief slid down my cheeks.

Jack held me close and presently I sat up and blew my nose. 'I can't believe how my life has changed since I came to Cornwall, Jack,' I said. 'And most of it is down to you.'

'Well, you're in for a few more changes before long, Lisa. I don't mean to wish Edith harm, but it looks like we'll be able to make plans of our own pretty soon.' But I told him I felt it was tempting fate to talk about that just yet, and anyway, snuggled up against his side on the big sofa, the present was enough for now and he said he'd drink to that and we clinked our glasses to the day's success.

But if we were more than satisfied with the course our lives were taking, Edith was obviously deeply concerned about her affairs. Her Mr Jones did not ring that evening. And all day long on Monday and Tuesday Edith visibly stiffened whenever the phone rang, sinking back in her chair in disappointment each time she learned it wasn't him. I was concerned at the effect of the strain on her. Already very frail and beset with bouts of sickness, I wished I could free her from her worry and foolishly suggested she might as well forget Mr Jones and put the house in the hands of an estate agent now she'd made up her mind to leave.

She turned on me fiercely. 'You don't know what you're talking about,' she raged and would have said more but needed a basin just then. My own annoyance soon abated; it's hard to stay angry when the object of your wrath is so very ill and helpless. She too said nothing further when I settled her back on her pillows, but the look in her eyes was one I'd not seen there before. It was a look of frustration and despair.

On Wednesday afternoon when Mrs Meadows came to relieve me, I went for a long walk, alone of course for Jack was at work. Apart from the pleasure of striding along in the warm air with the great bay offering a different view from each vantage point I reached, it gave me time to sort a few things out in my mind.

First, of course, there was my future. Our future. My son hadn't yet met Jack. Josh had planned to come down at Easter but was asked to crew on a boat sailing to Spain and I told him of course he must go; he could come and see me anytime. But I knew Josh would be glad I'd found someone and I was sure he'd welcome Jack into our lives for my sake, if not his own. In any case, he was a free young man and I felt he'd be secretly relieved to know I was happy in someone else's safe hands. The flat in London could pay for itself and the rental income could keep Josh until he graduated. And then we could take stock again. As for Katie, she seemed to be fine about Jack and me and glad to see her father so happy and cheerful while Maud was kindness itself and made no secret of her hope we'd soon be 'a proper couple and settled in.'

Jack's cottage too was ready and waiting and I'd already confirmed I could get a job in the local hospital. I'd spent very little of my wages since coming to Falmouth and I was still able to help with Josh's expenses, as I didn't want him starting his career with too large a student loan.

And now, the relief at not having Giles lurking somewhere in the background literally made me want to dance rather than walk along the path. But there were people walking their dogs and I settled for a brisk arm-swinging stroll.

I got back to the house an hour or so later and enjoyed a cup of tea with Mrs Meadows. Edith had chosen to stay in bed today and as we chatted the elderly woman, a widely experienced nurse, told me she thought our patient was visibly slipping away. 'There's something troubling her though. Even drugged, she seems to be struggling to stay awake.'

I nodded. 'She's been wanting to complete some business lately. And it's not going the way as she hoped.' I felt that was enough to satisfy her professional curiosity and explain Edith's burning restlessness.

She looked at me. 'You ought to catch up on some sleep yourself, my dear. Go on, I'm here for another couple of hours.'

So I went up to my bedroom, set the alarm clock and after my broken nights and the brisk walk I'd taken, I quickly fell asleep, relieved from knowing I needn't keep half an ear open for Edith's insistent bell.

That evening after Jack and I had finished our meal and were settled in the front room watching the news on the television, Edith summoned me upstairs. 'Get your man up here,' she said. And perhaps seeing my face, 'Jack. Ask Jack to come up here a minute.'

I called down to him and he came into the room, a little uncomfortable as always in Edith's presence, particularly since she'd become so ill. She waved to him to take a chair and told me to sit down for goodness sake, towering over her like doom.

I sat on a stool near the bed, alongside Jack. Edith stared at us, from one to the other as if she'd never seen us before and wished to memorise every detail of our faces. Later he told me the hair on the back of his neck stood up under her fierce glare.

Then she spoke. 'That man isn't going to buy my place now. He said he would ring. I don't know why he didn't, he was keen enough before.'

Jack looked at her with his direct gaze. 'It's because

of that break-in, Mrs Rogers. That pair wanted to keep a very low profile and I expect they're afraid the police might take an interest in the place now. And that's exactly what they don't want.'

She stared back at him. 'If you told me that before I needn't have been worried all this time.' Jack said nothing and Edith looked at her hands, which writhed and twisted on the edge of the sheet. Then she spoke again. 'I want you two to do something for me. I didn't want to ask before but now I must. It's very important and a lot depends on it. Will you do this thing for me?' She was staring now at Jack.

Jack looked back. 'Well now, Mrs Rogers. You'll have to tell us what you want first. Then we'll decide.'

She looked away from him to me. 'You must make him. Tell him it's important. Have you told him about the will?'

'No, of course not,' I retorted. 'Jack's not the least interested in your affairs, Mrs Rogers. But if it's something we feel happy about, I'm sure we'll both do what we can to help.' I didn't add what I felt, that it must be something pretty strange for her to go about it in this way.

She stared again at those restless hands. 'I've no choice then. I'll have to tell you. Have to trust you.' She looked up. 'Give me a drink, my mouth is so dry.'

I helped her while she sipped the cool water, aware of the rigid tension in her back against my arm. I shook up her pillows and settled her back. 'I better come straight

257

out with it then,' she said. And drawing a deep, shaky breath, she said, 'What I want you to do for me, is to get rid of Fred Rogers' old bones.'

CHAPTER THIRTY TWO

I felt the breath leave me as if I'd been punched in the stomach. Jack gave a slow, 'Whew.' Then he said, 'Look, you're going to have to tell us a bit more than that, aren't you?'

She stared at him indignantly. 'You don't seem very surprised. I suppose you're like all the rest of them that thought I'd done him in.' After what she'd just told us, I felt her outrage was a bit rich. But now she went on. 'It was an accident, see. I was down in the cellar filling the coal scuttle. There was always coal kept in the cellar until I had the central heating put in. I was using the big spade, easier than a footling little coal shovel to fill the scuttle. And he came down. He was in one of his tempers because he was overdrawn at the bank and I told him he must do like everyone else and sort it out for himself. He came at me and I was afraid what he'd do. He'd broken my arm once. Ask your mother. So I turned round and hit him with the spade. Over the head. He fell down and never moved.'

Jack and I were still, frozen. She went on. 'I couldn't think what to do. Only what people would say. In the shops, what it would do to my business. Who would believe it was an accident? I never meant to kill him, only stop him. So after a couple of hours thinking, I hid him. And you know the rest.'

She asked for another drink and lay back on the

pillows, spent. Presently she said, 'Until I got in contact with Charlie again, I never cared what would happen when I was gone. When they found out. But now I do care.' She turned to me. 'You've seen my will. You said you liked it. But if they find out, and they will, soon as a surveyor comes in to check the place over for probate, those nephews of Fred's will contest it. That's why I wanted those two men to buy the place. Those two crooks or whatever they were. They told me they wouldn't bother with a survey. And besides, if they ever came across his,' she paused, 'remains, they wouldn't go to the police. Wouldn't want to draw attention to themselves. I knew that from the start.

'But the thing is, I know the law. You can't benefit from killing someone. And though a lot of the money was mine, from my own properties, in the seven years before they declared him dead, I borrowed from the bank to buy some old run-down places that I could see would be worth hanging on to, worth going into debt for a year or two. And I sold them as building sites to a couple of big developers a few years ago. Made a couple of million pounds. And with investments I've more than doubled that since. But the lawyers could argue that as it was a joint account, half of that would be Fred's.'

I stirred. 'I see,' I said slowly. 'But at least they couldn't touch your share. Your will could still stand, surely.'

She shook her head weakly. 'You don't know those

nephews. They'd jump at any chance to overturn my will. I told them once it's all going to the cat's home and they said then they'd see about that. You know I've been generous to them,' she said looking at me, 'but if they found out about Fred, they'd do their best to get all the rest of it, the lot. And they'd rather the lawyers got it if they couldn't have it themselves. And they would, those lawyers, after years and years of wrangling. And Charlie can't wait that long. Go on, tell him.'

I looked at Jack. 'Mrs Rogers is leaving a lot of money to Charlie and his family. And a huge sum to the new cancer unit at Truro. And the same to a children's hospice. And there's a lot more besides.'

Her eyes glittered. 'So all I'm asking you to do, is get rid of what's left of him. And after thirty odd years it won't be a lot. It's not much to ask.'

Jack stood up and prowled across the room towards the window. He drew back the curtain and stared out for a while. Then he turned back. 'Not much to ask, Mrs Rogers. You're asking Lisa and me to help you cover up a murder. Or at least manslaughter. We could go to prison for that. Not much, you say.'

She would have sat up, stood up had she the strength, she was so furious. 'Don't be such a fool. Who would stop you? Who would find out? Just a little trip across the bay in that boat of yours and that would be the end of the story. And if someone fished up his bones, they'd think it was true, that he did drown that night like they decided in the end.' And she closed her eyes, totally

261

exhausted by the telling of her tale and the vehemence of her outburst.

Jack and I exchanged glances across the bed. Then she opened her eyes, sunken but burning still. 'Well,' she said, 'will you do it?'

The room was so silent I thought of the proverbial pin drop. Jack stood with his shoulders hunched as he did when wrestling with a problem. I knew I'd go along with whatever decision he made, for once unable to make up my own mind. At last he looked up. 'Big decision, Mrs Rogers. Give us a night to think it over, right?' She didn't answer his question but told me she needed a hot drink. Then she said, 'Did you tell him about his mother's place?'

I stared at her in confusion. 'His mother's place? What do you mean?'

Edith muttered to herself, irritated. Then she spoke directly to Jack. 'In my will I've left all my tenants their properties. I did it to spite the nephews.'

Jack looked astonished. 'You mean Mum will get her house?' Now I was the one who was startled and surprised because I never knew Maud was one of Edith's tenants.

Edith nodded. 'All of them. Most are old tenants, been paying rent for years. The luckiest are the new ones. Hardly paid anything yet. But I couldn't be bothered picking and choosing. Easier to make all the houses over to the tenants.'

Jack turned round and abruptly left the room and went

downstairs. After a bit Edith told me to go and see what he was up to. I found him in the kitchen, seated at the table, head bent. He looked up when I came in. 'It's blackmail, Lisa. That evil old witch up there. She knows the state Mum's been in lately over Rose.' And I remembered Maud fretting about Jack's younger sister in Germany, about to divorce her soldier husband and having to leave the army house. Maud would like to have her, but with three children there was hardly room.

Jack went on, 'If it was Mum's house, I could easily build on an extension. Extra bedroom. Granny flat. Whatever. Plenty of room for them all then. Christ, it's tempting. And she knows it.'

'Sleep on it, like you told her,' was all I could think of to say.

He nodded, but before we went back upstairs he opened the doors to the store cupboards and laundry and walked round, examining the walls, wondering aloud where the hell she could have hidden a body. 'It must be in the cellar but for the life of me I can't think where. I've been down there a lot and it's just an empty room.' He turned to me, 'Where does she keep the key, do you know?' But when we looked in the kitchen drawer the key wasn't there. He frowned, puzzled. 'Well, we shall find out soon enough if we agree to do what she asks. But I'll tell you this, Lisa my love. I'm sleeping in your bed tonight.'

I hugged him. 'Thank goodness for that. I was just

thinking I'd be scared to go to sleep in case of nightmares.'

We went back upstairs and Edith looked questioningly at Jack. 'Well?' she said.

'Like I said, Mrs Rogers, I want to sleep on it,' he replied.

'And if you decide no, I suppose you'll be going to the police?' Her voice was bitter.

Jack shrugged his shoulders. 'Of course not. What could I tell them? We've seen nothing. They'd think you were rambling from all the drugs. Or I was making it up myself.'

She seemed satisfied with this much at least. Then she said, 'Right. I shall expect you to tell me in the morning. You'll need to take a day off work,' she went on as if it was already decided, 'but I'll make that right with you. Go on, then. Goodnight.' We quietly left the room and I switched off the overhead light. When we looked back I could see by the soft glow of the bedside lamp, that Edith was far from sleep, lying on her pillows staring fiercely at the ceiling.

Close together in my bed that night, we talked for ages on the pros and cons of doing what she asked. The thought of all that money going to the hospitals carried a lot of weight with me. And Jack of course kept thinking what a difference it would make to his mother if the will went through unchallenged. Pros and cons. The list of pros was much longer. But though the list of cons was short, they were very serious cons indeed. As

Jack put it, 'God, Lisa, I break out in a cold sweat if I see a police car behind me in a traffic jam, worrying if my tax is up to date, or the MOT, whatever. Even though I know it's all OK. But with this job on my mind, I'd be a nervous wreck.'

But we were both enticed by Edith's words 'only a few old bones to get rid of'. And after all, what difference would it make after all these years? She would certainly not live long enough to face a charge of murder, or manslaughter or whatever. And I thought of Charlie's farm no longer going bankrupt in the drought. And the tidy legacy to Mrs Green, her previous nurse carer And all the rest...

I was up several times that night seeing to Edith who had another bout of nausea. And each time I went back to bed, Jack reached out his arms and held me close and though I quickly went to sleep, I know he lay awake worrying and fretting for much of the night.

It was raining next morning, heavy rain that put paid to Jack's working plans in any case. Edith looked pleased when I drew back the curtains and saw the raindrops tracking down the glass. 'Just the day for it,' she said with satisfaction as though we had already agreed to her request.

But at breakfast Jack was quiet. 'I've been thinking in the night, Lisa and it's all a lie, what she was saying.'

'What on earth do you mean?' I exclaimed. 'She'd hardly make up a murder, would she?'

He shook his head. 'No. But the way she said it happened. Whacking him over the head with a long-handled spade. You've seen how low the ceiling is down there, and they say he was a very tall man, so there's no way she could have brought a shovel down on his head. And what the hell could she have done with his body? People used to think she'd dumped him in the harbour, but if that was so, she wouldn't be asking us to get rid of 'his bones'. Jack grimaced at the last words and left his buttered toast on his plate.

'What are we going to do then, Jack? If you want to forget all about it and go off to work, I'll tell her. She was asleep just now.'

'I'm rained off anyway today, sweetheart as you know. It's almost as if we're being drawn into this thing despite ourselves.'

I shivered because that was exactly what I'd been thinking. Jack looked up at me. 'As soon as she's awake, let's tell her we need to know a bit more before we bite the bullet.'

Half an hour later, Edith's eyes glittered with triumph when we walked into her bedroom and put our questions to her. She knew we'd not turned her down completely and that the battle was probably won. 'Alright,' she said. 'I better tell you where he is.'
And with several pauses when she needed a drink or a rest, she told us of the hiding place which had held her grisly secret all these years.

CHAPTER THIRTY THREE

'The bottom part of this place is very old.' Edith said. 'A lot of different houses have been built on those foundations over the years, they go right back to when Falmouth started as a port. And in the cellar there was a trap door. People used to tip their slop buckets down it because there was no room along the waterfront for outdoor privies. And all their other rubbish went the same way. All the muck used to fall into the space behind the sea wall and eventually get washed away by the tide. But a lot would get stuck there and smell. So someone had the idea to build a sort of chute from the floor to a hole in the outside wall. Like a spout so everything went straight into the sea from the cellar except at low tide.

'Then, when Fred's father had the flush toilet put in, he got the hole in the outside wall blocked up, keep the rats out, he said. But they never got rid of the trapdoor. So there was this space still down there, like a funny shaped shallow well. Like I told you, we used to keep coal in the cellar and firewood and things. Tins of paint, all the normal stuff.

'So when Fred died like that, and I was at my wits end what to do, I suddenly remembered that hole under the floor. There were pallets on the trap door, like they still are now, they were there to keep my log pile dry in the flood tide. And the coal was alongside. So I had hours of hard work ahead of me that night before I could hide the body.

'First I had to move the logs away and shift the pallets. Then I opened the trap and looked down. I shone my torch down the slope to the sea wall. There was a bit of mud and stuff at the end. Nothing big can get through, only the water filtering in as the tide rises. I took his wallet out of his pocket to burn in the stove. He was wearing that posh watch of his, that Rolex. Worth a lot of money. But I remembered those watches can all be traced and I wouldn't be able to sell it. So I left it on him. Then I dragged him across and pushed him down the hole. I had some job on my hands. He was a big man, and heavy. But I was desperate and in the end I was able to push the trap door down on him. Then I dragged a pallet across it. Of course, now I had to pile all the coal on top and make it look like it'd always been there. And then I put the logs on the other pallets again, about a yard from where they used to be. I guessed the coalmen wouldn't notice it'd all been moved a bit, or the men who delivered the next load of logs.

'It all took hours and I was like a chimney sweep by the time I'd finished and brushed up the coal dust. There'd been a lot of blood too but most had fallen on the coal and I reckoned it wouldn't show.

'In the middle of it all I phoned the hospital to make it look like he was missing. And when I was finished, I had a bath and changed and set his boat loose. Then, early in the morning I went along to the police station and asked if they had any news of him. I told them I'd be at work if they heard anything. One of the policemen said he'd drop in here and see if Fred had come back and gone to bed, and I told him where we kept the spare key. I knew what he really wanted was to have a good look round the place. The cellar door wasn't locked or anything. They were able to look all over upstairs and down and I never thought they'd find anything. Lucky for me there was a spring tide rising up through the floor just as I finished the sweeping the dust around to make it look like it always used to and I knew when the water went down, the whole floor would be covered with silt and coal dust. No footprints.'

Edith's story was over. She'd sat upright against her pillows all the while as she spoke, stopping only for sips of water, her eyes burning and her shoulders rigid with tension as she relived the happenings of that terrible night. Now, spent, she sagged back and closed her eyes. Neither Jack nor I spoke, the pictures she'd painted were all too vivid in our minds. Then, at last she opened her eyes. 'Well, now you know it all. Where he is. And what happened. Will you do it?'

'When they blocked that hole in the outside wall, did they mortar it back?' Jack asked, frowning.

'No. No mortar. Let the water come through, they said, like the rest of the wall. All you have to do is pull out the stones. And then she,' she said, indicating me with a movement of her head, 'she can push out whatever's left inside the hole. There's a big old sweeping brush always kept down there, that'll do.'

'Oh no it won't,' said Jack. 'I'm not having Lisa involved in this.'

I started to protest and Edith shook her head angrily. 'You can't be in two places at one time, outside and in. If one person could do it on their own, don't you think I'd have done it myself years ago? And then I could have left this house that's full of him still to this day. She'll have to do what I said. Sweep it down the chute so it falls into a bucket or something and then cover it with the sand. And no one will ever know.' She looked at him sharply. 'I told you to bring more sand when you did the balconies. Is it still there?'

Jack stared at her. 'You were planning this even then!' He shook his head. 'But yes, there is plenty of sand down there.' He rubbed his jaw, thinking. 'The tide is low right now. I could check that wall I suppose. See if I can find the stones blocking the hole. Then I shall have to fetch my boat.'

Edith told me to go down and help him. 'You can come back and dress me when he goes for the boat. And here,' she said, 'you'll need these,' and she opened the drawer in her bedside cabinet and took out the keys to the cellar and the door to the jetty.

We went down the stairs, quiet and apprehensive. I pulled on my mac and Jack dragged on his waterproof and boots and we went outside and walked down the cobbles to the door at the end and unlocked it. When we stepped through, the force of the wind caught us, and the rain drove into our faces. Jack looked grim. 'Wait here,' he said. 'I'll take a look at that wall while the tide's low, and then I'll get the boat.'

He stepped on to the muddy shingle, sinking down several inches as he made his way along, peering up at the wall as he went. I stood waiting on the steps, hunched against the rain. Presently he looked round. 'I think I've found the place. The cellar floor must be a couple of feet above my head and allowing for a downward slope, the old opening should be about here.' He prized and tugged and then turned round with a barnacled rock in his hand. 'Yes, this is the place. There's a small lintel above. You go indoors out of the rain, Lisa, and I'll be in when I've opened it up.'

I did as he said and as soon as I'd closed the door behind me, Edith's bell summoned me upstairs. She wanted to know what was happening and since she was determined to miss nothing, I had to dress her. Jack came in before she was ready but she told me to go straight down and see if he needed any help.

He wiped his face and pulled off his wet coat. 'I've managed to get the stones out,' he said, and in answer to my unspoken question, 'All I can see behind where the stones were, is impacted mud. I didn't poke it about.' He gave a wry smile. 'And the rain is just stopping. No reason not to do a bit of fishing, they rise well on a day like this. What sort of container d'you think I should bring? I've got a couple of those plastic fishing barrels with rope handles. And some shallow trays, what do you think?'

I had been wondering myself what we would find hidden there below the cellar floor. I knew a large man's skeleton would take up some space. 'Bring the barrels,' I said. 'We can tip the sand on top.'

'Right. I'll take the van round to the slipway and collect the boat. Be half an hour or so. And once you've helped me load up, I'll take her out in the bay and dump the stuff OK?'

I shook my head. 'No. I'm coming with you. You can be teaching me to fish if anyone shows any interest. Only don't leave me behind, Jack. I couldn't stand the suspense.'

'But what about her?' he nodded towards the staircase and my heart lurched. I'd forgotten Edith. I bit my lip in frustration.

But when I went upstairs to finish dressing her, she read my mind in her uncanny way. 'You'll have to go along with him. I'll be alright. I'll wait in the front room. You shouldn't be more than an hour or so and I can manage on my own that long.'

I wasn't so sure about that but we could hardly ask someone to sit with her while we went about her grisly task in the cellar. I sped downstairs to tell Jack and he went off in his van to go to his mooring a mile or so away up the Penryn river.

I got Edith ready and brought her downstairs and gave her the tea and the thin bread and jam she requested to eat while sitting beside the front room window. Then I went into the kitchen and made a flask of strong coffee and as an afterthought, I took a half bottle of brandy from the kitchen cupboard and stood them both on the kitchen table.

I joined Edith and stood at the window of the front room, and it was a long anxious time before we were able to pick out Jack's boat chugging steadily towards us. There wasn't much movement out on the water and I chewed my fingers wondering if we'd be too conspicuous out there, one small boat going... where?

Then Jack moored below and a few minutes later came his tap on the door. I'd already made us both a mug of tea but he said leave it to cool and took the cellar key out of his pocket. 'Coming?' he said and unlocked the cellar door. I picked up the big torch which stood on the dresser and we went slowly down the steps and into the dimly lit space.

The pallets stood in their usual place, supporting the bags of sand and some cement. Jack turned to me. 'I've brought the boat right below the hole. Just enough water there to keep her afloat.' He rubbed his jaw. 'I've got the big barrels like you said, just in case we need a second one. And another bag of sand. Well, here goes.' And he set about lifting the sacks off the pallets and dragging them aside. The place where they'd stood looked no different from the rest of the cellar floor, covered as it was by the uniform layer of silt. Jack picked up the brush propped up in the corner and after two or three sweeps, the old trapdoor came to light.

'Moment of truth, eh?' he said. And visibly gritting his jaw, he raised the lid.

'Christ!' Jack stepped back and the trapdoor fell open with a crash. And I almost dropped the torch as my hand flew to my mouth and smothered the cry that left my lips. I'd braced myself to confront a broken skeleton and indeed what lay there was mostly bone. But to my horror, Fred Rogers' remains looked for all the world as if he was about to raise himself on his hands and knees and emerge from his narrow tomb. What I'd not expected was the hair which straggled over the head lying there on its side, the taut darkened skin, and the great teeth locked in a wild grin.

Jack dropped onto his knees to one side, and breathed hard, trying not to be sick. And I stood, appalled at what I saw but unable to tear my eyes away.

The body was lying on the slope, the head only a foot or so below us. But it was the hands that so horrified me, as the torchlight played over finger bones which were embedded in a crack of the stone. There was a gold ring on wedding finger bone. My training told me the airtight tomb was the reason for the amount of ligament and skin that remained, holding this upper torso still in its human shape. The skeletal arms were enmeshed in the remains of a jacket's lining; the wool of the jacket itself having long since rotted away. A watch hung on the lining's thread half way down one bony arm.

Jack was on his feet again and he quickly shut the trapdoor. 'Christ!' he said again. 'We can't do this, Lisa.' And he pulled his mobile phone from his pocket. I moved over to the steps, sat down weakly and closed my eyes. I heard Jack mutter through the roaring in my ears and bent my head between my knees. He dropped the phone and came to me, kneeling at my side and we clung to one another, unable to speak, unwilling to let each other go.

Presently Jack sat back on his heels. 'Bloody credit's run out on my phone. I can't believe it. It's like a curse.'

I took a deep breath. 'No Jack. Nothing's changed. We came prepared to shift his remains. Seeing them is hideous. But nothing can bring him back. All the arguments we went over last night still stand. The pros and the cons. Remember?'

He shook his head. 'I don't know. We need to think. And we both need a shot of that brandy I saw on the table. Let's go.' His arm steadied me as we made our way up the stairs and in the kitchen he poured a generous slug of the spirit into the mugs of tea. We sat with our trembling hands wrapped round the warming drinks and looked at each other.

'You're right,' he said at last with a sigh. 'I can't risk Mum losing her house because of me chickening out. But Lisa, love. I really don't want you to come with me. Once the thing is loaded, I mean.'

'We'll see,' I said. 'Just let's get it done first.'

We stood up to go and met Edith wheeling herself along the hall passage. It was hard to bring myself to look her in the face. I kept picturing that grinning head down below and the fingers embedded in the stones. *For he was alive when she'd closed that trapdoor.* How else to explain those desperate clinging hands? But Jack mustn't know what I suspected.

Edith's voice broke through my confused thoughts. 'I've got something here for you. When you come back.' She held up her cheque book. 'I'll get you cash if you want. You can name your fee.' Her burning eyes were fixed on Jack.

His tanned face was blanched and taut. He looked at her for a moment. Looked at the cheque book she held out. Then, 'I'd wipe my arse with your bloody cheque,' he said, his voice low and icy.

To me, he said, 'Come on, let's get it done. I'll cover it up with newspapers so you won't have to look. And I'll give a couple of revs on the engine when I want you to start shoving.' As he spoke he gathered a pile of papers from the storeroom. Then he went ahead of me down the cellar steps and when I glanced back, Edith was sitting in her chair, her mouth slack, and the cheque book pressed hard against her shrunken chest.

CHAPTER THIRTY FOUR

By the time I followed Jack down the cellar steps, he'd already opened the trapdoor again. The piled newspapers did indeed hide from my eyes what lay beneath. He picked up the brush once more and this time gave a tentative push against what lay beneath the paper. He breathed heavily. 'I felt it move. I shall have to go outside and make sure it all falls into those barrels. Oh my God, Lisa, I'm so sorry to have got you into this.'

I put my hand against his lips. 'My choice too, remember. Go on. I'll wait until I hear that engine rev, then I'll keep pushing and shoving until the space is clear. Go on,' I said again.

Those few minutes before Jack reached the boat and was ready for me to begin my work are burned in my memory. The dim room, and what lay at my feet. I couldn't get out of my mind the picture of how it must have been, the man's body, still breathing, crammed into that narrow space. Unconscious at first. How else could she have got him down there? But later coming round, trying to force his way out. And the final clawing of his fingers in the stones...

The revs of the boat engine brought me from my frozen trance. I pressed the head of the sweeping brush against the newspapers and after a bit, there was a movement. I pushed harder, trying not to look as the

277

papers slipped but despite my averted eyes, I glimpsed the shifting, sliding bones. Then I heard heavy thumps from the barrel in the boat below as it caught its grim cargo. I hoped with all my heart that the sandy dust pouring out of the hole would hide some of the grim shapes from Jack's eyes.

Once he called up to me to stop pushing while he moved the boat. Then his voice came through the opening again, muffled, telling me to go on. And there was another brief pause when I heard him being sick. Poor queasy Jack. But at last it was done and the sides of the narrow space were clearly outlined against the daylight coming through the opening above the water. I swept a lot of silt from the floor out through the hole; our cover story, if one should be needed, was that we were clearing Edith's cellar and the muddy dust hopefully would hide the fresh sand in the barrels. I looked round, tossed out the few bricks lying about and called to Jack that I was on my way. Then I closed the trap door firmly behind me.

I went up to the hall and grabbed my waterproof. There was no sign of Edith but I called out that I was going, picked up the flask of coffee from the kitchen table and shoved the brandy bottle into my pocket. Then I let myself out and hurried down to the jetty.

Jack brought the boat alongside and helped me in. He'd placed spare containers onto the jetty steps and the two big laden barrels stood in the bow of the boat, each over half full with what looked like sandy rubble, with a couple of broken bricks lying on the surface.

'OK?' he asked and I said yes, OK and we moved slowly away. I looked back at the wall and saw Jack had already replaced the barnacled rocks roughly into the hole he'd made. 'I'll check them properly later,' he said as he saw me looking at the wall. 'Just want to cover up the hole for now.'

The pelting rain had given way to a fine drizzle and the small boat rose and fell on the sweeping swell. Jack handed me a sou'wester. 'This was in the van. You'll need it if it starts raining hard again.' I pulled it down over my ears and immediately felt a little safer, hidden beneath the wide brim. Jack's rainhat too was jammed firmly on his head. I sat facing him and wondered if I looked as pale and shaken as he did. He stretched out his hand and pressed my arm. 'You're something else, Lisa. I don't know what to say.'

I managed a watery smile. Two fishing rods lay across the thwarts and all the paraphernalia of the fisherman besides. Innocent cover for our journey across the bay if it should be needed. But I was only too aware of the barrels behind me in the bow with their grim hidden contents.

'It was heavier than I thought,' Jack said after a long silence. And I nodded, remembering the heavy thumps I'd heard. The engine chugged quietly and after a while I turned my head and looked round the harbour with its familiar assortment of yachts and boats at their moorings. The drizzle was heavier now and I was more than grateful for the sou'wester. There were a couple of fishing vessels ploughing ahead of us towards the open sea and a big motor boat burrowed its way through the swell in their wake, all of us moving towards the mouth of the bay.

I clutched the seat as we rode a series of wakes from the larger boats which added to the uneasy swell and caused the boat to dip alarmingly and Jack raised a questioning eyebrow. 'I'm OK. Really,' I said, knowing the churning of my stomach was from nerves, not from the restless movements of the boat.

Suddenly the big motorboat changed course and headed towards us. 'Christ,' said Jack. 'It's the harbour people.' I looked again and recognised the navy and white of the harbour commissioners' craft. My heart started hammering in my chest and I clutched the seat and willed the boat to go away.

But it kept coming and when it was just feet away, a voice called. 'Hi, Jack,' and the waterproofed man seated at the helm throttled back as he spoke until our two boats crept ahead side by side. 'How's it going then?' the cheery voice went on.

'OK Adam. How about you?' I could hear the tension in Jack's voice and my nails dug deep into the wood of the seat.

'Hear you did Simon a bit of good the other day,' the man smiled. 'He won't say what, of course. Tight beggar, our Simon.'

'Adam is Simon's brother,' Jack said to me and trying

to keep his voice light, told him 'This is Lisa, my partner. Going to do a bit of fishing, we are.'

The boats were closer together now and I hardly heard the comments that Adam was making about our 'romance' because of the blood pounding in my ears. But I did hear the sudden change of tone when he spoke again. 'Here, what you got in those barrels then?' And he stood up, swaying with the movement of his boat, the engine idling. I saw Jack's throat tighten but he still managed to sound cool and offhand. 'Been clearing out Mrs Rogers' cellar. She's going into a home. Selling up.'

The harbour craft came alongside now. 'Going to do a bit of dumping in the harbour, eh?' Adam's voice was angry now, accusing.

Jack's voice, tightly controlled, replied. 'Well, yes. It's only some sand and sweepings from the cellar. Stuff that's been under water anyway every spring tide for years. I didn't think it would matter, putting a bit more sand down there.'

'That's not sand.'

Our boats were now so close that they rubbed against one another with a regular squeak of the fenders as we rose and fell on the restless water. Now and then the swell reached higher as if trying to shoulder us aside, a twisting, pivoting movement that left my stomach mid-air as we rose and fell. Then Adam suddenly reached across the gunwales and thrust his hand into the nearest barrel. But as he pushed his hand down into the sand, his boat swung away and he quickly pulled himself back and regained his balance, grabbing the rudder to correct the steering. He straightened up and said again, 'That's not sand.'

'Yeah, well, there's a couple of bricks in it. But it's mostly sand and grit. Like I said, I wouldn't tip any old rubbish in the harbour.' Jack's grin was stiff 'Still, now you've seen me, I'll have to go back to the slipway and load my trailer. OK?'

'Oh no. It's not OK, Jack. You know better than that. I shall have to put this in my report. You come along with me.'

The sweat coursing down both our faces might pass for rain, but as I huddled beneath the brim of the sou'wester I knew that one glance at my ashen face would arouse the man's suspicions still further.

Jack exhaled loudly. 'Alright, Adam. If I must. Give Simon a laugh when I tell him I got done for putting sand down the bottom of the harbour I suppose.'

The man in the other boat was suddenly still. 'When you seeing him then?'

'One night this week. He's taking me and Lisa out for a drink. Sort of thank you for the favour we did him.'

Another long pause. 'Well, I suppose one good turn deserves another. You can tell Simon I let you off this time. Go on, way you go. But don't let anyone else know. More than my job's worth, turning a blind eye to dumping.'

'Well, thanks, Adam. I'll tell Simon you've repaid the

debt in full. We'll buy you a drink yourself sometime. See you around.' Adam gave us an officious salute and then his boat roared away, leaving us rocking violently in his wake.

Neither of us spoke for a couple of minutes. My mouth was totally dry. Presently, as Jack drove the boat ahead once more, I pulled the bottle of brandy from my pocket with shaking fingers, and for the first and only time in my life, I swigged the spirit straight from the bottle. Silently I handed it to Jack and he too took a long pull. 'Thank you God,' he said fervently as we watched the navy and white vessel disappear into the drizzle.

We moved ahead slowly and after an age my heartbeat settled down to something approaching normal. The brandy too was doing its bit. I gave a sudden giggle. 'What?' asked Jack.

'Him. That Adam. Putting his hand in our barrel. Sort of lucky dip. Bran tub. Imagine his face if he'd pulled out...' but I could no longer speak, almost hysterical with laughter at the release of that unbearable tension.

Jack too began to laugh and we snorted and giggled for several minutes as we headed across the bay until Jack said let's have some of that coffee then, before Adam comes back and does us both for drunk driving. And the hot drink gradually settled us down and my giggles turned into the occasional smothered hiccup.

Presently Jack asked me to take the helm. 'Mist

coming down.' He fished a compass from his pocket and took a bearing. 'OK' he said when he was satisfied with his course and took over from me again to my relief. 'I want to get right away from where the guys drop their pots and the shore fishermen do a bit of angling. For obvious reasons. Place I've got in mind is a deep gulley at the foot of some rocks on the headland. Hardly likely to be found down there.'

Then we ran into what seemed to be a solid wall of fog. Shakily I asked Jack if he knew where we were. He checked our direction again with the compass. 'Yep. But I'm going to turn off the engine and row for a bit. We're in the lanes where the ferries pass and I want to be able to hear them coming. You sit at the helm, Lisa. If we hear anything, start up the engine again so we can get out of their way. Don't worry, love,' he said when he saw my face under the brim of the hat. 'I'll ship the oars and take over from you right away. But it's better to be careful. Don't want another upset, do we?' As he spoke he changed places with me once more and set the oars and began to row.

After the noisy chug of the engine, a blanketing silence came down, broken only by the creak and rattle of the oars and the slap of the water against our hull. I noticed there was much more movement in the sea now and waves came charging out of the mist so Jack had to keep swinging the bows to meet them head on.

Just as I began to say can't we just tip the stuff out and be done with it, Jack rested on the oars. 'Nearly there, I think.' He listened carefully and checked the compass again. And then through a sudden gap in the mist I saw a cliff face a few yards away, and on its top, amidst tufts of sea pink, a rock shaped like a cottage loaf. Jack turned when I exclaimed. 'A cliff, Jack!'

'Good,' he said. 'Just where I wanted to be. We call that rock up there, the Hat. The water down below is very deep. Just what we need. You stay by the engine, Lisa, while I tip this lot out.'

He used one of the oar handles to help lever the first barrel, heavy with its added burden of sand, and tipped it over the side. 'Good' he remarked grimly. Then the second barrel. But as he was levering it up to the gunwales, it slipped and the barrel with its contents splashed over the side. Jack had slipped the painter through the rope handles in case this should happen and though the boat rocked wildly as he leaned over, he soon got hold of the barrel again. With both arms under the water he tipped it on its side and gradually shuffled out the contents.

And that's how we saw some of the last remains of Fred Rogers going to his new grave, sparse hair floating above the skull, and bony arms held out as though about to swim away, the watch still caught in the transparent material of the lining. And then the remains sank slowly through the dark green water and disappeared from our sight.

Jack swished the barrel slowly to and fro to get rid of the last of the sand and then said, 'Whatever he did,

surely the poor bastard deserved a better end than this.'
And I nodded, a sudden lump in my throat.

Then Jack turned to me. 'I'm not a religious man,
Lisa, but aren't we supposed to say something? This is
a sort of funeral after all.' His words petered out.

I nodded and slowly got to my feet, Jack's arm
supporting me against the rocking of the boat though
here in the shelter of the cliff the swell was much less.
He pulled off his hat. I swallowed. I thought of Edith,
dying back there at the house and the deceit and hatred
that had led to this man's death. On the way here I'd
been wondering what we could say but when I tried to
remember the prayers and psalms from my convent
schooldays I could think of nothing that wasn't full of
love and forgiveness. And neither seemed appropriate
to this couple. So I said, "Oh God, only you know how
this man came to die.' I paused and as I went on my
voice came back from the cliff so close ahead, and
trapped by the mist, it sounded as if another woman
stood somewhere near, as the echo repeated my words
one by one. 'But we hope that now he'll lie in peace
and that out of our actions good will come. Amen.' And
when Jack repeated my amen, the echo came again,
clear and distinct, another ghostly voice. We stood in
silence as the boat drifted slowly towards the black face
of the cliff. Then Jack sighed and reached for an oar to
fend us off

'Come on,' he said quietly. 'Let's go.' He checked his
compass and started rowing but the mist was thinning

now and soon he started the engine again. I sat close beside him on our journey home and noticed how high the bow was now that the barrels lay empty on the floorboards. It seemed to take an age, that slow trip back across the bay, buffeted by the turbulent currents of the Roads. But at last Jack drew us in alongside the jetty and helped me ashore. 'I'll be with you as soon as I've moored the boat. Don't go down there, will you, Lisa? Best lock the cellar door, OK?'

I nodded and clutching the key went back into the house.

CHAPTER THIRTY FIVE

The first thing I noticed as I entered the hall was the smell. I had left Edith alone too long. I went along to the front room and found her in her chair with the window open and the room chilled with blowing mist.

She glared at me. 'I couldn't help it,' she began, but I said of course you couldn't and made soothing noises as I took her up to the bathroom and showered and changed her. Whatever she did, whatever she had done, she was still my patient and I knew better than most how ill and vulnerable she was.

Jack came back before we were ready and he went straight down to the cellar. Presently though, we all three sat in the warm kitchen and despite everything, we ate the soup I'd made.

Only once did Edith mention our trip. 'I saw that harbour boat stop you. I thought that was the end.'

'So did we,' Jack said wryly but he didn't elaborate and I found I'd no wish either to relive the tension of those dreadful minutes. He said to her, 'I've measured up down below and I'm going to take out the trapdoor and put a couple of concrete slabs across the hole. With a cement skim across the top it'll look just like the rest of the floor. Shouldn't be found for years.'

She looked pleased. 'Give me your bill,' she said. Then she turned to me. 'You can ring that Doctor West and tell him I'll go into that hospice place as soon as he says. Then you can have a bit of time off. I'll pay you to the end of the month. Better try and catch that doctor right away.'

So I phoned his practice and left Edith's message with the doctor's receptionist. Doctor West himself rang back a little later and asked if Saturday morning would be alright and Edith said it would have to be, wouldn't it. Soon Jack went off in the van and came back later and spent an hour in the cellar. When he eventually came up to the kitchen, he said he'd done what he planned. 'I've darkened the cement with a bit of dirt,' he said. 'It looks just like the rest of the floor now and by the time the next spring tide has left its mark, no one will guess it wasn't blocked up years ago. That's if any living person still remembers it was there.'

As soon as the falling tide had dropped enough, he went down again to the muddy shore and despite Edith's assurance, he used some mortar where it didn't show to make sure the stones in the wall wouldn't loosen in next winter's storms. And he said when he'd finished, the barnacled wall looked exactly as it had for years.

That evening, with Edith asleep or at least quiescent, Jack and I pieced together our thoughts on what had happened in that cellar. I'd not intended to tell Jack my suspicions, but he forestalled me. 'That trapdoor, Lisa. I took it away in the van. But as I was lifting it out, I saw what was on the underside. Scratches. Deep marks like you could make with your finger nails. A rough letter F.

And alongside a downstroke and a sort of half mark. He was still alive down there for a time. And she must have known, must have heard him when she was shifting all the coal on top the trapdoor. He scratched those initials in the wood in a last message to let people know what she'd done. As the floodtide rose, he drowned, Lisa.'

I shuddered as he spoke then nodded my head. 'Yes. I think so too. Those fingers of his, The tips of the bone were jammed into the crevice of the stone. But he must have been unconscious when she pushed him down there, though.'

Jack nodded. 'Yes, but do you see what it means? It was all planned ahead. She had to have that trapdoor cleared before she got him down to the cellar. Couldn't bank on having time to get it open otherwise if she only managed to knock him out. Which is what seems to have happened.'

I shuddered again and blanked out the thought that when she had him at her mercy, unconscious, she chose to wall him up in that ghastly hole.

Jack went on, 'She'd have had to trick him down to the cellar - maybe told him the wall was bulging. Something urgent anyway, something that would bring him down to where he'd never normally go. After all, it was only coal and wood down there. Women's work, something he never bothered with. Whatever. And when he came down the steps, she'd have had to strike him hard. Probably with the axe she said she used for chopping the kindling. Anyway, something with a short handle. Maybe she hit him more than once. She said there was a lot of blood.' He was quiet for a while then looked up. 'Did you,' he paused uncertainly, 'did you notice his skull at all? Marks of any kind?'

I crossed my arms across my chest, very cold as I shook my head, remembering only the glimpse of that wispy hair and the great teeth before I had violently turned away. 'No, Jack. I didn't look for anything like that. But he'd never have come round from a serious fracture, not enough to scratch his name like that.'

My skin was gooseflesh now. It all made a horrible sense, Jack's reconstruction. And I remembered what Edith had said. That he 'disappeared' not long after he'd told her how he'd got hold of Charlie's letters. That she couldn't bear it when he quoted them to her, jeering and taunting. Yes. She could well have planned the whole thing then, in her hatred and desire for revenge.

Jack shook his head as he spoke. 'All that about phoning the hospital in the middle of the night. It would need a very cool head to think of doing that if it all happened accidentally the way she said. But if she'd thought it all out carefully beforehand, then yes. A clever move. And going to the police station too, when she'd done all that work down in the cellar to cover her tracks. I imagine the police checked the coal pile to make sure there wasn't a body under it. But if no one knew of that weird hole under the floor, that's all they would have done. God, what a cold fish she was. Still is, come to that.' We were both silent a long time, I thinking of that grim funeral journey across the water with Fred Rogers' remains aboard and of the passionate woman whose hatred and love had driven her to such appalling lengths.

'What we did today Lisa, was not just covering up an accidental death, but a very nasty crime indeed. And yet...' He was silent for a while then he went on, 'Even now I don't regret it. Our part in it, I mean. What good would it do if it all came to light. And as it is...'

I gave a deep, shuddering sigh. 'I know. I've been telling myself the same thing ever since we agreed to go along with it. I just hope it won't come back to haunt us one day.'

'Don't say that!' exclaimed Jack. 'Come on. Enough of this talking, going round and round getting nowhere. Let's have a cup of tea and then go to bed. And just think, in a couple of days we'll be home in the cottage at last. And as soon as I've finished this job that I'm in the middle of, I'll be free. And so will you. So we can take a holiday. What about it? Spain? South America? We can make it our honeymoon. What do you say?'

He couldn't have hit on a better way to get rid of my morbid thoughts and though I had to get up several times in the night to see to Edith, at least when I did go to sleep, I wasn't troubled by haunting dreams or flashbacks of that hour of tension out on the waters of the harbour in the rain and the mist.

The following day the sun shone and Jack went back to work. Nurse Meadows came again in the afternoon and I told her Edith was going into the hospice next day. She nodded her head. 'Best place for her. I can see how quickly she's going downhill. And you look quite shattered if you don't mind me saying so. Are you going to catch up on a bit of sleep while I'm here?'

But I told her I'd like to go out for a while in the sunshine. I walked along to one of the beaches and sat down on the sand, sheltered from the breeze by a low bluff. The sun was warm and I watched a couple of young mums building castles for their toddlers, feeling relaxed and thankful to be out of doors, out of the shadow of sickness and death. Presently I lay back and closed my eyes and drifted into sleep, lulled by the murmur of the waves and the voices of the children and their mothers. It was a short sleep but I woke enormously refreshed and went on with my walk.

At last I turned back. Only one more night and then we would be back to Jack's cottage, and I'd be free of my responsibilities, free to start my new life with Jack.

During that last night in Edith's house, I woke and found I was alone in my bed. I sat up, heart thumping and thought I heard voices from Edith's room. Quickly I leapt up and ran along the landing. From the door I could smell the all too familiar sharp acidity of sickness. Jack was leaning across the bed with his arm round Edith's shoulders, holding the basin before her. I came over and took it from his hand to empty it and handed him the flannel and towel. He lowered her back on her pillows and gently sponged and wiped her face. Then she turned her head and gave him the most radiant of smiles, her eyes shining, her deeply etched face transformed. 'Thank you Charlie,' she said as she looked at him. 'You're always so good to me.' She closed her eyes then and seemed unaware of me as I tucked the sheet around her pathetically thin shoulders.

We went back to our bedroom together. 'I didn't hear the bell, Jack,' I said remorsefully.

'I know, sweetheart. You were out for the count.'

'But I feel awful. I know how it upsets you, sickness and that. And it's my job. You must make sure I'm awake next time.'

He squeezed my hand. 'It's OK, honestly. And after all the things I've been thinking about her, I suppose I needed that. Put things in proportion. Whatever has happened, whatever she's done, all she is now is a very sick old lady. And how about that, still thinking of her Charlie. right to the end.'

Next morning Maud came down to the house. I'd phoned to tell her Edith was leaving home today and she helped me pack some things in the case. I'd already called Darren Cornish the previous day and he said under the terms of my contract I could stay in the house until the end of the month. 'That's if you really want to.

But don't give the keys to those bloody nephews, Lisa. Drop them in the office when you're ready to leave.' He chatted for a bit, making me laugh despite myself. Then he told me the young girl who was in the process of buying her grandmother's house had called him, concerned when she heard Edith was dying. 'I told her not to worry, everything would be alright. Lucky for her we dragged our feet a bit, eh?' And I smiled to think of her face when she learned the house she wanted to buy for herself and her grandmother would be theirs as Edith's gift.

Maud said should we call the nephews and let them know what was happening. 'Not that they care,' she snorted as I phoned. One was away on holiday, I was told. The other said good, hospice the best place for her. Nothing in the house worth having anyway. Best to leave it to the solicitors to sort everything out. End of conversation.

Edith slept through much of the morning. She peered at me without recognition when I changed her and got her ready to leave. She knew Maud though. But soon I saw that it was a different Maud she spoke to; she was addressing a young girl, eager and willing to do her bidding. Maud shook her head and her eyes shone with tears as she listened to the quiet prattle which came from the dying woman's lips from time to time. At last the doorbell rang and Edith left the house for the last time. I went to the hospice with her in the ambulance and Jack and Maud followed in the Rover. We were all three quiet on the way home. We stopped at a pub Jack knew and had some very good food but we found it hard to enjoy our meal. Jack and I were pleased though, when Maud said Katie was coming to spend the night with her as neither of us liked the thought of Maud being alone with the day's sadness. We would see them both tomorrow. 'Sunday dinner at my place,' said Maud with something of her old cheer.

And, 'Home at last,' said Jack an hour later as he parked the car in the drive. He unlocked the front door. 'I never did sweep you off your feet and carry you over the threshold, did I?' he smiled at me.

I put my arms round him. 'You did you know. From the moment we met.' He swung my feet over the threshold anyway and then we stood and looked round the room, so familiar and welcoming. As he said, we were home at last.

CHAPTER THIRTY SIX

Jack drove me to the hospice several times in the following week but Edith gave no sign she recognised me. The last time I went, she appeared to be deeply unconscious, but I spoke to her nevertheless. Told her Charlie had phoned. That he was so sorry to hear she was very poorly. That he sent his love. And then I stood up. I touched her hand briefly and left the room. And we were not surprised, relieved in fact, when they phoned to tell us the following morning that she had died in her sleep during the night.

Darren Cornish phoned me at the cottage. 'My orders for funeral arrangements, Lisa. Strictly no mourners. And no religious rites. Simple cremation.' He went on to speak about getting the beneficiaries of the will together to hear their good news and suggested they might all meet at Edith's house. 'Appropriate, don't you think, for it to be the scene of something pleasant after all those years of gloom and doom.'

If only he knew, I thought. Then he told me I must come along and be hostess. 'You know where everything is. They'll all expect a cup of tea. So push the boat out, Lisa. Let them go away remembering a great party. Let them celebrate their good news in style.'

I smiled at the thought. Hard to imagine those rafters ringing with laughter and the sound of glasses cheerfully clinking. But yes. I would lay on a party for them to look back on for a long time to come.

Darren and his clerk had already listed the contents of the house for the nephews' benefit. 'We'll hire stuff for the party, glasses and all,' he went on. 'so those two stiff necked twits can't complain if something gets broken. And we'll get caterers in so you can be free to do the rounds. I'm her executor and I shall say it's what Mrs Rogers wished. Actually she did tell me to do what I liked as long as the cremation was as she ordered; that it must be completely private.' And I could almost hear the echo of her voice speaking to him in that chill puritanical way of hers.

The evening before they were all due to assemble, Jack and I went down to the house and I put flowers in all the rooms, using vases and pots from the storeroom that I supposed had hardly ever seen the light of day. We stood on the balcony for a while remembering all that had happened in this house, but our grim thoughts disappeared when we went back indoors as the delicate scent of the flowers wafted through the rooms.

And next day the house filled up with the mystified tenants. I heard one old man saying, 'I expect she've left us two bob apiece. Just like her to aggravate.' But his mouth opened the widest of them all when the terms of the will were read out. All the colour left Maud's face; we'd not told her what to expect and she was not the only one with tears running down her face by the time Darren had finished his reading of the will. The nephews left soon afterwards, but smiling at the news they'd heard. The freehold of the two shops was theirs; this house and a proportion of the residue of the estate and Darren assured them in my hearing that even after the considerable inheritance taxes were met, they'd be two wealthy men.

Then the champagne bottles popped and the two waiters scurried busily through the crush of people who filled the kitchen and front room. A few sat on the stairs alongside the stairlift and inevitably as the champagne flowed, the lift went into operation bearing a succession of laughing, singing men and women, whom I'm sure Edith would have said were quite old enough to know better.

Does happiness banish the ghosts of the past? I don't know. But when we locked up that night after the revels were over, both Jack and I felt the change in the atmosphere. Whatever she had done, whatever she had been, Edith had made some reparation at last.

Darren phoned the cottage again. Without informing anyone, and in accordance with her wishes, Edith had been cremated. After I put down the phone I wandered out into the garden and told Jack. We stood looking out over the sea, silent for a while. Then Jack said, 'So she had no one with her either. Only strangers to see her off. Like Fred.' I nodded my head, remembering the two of us standing in the boat above that watery grave.

And then I remembered those other voices in the fog, the ghostly echoes that sounded for all the world like another man and woman standing near. Perhaps for Edith too, there had been voices in the flames.

The next day, a Saturday, Darren Cornish turned up as Jack and I were sitting in the sun in the garden reading the newspapers and drinking coffee. I made him a cup. And after some small talk, he said, 'Edith told me to give you this when I could catch you both on your own.' He handed me a thin envelope.

Mystified, I opened it. Inside were two open return flight tickets to Australia. Speechless I passed them to Jack. The best he could come up with was, 'Well, well. How about that?'

Darren told us more. 'She said she hoped you'd take up the tickets. She doesn't mean for you to visit this old flame of hers. But she said she'd like you to go and have a look round the country with Jack, seeing she herself couldn't make it.' He put down his mug. 'Will you go?'

Jack answered for me as I was fumbling for a tissue to blow my nose. 'It's a bit of a shock, but yes, if Lisa agrees, then I'm all for it. I'm taking a couple of weeks off as soon as my present job is finished anyway. How about it, Lisa?'

I nodded. I had a lump in my throat. Presently I said, 'Make it three weeks, Jack. Once I start work again, goodness knows when we'll be able to take a decent break together.'

But later, after Darren had gone, I said to Jack, 'You know what you said about not taking any money from her. Not putting ourselves in the position of having been paid to clear that cellar. Won't these tickets count if anything should ever come to light?'

'Shouldn't think so. Especially after what Darren said about her having originally made the bookings for herself and you. And anyway, what could come to light? By now those bones will have been scattered by the movement of the tides. No. I think we can go and enjoy ourselves. Not that we're not enjoying ourselves already, eh?' And he pulled me down beside him on the grass to prove the point. And lying looking up at the blue sky that so matched his eyes, I felt the last of my worries slip away.

EPILOGUE

When we arrive back from our trip to Australia, summer is over and the trees are already turning brown. We are rested and full of memories of that journey we made through the outback. We did visit Charlie. A Charlie renewed and rejuvenated, so his daughter said, by the salvation of Edith's huge legacy. He spoke movingly of his lost love, a woman I hardly recognised as I remembered my late irascible employer and I wondered if he had any idea of the depths to which her love for him had driven her. But as his eyes shone with gentle tears, I was glad he would never have to know.

Jack is about to begin building a large granny flat for Maud. Meanwhile her grandchildren romp through the house and garden in a way that both delights and exasperates their mother and Maud.

Tonight we drop into our familiar local for a drink after a long walk. There is a lot of ribald laughter. A rich American has managed to mess up the self steering on his state-of-the-art new yacht and hit a rock. The wildly expensive vessel is fathoms down in a deep gulley. Jack joins the laughter and we turn to the television set which shows a diving platform over the spot, and the owner telling the cameras that, yeah, sure we can raise her up. These diver boys can do anything.

The camera pans across the bay, the water a deep and vivid blue under the autumn sunshine. It pans back and an icy shiver tracks up my spine. That rock is unmistakable. The cottage loaf, the Hat, as Jack called it. His hand reaches for mine and I see the gentle shake of his head as he signals reassurance. What if they do find the bones? He has already told me so many times that like Edith said, it'll only confirm the old story that he drowned. And Adam, the only person who saw us dumping something in the harbour, wouldn't dare say anything or he'd lose his job. And anyway, how would they know whose bones they are after all these years?

So now I sip my gin and tonic, grateful for its spreading warmth. But I keep remembering our last sight of Fred Rogers as he sank through the waves. The outstretched bony arms and clinging to the sleeve lining, that expensive watch of his. That Rolex. That traceable Rolex...

Acknowledgements

I need to thank my daughters for editing this novel, and also my sister, Pat Opie and my friend Molly Herman for their final proof reading of the book.

And also many thanks to Terry Lander, my publisher and his wife Mary for their remarks and corrections of my novel.

About the Author

After various occupations, Enid Mavor started teaching for some years. Upon leaving, she wrote her first novel, Portrait of Polwerris, which was then published. Several short stories were also published and broadcast on Radio Cornwall, together with some award winning poetry. Another novel will follow this book, Flood Tide, quite soon.